# Rowena Summers
# Daisy's War

CANELO

First published in Great Britain in 2001 by Severn House Publishers

This edition published in the United Kingdom in 2023 by

Canelo
Unit 9, 5th Floor
Cargo Works, 1–2 Hatfields
London SE1 9PG
United Kingdom

A CIP catalogue record for this book is available from the British Library.

Print ISBN 978 1 80436 544 1
Ebook ISBN 978 1 80436 291 4

Look for more great books at www.canelo.co

Printed and bound in Great Britain by Clays Ltd, Elcograf S.p.A.

1

# Daisy's War

Rowena Summers is the pseudonym of Jean Saunders. She was a British writer of romance novels since 1974, and wrote under her maiden name and her pseudonym, as well as the names Sally Blake and Rachel Moore. She was elected the seventeenth Chairman (1993–1995) of the Romantic Novelists' Association, and she was the Vice-Chairman of the Writers' Summer School of Swanwick. She was also a member of Romance Writers of America, Crime Writers' Association and West Country Writers' Association.

# Chapter One

The small boys stared open-mouthed as Daisy pirouetted in front of them, as grandly as any film star at the local fleapit. The girl playing with the rag doll on the mat merely sniffed and refused to look at her. Daisy was going to ignore her anyway. Stuck up little madam that she was. *Vanessa!* Who ever heard of a name like that for a kid from the slums? No wonder she had airs and graces and thought herself better than anybody else.

"So what do you think, then?" Daisy asked her small brother and the two young evacuee boys. "How would you fancy being looked after in your hospital bed by *Nurse* Daisy Caldwell?"

"You're not a proper nurse yet," Norman, the older of the brothers, said, scowling. "You're just a girl done up in a fancy uniform. Not like our dad. Our mum says he's got a proper uniform now…"

Vanessa hooted. "Your dad ran off and left your mum years ago, stupid. The only uniform he's wearing now has prob'ly got arrows on it, like them jailbirds wear in my *Beano*."

Daisy glared at her as the younger of the brothers howled, "Our dad ain't in jail! He's flying one of them bombers and killing Jerries, that's what he's doing, Nessa Brown, and you're a pig—"

I

"Oh yeah? Tell that to the fairies, birdbrain. And don't call me *Nessa*! Anyway, I bet your dad's rotting in some 'orrible jail – and prob'ly dying of consumption by now," she added for effect.

"Shut up, Vanessa," Daisy whipped out at once. "You don't know what you're talking about."

"Yes I do, clever-dick nurse," the girl said in a kind of triumph. "Me old gran died of it, so there."

All Daisy's pleasure in the brand-new probationer's dress she was wearing disappeared at once. She tried to remember that this irritating girl had no idea that Daisy's own best friend was suffering from consumption – or TB, as those in the know called it, she thought, with a brief surge of superiority – and that the outlook was bad. Very bad, as it happened. After such a good start, Lucy's chances of survival were less than possible. They were nearer to nil.

It was all so unfair. Why did Lucy have to die? What had she ever done to deserve it? Everybody knew the Germans were rough-riding it over half of Europe and killing people now, ever since that pompous Mr Chamberlain had produced his 'Note' six months ago and plunged them into war with Germany.

"*Politicians!*" Aunt Rose always snorted – having no time for them as a breed – "Always meddling in people's lives and usually getting it wrong."

But this was different. Lucy was different. She wasn't an anonymous face that Daisy didn't know. She wasn't one of the wounded soldiers who were starting to be sent to Weston General now, and cheerfully saying how much they liked to see Daisy's pretty face – even when some of them couldn't see at all through eyes that had been shot away or horrifically burned, and some of them had ghastly seeping wounds and not much chance of ever living a proper life again.

Daisy could cope with them – mostly – because it was her job, and she loved it. But Lucy was her best friend, stuck in a miserable sanatorium in deepest Wales, dying of TB at the age of seventeen; and there wasn't a damn thing anybody could do about it.

"Anyway, our dad's flying aeroplanes and killing Jerries, so that's all you know," Norman was shouting furiously now, rounding on Vanessa as his brother began to snivel. "Just like your boy, ain't he, Daisy?"

She snapped back at him without really meaning to, not wanting to think too much about the lack of communication from her young man right now.

"Maybe. I don't know. But I do know you'd better get this mess cleared up while I change out of my uniform. Then you can all help me get the tea started before Aunt Rose comes home from her knitting circle."

Vanessa looked scornful again. "Why would she want to sit around knitting socks for soldiers she don't even know? Why can't their mums do it for 'em?"

"For somebody whose mum never knitted anything for anybody as far as I could tell, you should think twice before you condemn other people," Daisy told her smartly, knowing Aunt Rose wouldn't like hearing her censure a twelve-year-old who was far from home and well out of her normal environment. But sometimes this one was impossible.

They were all far from home in Aunt Rose's motley household, she thought suddenly. Though it was hardly very far for her youngest brother Teddy and herself, moving down to Weston from their Bristol home after their mother had died.

3

It was just temporary, of course – they still had their old home in Vicarage Street to go back to any time. Except that temporary had somehow become more permanent than any of them had planned. You had to thank Mr Hitler for some of that – but not all of it.

It had been sensible for Teddy to be sent away after their mother's terrible accident. He had been too young at five years old to take it all in properly, and Aunt Rose and Uncle Bert had been only too glad to give him a loving home. But it had been Daisy's choice to come here too. Her older sisters were still in Bristol with their father, and Baz – well, Lord knew where her brother Baz was now, Daisy thought with a grin. Somewhere in mid-Atlantic for all she knew, with all his grand ideas of going to sea, but far more likely to be on a trawler in the Irish fishing grounds.

Her usual cheerful nature was returning fast after the little bust-up with the brats. Vanessa was sometimes the giddy limit, though, and Daisy had to keep reminding herself that she came from a broken home, as they called it. And if what the billeting officer said was true, it was unlikely there'd be a proper home for her to go back to at all, what with her flighty mother and her drunken father.

Which was *fine* if Aunt Rose had wanted her for a permanent lodger, but that wasn't really the plan. Daisy could more or less understand why her childless aunt and uncle had wanted to fill their house with children when the opportunity came, even if it had taken a war to give them what they had always been denied.

Evacuees weren't always welcome in every household, especially when you had to take them in whether you wanted to or not. Aunt Rose loved them all, though

Lucy's parents hadn't been too keen when they had been allocated a brother and sister from London at their farm.

Privately, Daisy thought this might be a blessing for when IT happened. She thought about Lucy's prognosis in capital letters now, referring to it as IT, unable to bear putting it into actual words.

"What we having for tea then?" Vanessa asked her sullenly, when she had changed out of her uniform and returned to the parlour.

"Bread and scrape and think yourself lucky to get it," Daisy said cheerfully, the way Uncle Bert usually did.

"Is that all?"

Daisy sighed. "Vanessa, why can't you try to be pleasant now and then? We all have to get along, whether we like it or not."

"You're so sweet, aren't you?" the girl snapped at her. "A proper blooming angel. Well, I'm not helping to get the tea and that's that. I'm not skivvying for nobody."

"I'm not asking you to be a skivvy, you idiot. Just cut the bread and don't be so pathetic."

"Why can't we ever have pie and mash like me mother used to buy down the pie and eel shop?"

Daisy shuddered. "Because we can't. Now, are you going to cut the bread, or do I tell Aunt Rose that you're being obstructive again?"

The girl stared her out. She was going to be a smasher when she grew up a bit, all high cheekbones and wide brown eyes like a blooming film star, Daisy thought, using one of the girl's favourite words.

"If I knew what blooming obstrucky meant, I might be bothered!" Vanessa said, flouncing towards the cutlery drawer and catching her finger on the edge of the carving knife.

She gave a piercing cry and clutched at her hand, wringing it up and down like a yo-yo.

"You really are a ninny, Vanessa…" Daisy began, and then she saw how the girl's face had paled.

"If there's blood I can't look," she whimpered. "Me old gran used to cough it up, and it was all bright red, like a lot of froth…"

"Sit down," Daisy snapped, knowing she was referring to the TB her grandmother had died of, and not wanting to be reminded too graphically of the symptoms that she knew only too well on account of Lucy. "Put your head between your knees and let me look at that finger."

She practically had to wrench the girl's hands apart, while Vanessa turned her head the other way. It was only a nick, but for somebody terrified at the sight of blood, Daisy knew it might as well have been a river.

"Don't move a muscle while I fetch some Vaseline and sticking plaster from the medicine box, and you'll soon be as right as ninepence."

"Don't tell them boys then," Vanessa muttered next.

"Of course not. Girls have to stick together, don't they?"

She dared her to argue with that and got the merest hint of a smile in response. But she really was deathly white by now.

"There's nothing to be ashamed of in being afraid of the sight of blood, Vanessa," Daisy told her.

"I ain't afraid…"

"Everyone's afraid of something. It's natural."

Vanessa glared at her. "Oh yeah? What are you afraid of, then?"

"I'll tell you a secret. When I was a little girl I used to be afraid of clouds."

6

Vanessa hooted. "*Clouds* can't hurt you. Who ever heard of anyone being afraid of clouds?"

"Well, you just heard it. I thought they were monsters in the sky, just waiting to come and gobble me up," Daisy went on evenly. "Until my mother told me differently. She could always see good things everywhere."

She waited, knowing Vanessa wouldn't be able to resist asking.

"Go on then. What did your mother say? She sounds like a blooming saint."

Daisy ignored that. "She used to tell me that clouds were like castles in the sky, and if I looked at them for long enough I'd see them too. And she was right."

"I think that's daft."

"It's no more daft than being afraid of a little bit of blood from a cut finger. What would you do if you *really* hurt yourself?"

She saw the girl shudder as she finished taping the cut finger and spoke more cheerfully. "Oh well, it's one way to get out of slicing bread, I suppose, and I won't tell anyone your secret if you don't tell mine. So don't go bragging that you got the better of me!"

"Would I ever?" Vanessa retorted as she flounced off, and they both knew very well that she would.

Daisy began savagely slicing the bread herself, knowing that Aunt Rose would be tired after her afternoon out – and more likely from an afternoon of cheerful gossiping.

It was a regular occasion that was part social and part war work, but one that Rose and the knitting circle hugely enjoyed as they put the world to rights far better than any politicians ever could, in their opinion.

Daisy caught sight of herself in the mirror over the mantelpiece, and paused to smile for a moment, remembering her appearance in her new uniform.

*Not bad, Daisy Caldwell*, she told herself mentally. Not bad at all. Even if there were some who had thought she would never stick at it, and that her fads had come and gone as frequently as changing her stockings. But she'd proved them all wrong, and she blooming well knew it!

–

Two other young ladies were also assessing themselves in a mirror that afternoon. Daisy's oldest sister Imogen and her best friend Helen Church were in Immy's bedroom in Vicarage Street and scrutinising their appearance with less admiration than Daisy had done.

"Do you remember that night at my mother's fundraising ball in Bath last year, Immy, when we both looked such a treat?" Helen said dolefully. "Well, *you* looked like an absolute angel as usual, of course. Uniforms are such a miserable colour, and they don't do a single thing for my complexion."

Immy laughed as her friend ruffled her hand through her blonde curls.

"You'd look a treat in anything, and you know it..."

"Oh well, you would say that, but it doesn't. Anyway, James will probably turn somersaults when he sees you, regardless of this beastly khaki. They say girls go dotty over men in uniform, so let's hope it applies the other way round as well."

"I wish I could let him know what's happening," Immy said wistfully; "but since I haven't the faintest idea where he is right now..."

"He'll write when he can, you know that. You needn't fear that any French mam'selles will get their clutches into my brother, darling."

"I hadn't given such a thing a second's thought, actually, so thank you for putting the idea in my head!"

Helen stared at her. "Good Lord, you aren't taking me seriously, are you? Anyone with half an eye could see that James is totally besotted with you."

"Anyone with half an eye can't see much of anything," Immy replied smartly, pulling a comic face and crossing her eyes.

They both began to giggle, and then sobered up as they heard the creaking floorboards from the converted rooms above that had been turned into a self-contained flat for paying guests.

It no longer contained the two elderly widows who had lodged there for a year, since they'd both decided to get out of Bristol before Hitler's bombs made an unholy mess of it, as Immy's father put it. The flat was now the middle Caldwell sister's domain.

Immy still had to remind herself that Elsie was no longer a Caldwell, but a Preston, since she and Joe had married in haste at the very beginning of the war, six months ago. It wasn't *indecent* haste though, she insisted quickly, even though Elsie had become pregnant a few months later, raising a few eyebrows.

"And why not, when two people are as passionately in love as those two lucky stiffs?" Helen had said stoutly, sounding far more worldly than she really was, and knowing little about the mysteries of love-making or childbirth, for all her sophisticated outlook on life.

But together they had consulted the brown-paper-covered book that Immy's brother had failed to hand back to his school chum, to be read strictly beneath the bedclothes, and explaining things far more frankly than a young boy or an unmarried girl had the right to expect.

Or maybe not. To someone with a logical mind like Imogen's, it always seemed faintly bizarre that school-teachers instructed people on dull old dates in history and expected you to recite them parrot-fashion, and yet never dreamed of telling pupils about the most fundamental thing of all…

"Where have you gone now, Immy?" she heard Helen say, as her eyes misted over. She brought them back into focus and met the knowing gaze of her friend.

"Or do I need to ask?" Helen went on. "Dreaming about James again, I suppose, and wishing he was coming home on leave soon, like Joe." She gave a mischievous grin. "Do they still *do* it, do you think? Are they *allowed* to, when she's expecting?"

"How should I know?" Immy said crossly. "It's none of our business, anyway, so don't even think about it."

"We could always ask Daisy. I never thought she'd be so knowledgeable about stuff like that, but I bet she even knows all about delivering babies by now."

Immy laughed. "I doubt it! Whatever else Daisy does in that hospital of hers, I'm sure she'd be far too squeamish to be present at a birth! I'm sure her best role is offering tea and sympathy to the wounded servicemen and revelling in being a perfect little Miss Nightingale."

Helen spoke shrewdly. "You're proud of her though, aren't you?"

"Of course I am. We all are. Who ever thought Daisy would forget her flighty ideas of going on the stage and turn into a really dedicated nurse? Actually, I'm glad she didn't try to follow in Mother's footsteps. It would probably have broken Father's heart to support her in the theatre, which he would certainly have done, of course. But I know he couldn't have borne watching her perform on the very stage where Mother used to."

As she spoke, she was momentarily transported back to the halcyon days when their sweet-faced mother had danced and sung on stage, enchanting everyone who saw her. Frances Caldwell had been a star, beautiful and ethereal, and while her three daughters had inherited her beauty, no one could replace her in her children's eyes, nor their father's either. It had devastated the whole family when the cruel illness that had deprived her of her senses had driven her to the edge of the Avon Gorge and seen her plunge over to her death.

Even now, eighteen months later, the memory of the way she had almost floated towards the edge of the precipice in a weird kind of slow motion that no one had been able to stop could still make Imogen shiver with horror.

"So are we going to parade in front of your father, or shall we get out of uniform and pretend everything's back to normal?" Helen's bright voice broke in.

"Let's change," Immy said swiftly. "It will be soon enough to remind him when we have to report for duty after the weekend."

Helen gave her a quick hug. "I'm really going to miss you, Immy. Whatever happened to our plans of joining up together and staying together? It would have been such a lark. And now we're reporting to different units and being sent Lord knows where."

"Well, I'm sure *you* needn't worry. Your father's got influence, and I daresay you'll get a cushy job. Mine's just a shopkeeper..."

"But you've got the brains, darling," Helen told her lightly. "Just like that little sister of yours. And Elsie's got her man."

Elsie Caldwell Preston wasn't feeling anything like as perky as everyone said you were supposed to feel when you were expecting. In fact, if anyone had bothered to ask her right now, she would have told them she felt decidedly wretched. Doctor Wolfe had told her she was definitely two months pregnant, if not a little more, and of course she was delighted about the fact – and more than a little scared.

If only Joe had been here to share this time with her – if only these were normal times, instead of months into a war that seemed to have been forecast for ages beforehand, and now seemed be going nowhere... but where people all around her were joining up and taking part, while all she had to do was sit and twiddle her thumbs and feel utterly frustrated...

She felt the weak tears fill her eyes and told herself she was being a fool. It was also a little shaming, as if she resented the fact that she was going to have their baby, which of course she didn't. It was just that she had never felt this way before. She had never felt so helpless and so vulnerable – and so alone, without Joe's support.

Even here, in the little flat that her father had put at their disposal for as long as they wanted it, she was alone. She was terribly proud that Joe had enlisted the minute he could and hadn't waited for conscription, and of course she adored him and was deliriously happy to be married to him... but being married also meant that she couldn't do her bit for the war effort like her sisters and her brother Baz, and being pregnant meant she was going to grow fat and ugly…

Without thinking she put her hand protectively over her belly, where the uncomfortable stitch was starting to nag at her again. But with the thought of becoming fat and ugly came more of that swift shame, because it seemed to imply that she didn't want this baby.

And she did. Of course she did. It was something precious that belonged to her and Joe alone. Something they had made out of their love for one another. Some*one*. A real little person.

Sometimes, in the long hours of the night when she couldn't sleep, she tried to imagine the baby's face. Tried to see herself bathing it and feeding it and dressing it. Tried to imagine it as that living, breathing little person, instead of the rather hideous diagrams the midwife had given her that showed a baby's progress inside a mother's womb.

She didn't want diagrams of that odd little froglike creature with its sightless eyes and half-formed limbs. She yearned to hold the real thing in her arms, to have it here and now, as a sort of living proof that Joe was still near, still beside her in his baby son or daughter, like a talisman…

She shivered, not wanting to admit to anyone how fearful she was for Joe. It wasn't the way women were supposed to behave in wartime. They were supposed to be strong and stoical and keep the home fires burning and all that stiff-upper-lipped patriotic business. But it wasn't so easy in the chill of the night when you remembered all you had read in the newspapers that day about the way the war was going, and the wireless bulletins that were so depressing.

She tried to be more positive, but she didn't have her sisters' capacity for it, and never had had. Elsie was quieter and more of a thinker than Daisy, who plunged into everything with equal enthusiasm. She was far less strong than Imogen, whom they all looked up to as the older, clever sister who could do no wrong.

Elsie was a failure in her own eyes, and even though Doctor Wolfe had told her these odd moods might trouble her at times, she knew none of it would be half so bad if only Joe was coming home for good instead of forty-eight-hour leave in a few weeks' time. If only Adolph Hitler hadn't started this hateful war...

She jumped as she heard the knock on her door and called out to someone to come in, her voice choking.

"For pity's sake, Elsie, what's wrong?" Immy said in concern, seeing how flushed her sister looked. "You had a letter from Joe this morning, didn't you?" All must be well with him, or Elsie would have told them by now.

"I just feel so miserable without him," Elsie burst out. "I know I'm being a misery, and I'm not the only one to be left alone in wartime..."

"Far from it, darling," Immy said drily.

"But I keep getting this wretched nausea all the time, and you know how I've always hated it."

"Are you following the midwife's suggestions about sipping warm water before you get out of bed in the morning, and eating a dry biscuit or two?"

Elsie gave her a wan smile. "Of course I am. And are you practising to take over her job now with all this new-found knowledge?"

"Not likely! I just want to help, and if she thinks it will work, you should try it, Elsie. If you have our old spirit stove by the bed you can heat up some water without moving a muscle. I'll find it for you."

"Oh, I'm sure it was thrown out long ago," Elsie said, still feeling contrary and not prepared to be pampered.

"No it wasn't. It's in the air-raid shelter with the rest of the emergency supplies, but right now I'd say your need is more urgent than waiting for one of Hitler's bombs to fall on Bristol."

"And I hope you're crossing your fingers when you say that," Elsie said.

## Chapter Two

Daisy hadn't heard from Lucy for several weeks now, and she felt alternately guilty and annoyed with herself. Guilty because she didn't have the nerve to go to the Luckwell farm and ask Lucy's mother what the latest news was; and annoyed because she was a nurse and should be professional enough to deal with whatever she had to face.

She was capable enough when the wounded were brought in from the special trains, and had proved herself on more than one occasion, even when some of the older nurses were trying desperately not to retch at the sight of the men's suppurating wounds and the sickly-sweet gangrenous smells that came from some of the poor devils. But Daisy knew she wasn't completely professional yet. She hadn't had enough experience to be able to hide her feelings when it was her best friend involved in a horrible debilitating disease. She wondered how any normal seventeen-year-old girl coped with being in a sanatorium with old men and women dying of consumption. Being handed out regular sputum dishes and having the disgusting mess examined and assessed was humiliating enough, without watching the rest of them go through the same procedures, and knowing that, at the end of it all, most of them went out of there feet first.

Daisy shuddered; but she had decided that being a nurse was her vocation from the day when Lucy had been in danger of being crushed by her horse and Daisy had had such praise heaped on her for keeping her head in the midst of a panic, knowing exactly what to do for her shock and sprained ankle.

Minor things, she thought now, dismissing them. Like taping up Nessa's cut finger and reassuring the patient with her own childish tale of being afraid of clouds… which was perfectly true. They were all minor things that anyone could cope with who had an ounce of gumption.

But this was something else. Something that was tearing the Luckwell family apart, and Daisy too. Even Aunt Rose, who had known Lucy and her family far longer than Daisy had, usually came back from her visits to the farm with a grim face. At those times, Daisy guessed that even Lucy's no-nonsense mother had been unable to resist spilling out all her anguish to her old friend.

"It's just not fair!" she said out loud, forgetting where she was for the moment.

The young soldier whose leg she had been binding looked at her in astonishment, not knowing how her thoughts sometimes went off at a tangent while she did the routine jobs on the ward.

"Crikey, nursey, you've got a bee in your bonnet today, aincher? What ain't fair, for Gawd's sake? I mean, we all know this bleedin' war ain't fair, and my having half a leg on the port side ain't fair, but a pretty young miss like you shouldn't have anything troublin' you, unless it's the fact that you and me can't go dancin' tonight, what with my iffy leg and all…"

Daisy laughed at his nonsense. "Stop it, Private Webb. There's nothing wrong with your leg that a few weeks' treatment won't cure, and you'll be up and dancing with the best of them in no time."

"How about it then?" he asked slyly. "There's nothing in the rules that says a nurse can't go dancin' with her patient, is there?"

"Not that I'm aware of…"

"Except that a bobby-dazzler like you is sure to have a boy somewhere, I'll bet. Come on now, what's his name?"

"You're a terrible flirt, Private Webb, and I'm not telling you," Daisy said with a giggle.

"Ah-hah, so there is somebody then! Just my luck when I'd found the girl of my dreams." He put his hand over his heart dramatically.

"Stop it, for goodness' sake, or you'll have Sister after me," Daisy told him, finishing off the leg-binding and admiring the neat job she had made of it.

"All right then, but remember to save the last dance for me," he called out after her as she swished away.

She grimaced at the task the nurse at the next bed was performing, knowing that her patient wouldn't be dancing ever again, or doing anything else, for that matter. His number was well and truly up, and he hadn't even had a single visitor, Staff Nurse Hetty had said indignantly, even though they'd informed his relatives. Some of them just couldn't face it, she had added derisively.

Remembering those words, Daisy resolved to cycle over to the Luckwell farm as soon as she had finished her shift that day. The sanatorium in Wales was too far away for Lucy to receive regular visitors from home, and farming folk couldn't just go off whenever they wanted to.

There were always cows to be milked and livestock to be fed; and anyway, it was forbidden for Daisy to visit Lucy, when she was working in a hospital herself where patients had open wounds and were so susceptible to infection. But she owed it to the Luckwells to visit them as often as possible, as she had promised Lucy she would.

–

At least her friend was well away from any dangers of bombing, Daisy thought ironically, as she left the hospital on that blustery March afternoon, bending low over her handlebars as she cycled towards the rural part of the town beyond the miles of sand and seafront. She could have kept to the inland streets and avoided this always windy part of Weston, but she liked to come this way, because it was where she had literally bumped into Cal for the first time.

The stinging in her eyes now, as the sand was whipped up by a strong gust of wind, had as much to do with wondering where the dickens the Air Force was sending him, as with the saltiness of the sea air. Daisy was in love, and although she didn't exactly envy her sister Elsie for expecting a baby so soon after being married, she certainly envied her the closeness with Joe that had produced it.

You didn't say so to anyone, of course. Such thoughts were best kept private or else you might be thought of as fast. But when you were a nurse, you were privileged to witness sights and sounds that other people weren't; and she had listened to more than one soldier's confession about how much he loved his girl, and the things they did together, while wondering if they would ever be able to do them again. She had washed and dried every part of their bodies, and joked with them over sizes and shapes, and wept secretly at their desperation that things might never be the same again for many of them – and not only in the baby-making department, either, as Staff Nurse Hetty called it, but in losing confidence in regaining their old jobs, or in facing their families or going home a wreck of a man.

It was tragic in many ways, and Daisy had already vowed fiercely that if Cal came safely home again – which of course he *would* – if he asked her to give in to him, she would. She definitely *would*. Only a hard-hearted harpy would send a man away to war without giving him what he craved the most…

The fact that Cal had never been anything but the perfect gentleman made such a vow easy to keep, of course, and he had never even touched her bosom except very tentatively on the outside of all her clothes; but Daisy wouldn't think about that. She was a romantic – she was Guinevere to his Lancelot – and she loved him so much, she would give him anything.

"Here, watch where you're going, miss," she heard someone shout, and swerved to avoid the small column of air cadets marching along the seafront.

She heard them snigger and one of them made a rude gesture towards her, making her face burn. *Snot-rag*, she thought crudely, using one of Uncle Bert's least attractive expletives; but then her face softened as she watched them march away, with their leader barking orders at them. Cal had been one of them not so long ago, and they would all be sent far from home, the same as he had been. She and Lucy had taken a special delight in riding their horses as close to the Locking Camp periphery fence as they had dared, where they could watch the air cadets doing their training. It all seemed a very long time ago now. It seemed as if all of them had aged a hundred years instead of less than one.

–

"Daisy, my lamb, 'tis good to see you," Mrs Luckwell exclaimed at once, when she arrived hot and breathless at the farm. "Your auntie's always telling me how busy you are these days with your nursing, so I'm glad you can spare a bit of time to come and jaw with us."

Daisy knew it wasn't meant as a reproach, but right now she was sensitive enough to see it that way.

"I've been meaning to come for ages," she said quickly. "I'm sorry it's been such a long time, Mrs Luckwell—"

"There now, you mustn't think there's a need. Lucy wouldn't want to think you felt obligated to us on her account."

"I haven't heard from her for a few weeks," she said, when she had been given a large glass of home-made lemonade and a slice of Mrs Luckwell's seed cake. "That's why I'm here really. What's the latest news?"

"Not so good, my dear." She spoke without expression, which to Daisy's trained ear meant that 'not so good' meant 'pretty bad'. "Some days I almost wish the Good Lord would – but 'tis wrong to think that way. He'll choose her moment in His own good time."

For a moment Daisy didn't follow. When she did, she was shocked.

"You don't mean you want her to… to…"

"To die? Daisy, love, you must have seen plenty of folk going from this world to the next by now, and 'tis often more of a blessing than a sadness."

"But those are *old* people. Or badly wounded soldiers who haven't got a hope of surviving. Lucy's your daughter. My friend. She's only seventeen…"

"And she's dying slowly. By inches, you might say. If 'twere one of our beasts, we'd have it put down painlessly and there'd be an end to it."

Daisy didn't know to answer her. Uncle Bert said often enough that farming folk had a different philosophy from the rest of them. Animals were part of their lives, to be fatted and slaughtered when necessary, and they couldn't afford to be sentimental over them. In farmers' eyes, people were not so different. Unless they were talking about a *daughter*...

"I've shocked you, haven't I, Daisy?" she heard Lucy's mother say quietly. "But you mustn't think we don't care. It's a kind of safety valve, see? And once it blows – well..."

Whatever else she was going to say was interrupted by the door being flung open and two small figures rushing inside, followed by one large one. The brother and sister stopped as soon as they saw the visitor with the bright-red hair that Daisy tried in vain to keep tidy at the hospital, while the older fellow's face split into a wide grin.

"We ain't seen you around here lately, Daisy. Ma was saying the same thing t'other day, weren't you, Ma?"

"*Ben!*" Mrs Luckwell chided her bumbling son. "If you can't say something pleasant..."

Daisy saw how his face reddened. He wasn't the brightest of young men, and she had always felt a mite sorry for him. "It's all right, Mrs Luckwell. I know it's been a while. So how are you, Ben? Taking to baby-sitting, I see."

"We ain't babies," the boy with the cockney accent said indignantly. "We've been doing a special job, feeding the pigs."

"I can tell that by the smell. And who are you?" Daisy asked him, knowing very well that these were the evacuees Lucy's mother hadn't wanted, but whom she was fussing over now like the proverbial mother hen.

"I'm Cyril Jenkins and this is me sister Tess. Are you a nurse or summat?"

"That's right," Daisy told him. "You're a bright boy, aren't you?"

"Nah. Knew it by the uniform, didn't I? The nurse used to come to our 'ouse every day to stick a needle in me mum before she died."

"Oh." He said it so matter-of-factly Daisy didn't know what to say. He must be around seven-going-on-forty, she thought, seeing the wise old eyes in that so-young face. Tess looked even younger, but she spoke up suddenly.

"Our mum had the sugar, miss."

"She means—" Mrs Luckwell began under her breath.

"I know what she means," Daisy told her.

She knew that in the worst cases, sugar diabetes could bring on a coma and even death, and maybe this was what had happened to the Jenkins mother. She sympathised with these two, having lost her own mother, though in very different circumstances; and her little brother Teddy hadn't been much younger than them when it happened. She switched her thoughts abruptly.

"I'll have to be going, Mrs Luckwell," she said next. "But if you ever want these two off your hands for an afternoon sometime, shall I ask Aunt Rose if they can come to tea with our little crowd?"

"That would be nice," Mrs Luckwell beamed. "Providing young Vanessa don't put on her airs and graces. These little 'uns have had enough trouble in their short lives, what with their mum dying, and their dad wanting 'em out of the way for the duration."

Everything had changed since the war began, Daisy thought, pedalling back towards the town and up to Aunt Rose and Uncle Bert's rambling old house. Families were being split up all the time, and if you didn't know the full circumstances – who could blame the Jenkins father for wanting his two little ones out of the way when bombs were falling? Most children were being sent to the country for safety, well away from London and the south-east counties.

It made her start thinking about how her own family had been split up, long before the war came. It had all begun with her mother's death, and the fact that her father's once proud business had been bought up by a northern emporium. What a disaster that had seemed at the time, and how it had all faded into far less importance now. Weirdly so, thought Daisy, especially since if it had never happened, then Elsie would never have met Joe and got married, and her father wouldn't have become the manager, if not the owner, of his shop once again, since all the young men had gone away to war anyway. It was definitely weird, the way things worked out.

Aunt Rose would have said there was an Almighty Design in all these things, of course, along with her churchy friends; but Daisy wasn't so sure of any of that any more. Not since her mother had died, and not since the war had started that nobody wanted, and definitely not since she had seen some of the hideous injuries she was faced with every single day.

A loving God shouldn't allow these things to happen, and Daisy wasn't sure she believed in anything except the need to survive. She dismissed all those moments that were almost like revelations when some poor dying soldier prayed to God to let him go… and more than one of them had sworn that they glimpsed this long white tunnel and some heavenly light at the end of it…

It was all a myth, and you might as well believe in fairies. Daisy didn't believe any of it – nor the way some of the older nurses swore they had seen guardian angels hovering near their charges in the still of the night… It gave Daisy the shivers, though it was a non-belief she didn't dare to share with anyone else, least of all Aunt Rose, who would be horrified at such blasphemy.

When she heard the sounds of children's shrieks and laughter, she realised she had already reached the house. She opened the gate with relief, glad to put all these uneasy thoughts behind her. Aunt Rose told everyone approvingly that she was growing up into a sensible young lady. But Daisy wasn't at all sure she wanted to be sensible. Not if it meant facing things beyond her understanding.

She was basically an optimist, but there were also darker moments when she sometimes felt she spent far too much time with sick people who wanted help in moving from this world to the next, as they put it, instead of having fun, the way any normal seventeen-year-old should. And that was a fine way for a nurse to think, she thought in sudden anger – and not a little shame.

"We've got a visitor, and you'll never guess who it is," Norman was yelling at her now, prancing around with his brother like two small whirling dervishes.

"Me mum's come to see us," Ronnie shrieked. "She's having a cuppa tea wiv Auntie Rose and Uncle Bert."

"Good Lord," was all Daisy could say.

She saw her brother Teddy playing with George in the corner of the garden, and the dog was going wild, leaping up and down after the yo-yo Teddy was teasing him with. There was no sign of Vanessa.

"Me mum's going to take us 'ome soon," Ronnie said confidently.

"Is she?" Daisy said, doubting it. What kind of a crazy woman would take her kids back to Kent, with its proximity to London, when they had the comparative peace and security of the south-west countryside?

She went inside the house, to find her aunt and uncle in the middle of a fine old harangue with a blowsy-looking woman in a shabby coat and down-at-heel shoes. She was shouting at Aunt Rose, whose face was getting redder by the minute, Daisy noted, and seemingly out of her depth for once.

"I know you've done your best for 'em, missus, but they're my kids, and they'd be far better off with me than with you. My sister's got a place in Wales with her young man's fam'ly now, and we can all go there for the duration."

She glared at the older couple, daring them to dispute her words. But why would they? wondered Daisy. Unless the woman was lying, and there was no place in Wales for them at all. She certainly had a shifty look about her and didn't ever meet anyone's eyes for more than seconds. The evacuee boys were often more like defensive little devils than angels, but Daisy knew her aunt wouldn't want to see them hawked around the countryside on a whim.

Without thinking twice, she put in her spoke while Aunt Rose was still drawing breath.

"Don't you have to go through the proper channels before settling the boys somewhere else, Mrs... uh... Turvey?" she said, groping in her mind to remember the boys' surname. "I know that's what my aunt and uncle had to do when Vanessa came to stay with us. The billeting officers are very particular about checking each property to see that there's enough accommodation, and that there are suitable hosts for looking after the children."

She knew she shouldn't be taking charge like this, and she didn't quite know where all the words came from. She only knew that she looked and sounded authoritative in her uniform with her usual tangle of curls tamed and swathed on top of her head for neatness and hygiene, since she'd gone straight from her hospital shift to the farm. Her uncle took his cue from her now.

"My niece is quite right, Mrs Turvey. It's good news that you've come to visit the boys, but we're responsible for them now, and we couldn't relinquish that care without checking firstly with our own billeting officers, and then they would refer the transfer request to the billeting people in Wales where your sister lives.

"I think you'll find that's the legal requirement," he added, having no idea whether it was or not, and pretty sure that no such thing applied to any case where a child's own mother wanted to remove him. But he counted on the fact that Mrs Turvey wouldn't know that. It was obvious that she wasn't an educated woman, and heaven knew where her husband was in all this. She might want custody of her children back for some other reason, maybe to get extra housing assistance, or to plead poverty with her local council, or even to get extra rations.

The Lord knew her reasons, and He wasn't telling, Bert thought grimly, but there were plenty of devious goings-on these days. He also knew how attached Rose had got to all these children filling their empty old house, and he wasn't having two of them taken away from her without being sure the cause was genuine.

Besides, in all these months the Turvey woman had only written a couple of sketchy letters to her boys and not even sent them a Christmas card. He hardened his heart against what some would have seen as a loving mother's request, and then Rose spoke up crisply.

"So what do you think, Mrs Turvey?" she said, her equilibrium restored as she saw the indecision in the woman's eyes. "Naturally, you must do as you think best, but Norman and Ronnie are quite settled now, and it would be a shame to disrupt them all over again. Of course, the bed-wetting did take quite a while to over-come," she added, as if as an afterthought. "But if it starts all over again, I'm sure your sister and her young man's family will be understanding."

Mrs Turvey gave a small shudder. "P'raps I should think about this some more before I decide for sure. I'm told the house in Wales ain't very big, and it may not be so suitable."

"I think that's a very wise decision," Rose said. "Now, another cup of tea before you go?"

–

It was inevitable that Ronnie would wet the bed that night. It hadn't happened for weeks now, but Daisy told Elsie on the telephone that weekend that you couldn't blame a mother for wanting to see her boys, even though it meant a certain amount of emotional disruption. Daisy had recently begun a course of instruction on emotional disturbance, though mainly with regard to servicemen having to face civvy life again, whether it was limbless or sightless – or even having a complete mental breakdown.

"Some of these poor kids don't know where they are these days," Daisy went on, with seventeen-year-old wisdom.

"Ah, you're really enjoying playing Miss Nightingale, aren't you, Daisy?" she heard her sister say, with an unmistakable smile in her voice.

"It's what I do, isn't it? You'll be glad of someone like me in a few months' time, earth mother, so don't scoff."

"Would I dare? I'm only teasing, darling, you know that. Actually, I'd be glad of someone like you right now, if you could tell me why I keep feeling so horribly nauseous all the time."

"Have you told Doctor Wolfe?"

Elsie sighed. "Oh, he has enough to do without a perfectly healthy expectant mother fretting over the slightest thing. Besides, I'm under the midwife's care now, and she says it's perfectly normal at this stage. And before you ask, I've done everything Immy suggested, including having the camping stove by my bed and sipping hot water every morning before I get up. It works – but I'm sick at night too, so what's your diagnosis for that, oh great doctor?"

Daisy grinned. "I'd say Immy's missed her vocation, if she's advising you on morning sickness! How is she, by the way? More to the point, *where* is she?"

"Oh, somewhere in Oxford now, I believe," Elsie said vaguely. "All set to be a driver for some army bigwig."

There was no mistaking the misery and frustration in Elsie's voice now. This was supposed to be one of the happiest times in a woman's life, wasn't it? Daisy thought. She tried to cheer her up.

"Never mind, Joe's coming home on leave any day, and I'm sure you won't be worrying too much about morning sickness then!" she added daringly.

"I hope not. It would be too awful – but I'm not going to talk about such things with you, little sister, so stop fishing!" she said with a laugh.

After they finished talking, Daisy set about tidying her room as she always did on a Sunday evening when the whole household had come back from church. They were quite a little crocodile now, she reflected, with the boys bellowing out the hymns, and Vanessa pooh-poohing the whole thing, despite the fact that she always joined in lustily, and had quite a sweet singing voice.

By now, Daisy's own voice had been discovered, courtesy of Aunt Rose's insistence, and she was in the choir, despite any feelings she may or may not have about the ethics of joining in a service in which she had no real belief; but she enjoyed the music so much that she went along anyway. It wasn't treading on her mother's professional toes, either, since Frances Caldwell had sung modern ditties on the stage and danced like an angel.

Daisy paused in the midst of her tidying, burying her nose for a moment in a soft mauve cardigan that reminded her of one of her mother's. It didn't do to dwell on the past these days, when they all had to get through difficult times, but when the past held the sweetest memories, it was hard not to yearn for them.

That must be the way Elsie would be yearning for her Joe right now. The thought was in Daisy's head before she could stop it. She didn't *want* to imagine what they did. She didn't *want* to admit to anyone that she knew very well how a man's body looked, because it was part of her job to know and understand the workings of bodily functions. She knew about sex. Not that she had ever experienced it, of course, but she knew the mechanics, which sounded so clinical; but that was the way the medical books explained it. Some of the older nurses were more explicit, though, she thought with a grin.

She didn't really *want* to wonder how it would be for her and Callum Monks, if he ever came back into her life again. But sometimes she did, however guiltily. Sometimes she just couldn't help thinking of those pleasures of the flesh, as they were referred to in the Bible, if only to take her mind off the awful things she had to do in the hospital, and to remind herself that she was young and in love, and a perfectly normal and healthy young woman.

"Daisy! What on earth are you doing up there?" she heard Aunt Rose's voice call out from the parlour below. "We're all waiting to have a game of charades before the little ones go to bed."

That just about summed up her life, she thought ruefully, feeling the heat in her face. Longing for something she couldn't have, without ever knowing quite what it was… and spending the next hour or so in the company of bawling, squabbling infants and her doting relatives, playing a game of charades.

# Chapter Three

Imogen Caldwell, now Private Caldwell, reported for duty at the army unit just outside Oxford with a mixture of excitement and apprehension. It was one thing to drive to Weston and back in the big old family Rover car that was mostly relegated to standing in the road with no petrol in its tank now. It was quite another to have been assigned as official driver to a Captain Grayson Beckett, Royal Engineers, whom she was about to meet that morning. She couldn't deny that she was a little fearful. The last time James had been home on leave and she had told him of her intentions, his comical descriptions of officers had made them sound like ogres.

"They either have barking voices you can hear a mile away, or they talk with a mouthful of plums, don't-ya-know, and they look down their noses at you as if you've just crawled out from under a stone. You don't want to have any truck with officers, Immy!"

"I don't have much choice if I want the driving job, do I?" she had said, feeling ridiculously irked by his teasing words. "Unless you think I should join you as a co-driver in your blessed tank?"

He had sobered at once, hearing the uncertainty in her normally strong voice. He gathered her to him, murmuring against her hair, glad that she couldn't see his eyes and the knowledge there.

"That's the last thing I want, darling. Bertha's a one-man tank, and you're a one-man woman – I hope."

"Of course I am." She had wrenched away from him. "You know that, don't you? You don't think I shall start falling for a fancy officer's uniform, do you?"

James laughed softly, confident of her feelings for him. "I do not. And I'm only teasing. I'm sure your officer will be a perfect gentleman, sweetheart, so let's forget him, and think about more important things – like you and me."

She had capitulated at once. Safe in James's embrace then, with his kisses warm on her lips, it had been easy to forget her qualms. But now he was far away, and she was here, about to knock on the door of this office, not knowing what was awaiting her on the other side of it.

"So you're Private Caldwell," the officer said with a smile. "Do sit down, and don't look so scared. I'm not known for eating young ladies."

Imogen sat. He wasn't at all like she had expected. For one thing, he wasn't young, and he wasn't old. About her father's age, she guessed, which presumably meant he was a regular soldier and hadn't been conscripted because there was a war on. He had a round, jovial face, and the buttons on his jacket were slightly strained as if he had eaten too well lately.

"Well? Do I pass the test?" he asked, his well-bred voice having just a hint of the south-west in it that reassured her immensely.

"I'm sorry, sir. I didn't mean to stare," she said, acutely embarrassed at knowing she had been doing exactly that.

"That's all right. Since we'll be spending plenty of time together, it would be a tragedy if we hated one another on sight, wouldn't it? Now then," he went on more briskly, shuffling papers about on his desk, "let's get down to business, Private Caldwell. You're from Bristol, I believe, which is not so far removed from my home in Devon, so we have something in common. And you're a competent driver, I take it?"

"Yes, sir." She was on safer ground now, sure of her abilities. "I'm also a typist and I'm good with figures," she added for good measure.

"Good God, have I found myself an angel?" Grayson Beckett said with a smile. "I have a secretary who sees to all my admin work, but there may be occasions when your other talents come in useful, Private."

Immy's heart missed a beat at the word, but there was nothing in the least suggestive in his manner, and she was certain he meant exactly what he said. She hadn't realised she was still so sensitive over innuendoes – ever since her best friend Helen had been taken in by Joe's cousin Robert and nearly come to grief.

At the time Immy had stormed the hotel where Robert Preston was staying, and dealt with him very efficiently, but the legacy had left her wary of double meanings. Thankfully, she realised now that Captain Beckett hadn't meant any such thing. Her other talents were simply that.

He stood up with a smile and held out his hand to her.

"You'll want to settle in to your quarters today, Private, and I'll see you here at nine-thirty hours tomorrow morning."

"Yes, sir," Immy said smartly, shaking his hand and then stepping back a pace before saluting.

"Actually, it's a bit of a lark here," she told her father on the telephone later that day. "It doesn't feel as if we're in the middle of a war at all, though some of the other girls have heard rumours that the regiment's being sent to France soon. But you know what rumours are."

Quentin Caldwell didn't take her levity so complacently. "Just take care, Immy. Personally, I'd rather have all you girls safely home in Bristol."

"I know, but we have to do our bit nowadays, don't we, Father? And I always wanted to travel, didn't I?"

She wasn't aware that she had, but it seemed as good a way as any to put his mind at rest. And to change the subject quickly. "What about Baz? Have you heard from him lately?"

Her father snorted. "He's talking about joining the Navy now, the young idiot. He's far too young, of course, and he's impatient for the war to last a few years so he can enlist. He doesn't know what he's talking about, and I've warned him not to push his age on so that they take him. He's working on a trawler now, and I even had to hear that news from the old ferryman he used to work for. His letter to me came a few days after I happened to meet old Enoch."

Immy wasn't sure whether pride in his son's ingenuity or annoyance at his deceit was uppermost right then.

"He'll do all right, Father. Baz always did," she said.

When they finished speaking, she put down the telephone carefully. If things had been different, she would have added, *Give my love to Mother.* But if things had been different, the country wouldn't have been at war with Germany, and she wouldn't have been wearing a khaki uniform and about to bunk in with five other girls in a communal barracks where there was little chance of privacy.

The thought of it gave her a small shiver, and she told herself she mustn't be snobbish. She was used to sharing life with her two sisters, and to a certain extent her close friend, Helen; but sharing with strangers was something that none of them had ever contemplated. The old saying that war made strange bedfellows was certainly true, she thought – not even sure that she had the words right, but they rang true enough, and that was all that mattered.

In the barracks, apart from her bed, she only had a locker for her clothes and personal things – somewhere to keep her precious letters from James, including the one that had come only that week that was heavily censored, but marked 'somewhere in France'. Which was one of the reasons she hoped the other girls were right, and that she too would be going to France.

"Fancy a game of dominoes before lights-out, Caldwell?" one of them called to her. She didn't really, but she joined them, if only to be sociable.

–

In Weston-super-Mare that evening Bert Painter was finding it hard to be sociable to the three evacuees in his care. Rose could overlook their annoying little habits, but he didn't like lies and he couldn't abide the sneaking little tales they told on one another. The two Turvey boys were still young and impressionable, but the Brown girl should know better. And one of them had taken two pence from the mantelpiece. It wasn't so much the paltry amount, as the lies they were all intent on inventing about it.

"If one of you doesn't own up, then all three of you will have to be punished," he snapped, wishing Rose was here to deal with this, instead of out at her church choir meeting with Daisy.

Teddy was snuggling in a corner, hugging George as if he would smother the dog, while the other three young-uns squabbled amongst themselves, each accusing the other.

"You're worse than bloomin' Hitler," Vanessa burst out finally. "I didn't take yer bloomin' money, so it must be one of them."

"Well, it weren't me, pig-face," yelled Norman. "And if it weren't you and it weren't me, then it must be our Ronnie."

His brother went a dull shade of puce, and they all saw the tell-tale dark stain begin to creep over his shorts in his fright at being accused.

"I ain't got it!" Ronnie shrieked. "I ain't no pick-pocket."

"Now look what he's gone and done!" Vanessa snapped. "He's gone and peed himself again."

"I hate you!" Ronnie screamed at her, tears bursting out of his eyes now, as he threw himself flat on the floor and banged it with his head.

"Silly little devil will end up with a head like a bloomin' hangover if he ain't careful," Vanessa crowed knowledge-ably.

"Be quiet, Vanessa, and leave him to me. You're just making things worse," Bert shouted, hauling a bleating Ronnie to his feet as the door opened.

"What on earth's going on in here?" Rose gasped. "Daisy and I could hear you all along the street. Has there been an accident?"

"Only the usual," Vanessa said sulkily, unable to resist the barb.

As Ronnie looked imploringly towards Daisy for sympathy, she took him out of her uncle's grip and cuddled him, ignoring the bitter smells that wafted up from shorts that had known previous wettings and were never quite rid of them, no matter how many scrubbings they endured.

"Come on, sweetie, let's get you cleaned up and into your pyjamas, while Auntie Rose sorts out the rest of them," she told him.

"Is she going to hit me?" he said fearfully.

"Of course not," Daisy said quickly, wondering how often this had been the case in times past.

"Well, I didn't take the money…"

"What money is this?" Rose said at once.

"On the mantelpiece. The two pence that you always leave there for the newspaper boy," Bert said shortly.

"I paid him before I left," Rose said. "Is that what all this rumpus was about?"

"*See?*" Vanessa yelled at Bert, her eyes flashing triumphantly. "'Tweren't us at all. I *told* you it bloomin' well weren't!"

"And how was I supposed to know that?" he said angrily.

"You'd better say you're sorry, Uncle Bert," Daisy said softly.

"Well, of course I'm sorry…"

"Not to me. To them."

It wasn't her place to challenge him, and she didn't really know why she was doing so. She just knew how they must all feel, to be falsely accused when they were all so vulnerable; and from the way Ronnie was shuddering against her, dampening her frock in the process, she knew how hard he had taken all this fuss. He might like to appear like a little toughie, but he was only a baby…

"I'm sorry, children," her uncle said to them all now, struggling to keep his dignity. "I was wrong, but if we can all be all friends again, now is as good a time as any to tell you what we've got planned for tomorrow. Since the weather's so fine, we're all going to start on a project when you get home from school."

"What's a project?" Norman asked suspiciously, as Teddy came out of the shadows, releasing a relieved George, and Ronnie stopped shuddering.

"We're going to dig for victory," Bert declared. "Auntie Rose and I have decided we're going to dig up the back garden and plant vegetables, and you can each have a little plot to grow your own."

"Is that all?" Vanessa said scornfully. "I hate vegetables anyway."

"You'll go hungry then," Bert told her.

He stared her out, and she finally shrugged and went back to the *Beano* she had been reading, while Daisy took Ronnie upstairs to get him cleaned up, told him he wasn't in disgrace, and that, if he wanted her to, she would help him dig his very own garden plot.

He threw his arms around her neck. "I love you, Daisy," he whispered.

"I love you too, Ronnie," she told him.

Then, still snuffling, he hesitated before asking: "Daisy, what's a plot?"

On days like these, Daisy decided she definitely wasn't going to have children. They were exhausting – and if she felt like that at seventeen, she thought weakly, heaven knew how older women coped with having them and looking after them. Heaven knew how Elsie was going to cope, but maybe it was different when it was a baby that you and your husband had made because you were so much in love. Just like her and Cal... or at least, how she believed it was for her and Cal.

Sometimes she wondered if it was all a fantasy. Maybe she was just enjoying the fact of being in love without thinking beyond the excitement of meeting him on the beach, and writing long letters, and hearing his voice on the telephone. And when none of that seemed to have happened for ages, even pining away for him had its own poignant charm.

Being a romantic, Daisy could see the sweet tragedy of it all, of being Juliet without her Romeo... but that was as far as the imagination went, because she certainly didn't want to end up like *them*. She and Cal weren't exactly star-crossed lovers... they weren't lovers at all, in the real sense of the word.

She pushed the erotic thought out of her head. Sometimes she wondered if her nature was too shallow for her to *really* be in love, the way Elsie and Joe were in love. The way Immy and James were in love. Sometimes she thought she was far more like Helen Church than either of her sisters – happy to flirt and play at being in love, but never seriously thinking of what settling down meant.

She pulled a face at her reflection now, as she pulled the confining pins out her hair and shook it loose. *Settling down* had such a middle-aged sound to it, and she was far from ready for that yet. Even though she was sure she did love Cal, and absence was supposed to make the heart grow fonder, she wasn't at all sure that her earlier thought of *giving in to him* was such a good idea now. At least not until she was much, much older. It was just too final a commitment, and once a person had carnal knowledge of another person, it would be going against all the Bible's teachings not to be true to him for ever.

Anyway, perhaps he wouldn't even ask her.

She turned away from the mirror, flopping down on her bed and staring up at the ceiling, and feeling more restless than she had any right to be. She was here in a loving home, full of people that she loved, doing a job that she loved, and yet something was missing. Not her darling mother or the rest of her family. Not even Cal. It was something else. Something that everybody else had, and she didn't. And she wasn't thinking of *that*, either.

After a long while, she sat up slowly, realising exactly what was missing. Since she had never been one to waste time wishing for something if she could do something about it, she knew exactly what she had to do.

–

"No, Daisy, you're far too young, and I forbid it," her father said, when he came down to Weston to visit them that weekend, hot and bothered from taking the train in order to save precious petrol in the car.

Daisy looked up, flushed, from the patch of earth she was forking over for Ronnie, since he'd got fed up with the whole idea of making a vegetable plot for the moment, and had wandered indoors looking for Teddy and George.

"How can you say I'm too young! Baz is younger than me and he's already gone to sea."

"And you know my feelings on that," Quentin said grimly. "But my dear girl, you're already doing a fine job of nursing in a hospital and seeing sights no young girl should be subjected to, in my opinion. So why on earth would you want to join up and do exactly the same as you're doing now? I can't see the point, darling."

"*I* can, Daddy. I know I'm a good nurse, but I'm stuck here, and I want to be in the thick of it…"

"Oh, for pity's sake, Daisy, listen to yourself," Quentin said, quickly losing patience. "War is not a game, my dear, and you're not Florence Nightingale."

She flinched, hating him for belittling her, especially as the precocious Vanessa was probably skulking somewhere near, listening to every word.

"I'm not pretending to be any better than any other nurse, Daddy," she went on, struggling to keep calm. "I just feel that I want to go farther afield. I never thought war was a game, and I see the evidence of it every day on the wards, remember."

"And you just remember that you'd need my agreement before you did anything so foolish as enlisting, Daisy. If not legally, then out of respect for me."

She wouldn't mind betting that Baz wouldn't wait for his father's approval. But boys seemed able to get away with anything.

She couldn't hide her anger and frustration now, but the idea had been growing inside her for days, and she hadn't even recognised it for what it was. Nor could she hide – except from everybody else – the other, more shameful reason for wanting to get away from here and everyone she knew. In the midst of the undoubted excitement and drama of wanting to be in the thick of it, despite all its dangers and heartbreaks, there was something far less noble lurking in the back of her mind.

If she was away from home – even out of the country – then when the inevitable news came through about Lucy, then maybe she wouldn't feel it quite so personally and emotionally. It was cowardly, and she knew it, and it was something she would never have dared to admit to anyone else.

"I never imagined you wanting to be a boy, darling," she heard her father say more whimsically, as if he realised how tense she had become, without ever guessing the truth of it. "You're far too much your mother's daughter for that."

She felt her eyes mist at once, knowing this was a kind of emotional blackmail, but loving him all the same for being able to talk about his wife in that calm manner, and for comparing her in any way to her delicate, beautiful mother.

She hugged his arm and told him she certainly wouldn't want to be tossed about on the ocean, thank you very much! And resisting the thought that, to get anywhere out of England at all, it would mean going by ship, unless you were Cal, of course, and flew aeroplanes…

"So shall we just give ourselves time to think about it, Daisy?"

"All right. It was only an idea, anyway," she mumbled, knowing it was more than that, but satisfied for the moment that he was even considering it.

"And at least I have one daughter safely at home," he went on with a smile. "Elsie's busy sewing for the baby now, and of course, with her skills, the child will have the best layette outside the royal family!"

Daisy laughed, sticking her garden fork into the little patch she had dug for Ronnie, and deciding that it was enough work for one day, especially as the little wretch had left most of it to her. She linked arms with her father as they strolled indoors to join the rest of the family.

"It's a far cry from creating hats for the city gentry though, isn't it, Daddy?"

"It is, but I doubt that Elsie thinks she's got a poorer bargain, my love. Joe's home on leave this weekend, which is why I decided that now would be a good time for me to let them have the whole house to themselves."

–

Safe in her husband's arms during these precious few days and nights, Elsie wished that times like these could go on for ever. They couldn't, of course. There was a war on, even though it didn't seem much like it lately, and everyone was calling it the phoney war and wondering when anything was going to happen.

It was short-sighted to be having such thoughts, of course, because everyone also knew that war was very much a reality in Europe. Hitler's planes were bombing cities and towns, and by now, nearing April, the enemy's grip was being firmly felt all over Europe. Finland had capitulated to the mighty Russian Red Army, and all the Scandinavian countries were in imminent peril.

Elsie's geography had never been particularly good, but like everyone else she felt it her duty to know what was going on, and to follow the events of the war on the wireless and in the newspapers, even though it had hardly touched her personally. Apart from Joe going to war, and there was nothing more personal in her life than that...

"Come back, my love," she heard Joe whisper in her ear as he felt her shudder. "What were you thinking about?"

She swallowed her fears for him, in case saying them out loud was tempting fate. And although it wasn't patriotic, she didn't want him to go away, she thought passionately. She didn't want him to fight, nor even to be a hero. She wanted him here always, with her and their baby. It was where they all belonged. Soon – far too soon now – they would be saying goodbye again, and this time she was very sure he would be heading for France. If the fighting wasn't on their own English soil – and thank God it wasn't, she added silently – then the servicemen fighting for God and country had to go wherever the fighting led them. She knew it, but it didn't make it any easier.

As if his thoughts echoed hers, she felt him rest his hand lightly on the soft swell of her belly beneath the bedclothes on that sunny Sunday morning.

"You don't need to worry, you know," he said softly. "Didn't you know I've got a charmed life?"

She swivelled round in his arms to lie as close as possible to him, feeling his flesh warm against her own, almost as close as if they shared the same skin.

"Can you guarantee that?"

He bent his head to kiss her throat, and his mouth went lower, making her catch her breath with a rush of ecstasy, recognising the swiftly rising desire in him, matching her own. His voice was muffled as he spoke against her breast.

"How can it not be so, when I've got my darling wife to come home to?"

"And our baby," Elsie breathed raggedly.

"And our baby," Joe said, moving slowly downwards beneath the bedclothes to kiss the mound of the child growing there.

She gloried in his love-making, in his gentle, considerate approaches, and the unhurried manner in which he made her ready for him. He was everything she had ever dreamed of in a husband and lover, and each time he made love to her she wept a little, simply because it was all so perfect, and she adored him so much.

Sometimes she was almost afraid that such happiness couldn't last, and that someday there had to be a reckoning for it. But those were crazy, demonic thoughts that normally came in the dark sleepless hours before daylight when the baby was lying awkwardly, and the blissful dreams of Joe were interrupted by darker ones of tragedy and death.

But they were for another time. Not now, when Joe's hands were seeking her warm moist secret places, and she could feel him hard against her, and herself responding as she always did.

"Joe, I love you so much," she gasped out, burying her face in his neck. "I wish – oh, I wish…"

As she felt him enter her and start to move within her, he stilled her words with a deep and passionate kiss. Without the need for words, she knew her dearest wishes were the same as his, and that one day, God willing, they would be together for always.

# Chapter Four

War might be raging in Europe, but as the phoney war in Britain seemed to be making people complacent, many evacuees were being taken back to London and the Home Counties and causing disruption in more than one household.

"It's a big mistake," Bert Painter said, reading aloud the latest newspaper account of the reversing trend. "Old Adolph's got his sights set on England, sure as eggs are eggs, and when he's done with marching through Europe, he'll be looking to invade us. Stands to reason. Poor little kids won't know whether they're coming or going if they end up being sent back to the country all over again. And to different families, probably."

"You don't really think that, do you, Bert?" his wife asked anxiously.

He looked at her sternly. "Now look here, Rose, you know as well as I do that we've only borrowed these little tartars. They've got homes and families of their own to go back to, and it's foolish to get too fond of any of them."

"Tell that to the fairies," Rose scoffed. "You're just as fond of them all as I am, so you don't fool me on that score, Bertie. You're the one who takes the boys out as often as possible, teaching them how to catch fish and playing sand football with them at the beach."

"So I do," he admitted. "And it's something we all enjoy; but they'll be different children by the time they go back to the big cities, won't they? They'll have learned our country ways. Pity it will all have to end."

"Oh, you think it'll be a pity when the war ends, do you?" she said archly.

"I damn well do not, and you know it, woman," he growled. "I was thinking of you and how you've let yourself become far too attached to them, that's all."

"And I suppose you haven't, you old softie?" she said with a laugh. "Anyway, I doubt that ours will be taken back just yet, now that Mrs Turvey's given up the idea of taking her pair to Wales," she added beneath her breath in case any of them was lurking near. But none of the children was up yet, and Teddy practically slept the sleep of the dead until somebody woke him.

"A good thing too. The woman looked no better than she should be," Bert said in response, in what Rose always thought was the daftest statement ever. But it always made her lips twitch, and they were in a more harmonious mood by the time Norman and Ronnie came rushing into the room with a shock announcement.

—

"What do you mean — all her things have gone?" Rose demanded, as Norman hopped up and down with importance, and Ronnie crossed his legs desperately. Fear or excitement always had the same result with Ronnie.

"She's gone back 'ome," Ronnie shrieked, his self-control finally giving up as the waterworks started at both ends. "I wanter go 'ome as well."

Daisy appeared in the doorway, still half-asleep after her night shift at the hospital and none too happy at seeing

Ronnie's darkening trousers after all their efforts to get him dry.

"What's all the noise about?" she snapped.

As Rose rushed out of the room and up the stairs to find out the truth of it all, her uncle told her quickly.

"The boys say that Vanessa's things are missing, and she's gone home."

Daisy stared at him. "She can't have gone home," she said, her thoughts still muddled from being woken up rudely by all the shouting. "She's got no money and she wouldn't know where to go."

But they all knew that she would. Vanessa's East End nous made her far more canny at twelve than many older girls. In her own self-opinionated words, *she knew what it was all about*. She had been doing odd jobs at a local corner shop after school and saving her money for what she said her old gran always called a rainy day. This could just be it.

"The railway station," Bert said now. "She'll obviously have tried to catch a train to London."

Rose came back to the room, her face white. "It's true, Bert. All her clothes and comics are missing and her gas mask too. The little minx…"

"That's not what I'd call her," he said, his face darkening furiously now. "I'm getting down to the railway station now and then on to the police. Lord knows when she left the house, and anything could have happened to her."

Daisy was fully awake now, abandoning any thought of sleep. "Shouldn't we let the billeting officers know as well? They'd have her home address and other contacts. I could do that, if you like."

"You're right, my love," Rose said. "You see to that and I'll clean up Ronnie and get Teddy downstairs. Then we'll have some breakfast and get the house back to some kind of order. It's no use all of us panicking. She might not have gone very far at all and I'm sure she'll be back with us by dinner-time."

She didn't believe it, but she said it to calm down the two young boys, who were looking terrified now that the first excitement had died down. Vanessa had been a thorn in all their flesh from the day she had arrived, but the thought of where she might be now was something Rose didn't care to think about. You heard such awful tales…

"Do you think Nessa's dead?" Norman whispered.

"Of course she's not dead," Rose said briskly. "What an idea! She's being a very silly girl and I'm sure her mother won't be at all pleased that she's given us such a fright."

"Ain't we going 'ome then?" Ronnie howled in searing disappointment.

Rose gave him a hug. "What, and miss Uncle Bert taking you out on Saturday? Uncle Quentin's coming here for the weekend as well, remember, so you'll have two uncles fussing over you."

As she took him upstairs to wash and change him, she knew it wasn't much consolation. No matter what the potential danger, the poor little devils would have much preferred to be at home with their own families, instead of living with strangers. A few months away from home had done nothing to change that, and she was full of sympathy for them.

All the same, she thought more practically, she wished someone would give them a magic cure for Ronnie's evil-smelling undergarments…

Long before Vanessa's disappearance had been discovered, she was sitting beside a cheery driver in a long-distance lorry that was taking her back where she belonged, and even though she was a bit sorry for the fuss it would cause, she couldn't control her excitement at going home. She knew she could pass for much older than she was, especially with a bit of Daisy's lipstick that she'd borrowed, and she had invented a story for the driver about only visiting here for a week or so. She knew her mum would be glad to see her, and if they were short of money, she could always get a Saturday job at the market. Just thinking about it reminded her how much she had missed the jostling streets of home, and she was never going back to the bloomin' country again.

"If the girl's gone back to London, we'll find her," the billeting officer told Daisy. "I'll put a call through to the appropriate department at once, although if her mother accepts her back, you realise that will be the end of it. We don't force these children to come here, Miss Caldwell, and if they're unhappy, there's nothing we can do about it."

"I hope you're not implying that she wasn't well treated at my aunt and uncle's home," Daisy snapped, far too tired to play games with this frosty-faced woman. She should be in bed, not chasing about the town after the ungrateful Nessa Brown.

"Knowing Mr and Mrs Painter, I'm sure she was treated very well," the woman conceded. "But the fact remains, if these children and their parents want to stay together, there's nothing we can do about it."

"But you'll be sure to let us know that she arrived back safely, won't you?" Daisy persisted.

"Naturally. Now, I suggest you go home and let us get on with our job. You'll be informed as soon as we know anything."

Daisy left the Town Hall, feeling snubbed at the woman's unspoken criticism, but not without a sudden grudging admiration for Vanessa's self-confidence in even considering travelling all the way back to London on her own. It made her own move down to Weston with her aunt and uncle seem so much less of an adventure than it had seemed at the time.

Not that the evacuees had ever had any choice, she thought, pitying the smaller ones sent off to Lord-knew-where with their name labels pinned on their chests, and all their possessions in carrier bags or cardboard suitcases with their gas masks slung around their necks. Like a lot of unwanted parcels. Newspaper and cinema pictures of them, herded together on railway stations before the war had even begun, had been heartbreaking – and a major cause of Aunt Rose's determination to take some of them in.

Remembering Aunt Rose now, as she stood outside the Town Hall fuming, sent Daisy back to the house at once, to report her news. Her uncle had returned from the railway station, where no one had seen a young girl waiting for an early-morning train. Even if they had, they would probably not have registered that she was a runaway. Vanessa had the knack of self-composure, and the only time Daisy had seen it slip was at the sight of blood when she had cut her finger on the bread knife.

For a moment she felt a chill run through her. Vanessa was obviously making her way back home to the East End of London; and if the Germans broke through all the south coast defences and started bombing London,

Vanessa might very well see a lot more blood than she had ever seen in her life before…

She stopped surmising and went to make a pot of tea for them all. Her tiredness had vanished for the moment, and it was more important to keep cheerful for the sake of the three small boys, especially Ronnie, who was still bitterly jealous of Vanessa, and didn't see why he and Norman couldn't go home too. They were going to have trouble with him if they weren't careful.

"Who wants a game of Ludo?" she asked brightly.

Before they could answer, Daisy turned in relief as she heard her father arrive at the house, and the news was quickly related to him. The appearance of a new arrival was a diversion for the children, and while they all chattered noisily, Daisy left them all to it and went back to bed for a few hours.

Knowing they would find it hard to sleep, the boys had been allowed to stay up later that evening and were still awake when the billeting officer telephoned to say that Vanessa Brown's mother had been in touch. Her daughter had come home, and although she'd given her a pasting, she was keeping her now, and it was no thanks to these country yokels for letting her wander about all over the place.

"I'm just repeating what was told to me, and I gather Mrs Brown is none too pleased at us for letting the girl make the journey on her own," the woman said, as if Rose couldn't read between the lines. "Just as if anyone would have allowed it if we had known her intentions! Some of these people have no gratitude, but I suppose we have to learn to put up with a lack of manners in wartime."

"And that seems to be that," Rose reported to Bert and her brother when she put down the telephone. "Vanessa is back where she belongs, and it seems that we count for nothing after all."

She was far too stoical to cry, though she felt remarkably near to doing it at that moment, partly out of an unnecessary feeling of failure, and partly with indignation at the girl's ingratitude. Her brother patted her hand.

"Now you know that's not true, Rosie. All these kids have got a good life with you, and if that little madam's foolish enough not to know it, then there's nothing more you can do about it, except to be sure you did your best."

"Just what I've been telling her," Bert agreed. "So let's change the record, shall we? What about you, Quentin? Is the shop still doing good business?"

Quentin pulled a face. "Hardly. Folk aren't buying much in the way of fancy goods these days, except for cloth for blackout curtains, of course, and tape to put across the windows to keep out bomb blasts. But even the demand for that has dwindled since we haven't had a whiff of any bombs."

"My goodness, Quentin, you do sound gloomy!" his sister exclaimed. "And it almost sounds as if you want the bombs to fall."

"That I don't! But I can't pretend that it won't happen in time, just like we've always predicted, what with the docks at Avonmouth and the aircraft factories at Filton. Sometimes I wish they'd just get on with it and let us do our bit, that's all. It's like a battle of nerves, wondering when it will happen. Oh, and did I tell you I've joined the AFS? In my spare time, of course."

"What's the AFS?" came Teddy's curious voice from the fireside rug where he was quietly tickling the adoring George's ears.

"It's the Auxiliary Fire Service, son."

Teddy perked up at once. "Are you going to drive a fire engine?"

"Well, I probably won't drive it, but I'll be able to ride in one if there's a fire somewhere in the city."

"Can I come with you?"

Quentin laughed, ruffling his hair. "I don't think so. It won't be play-acting, Teddy, not like the little red fire engine I bought you for your birthday."

If the enemy finally did set their sights on Bristol – as he knew in his heart they must – then none of them would be play-acting.

"So how is Elsie?" Rose said, changing the subject quickly.

"Blossoming, of course, since Joe came home on leave. And Imogen wrote to say she's now an official driver for a Captain Grayson Beckett."

"My word. Whoever would have thought it? It's a far cry from all your girls working in the family business, isn't it, Quentin?" Bert said. "And young Baz too – not that he was ever cut out to be a shopkeeper. I always said as much, didn't I?"

"You did," Quentin said crisply. "And as usual you were right. So what are we going to do with these three young-uns to keep them occupied tomorrow, Rose? What's the plan?"

"Well, to keep their little hands from digging up their vegetable seeds to see if they've started growing yet; and before we had all this fuss over Vanessa, Bert thought you and he could take them all to the beach."

"Well, there's nothing stopping us now that we know she's all right. You should come too, Rose. There's no sense in staying indoors and moping. There'll be time enough for that when you've really got something to pipe your eyes for."

He didn't say it with any real meaning – just to jolly her along – but for a moment his eyes clouded, as if seeing into a future he didn't want to acknowledge. There might be those who thought this war was going to be over soon, and that it wouldn't come home to England, but Quentin didn't believe that. Nor did any of them who had seen it all before...

"Let's all go," Daisy put in quickly, seeing the strained look in her father's eyes. "There's no point in brooding just because Vanessa Brown preferred to be in her own home than here with us, is there?"

"And there speaks a sensible girl," Rose said approvingly.

Two weeks later a letter arrived addressed to Mr and Mrs Painter. Rose opened it, to find Vanessa's badly spelled apology inside.

> *Dear Aunty Rose and Uncle Bert,* it said,
>
> *I know I did wrong to run out like that, and me mum said I had to write and say sory for any upset. It weren't that I didn't like you all, I just wanted to come home where me frends are. I've got a Satday job down the market now and am earning a bit to help out. Mum says she's glad of it, even if she weren't too plesed when I turned up like a bad penny. The lorry driver had a bloomin' fit wen he knew how old I was too. That's all reely, excep mum says can you send me rashun book as soon*

*as yesterday, cos she can't feed me proply without it.*

> *Yours respecfully,*
> *Vanessa Brown*

*PS this is my address for the rashun book.*

If Rose hadn't cried before, her eyes were decidedly moist now, though she dashed the tears away with an angry gesture as she thrust the letter under Bert's nose.

"The silly little girl," she said, sniffing. "But I suppose it's true that there's no place like home, even if it's a miserable-sounding place like 27 Hollis Mews."

"You don't know that it's a miserable place. It might be very select."

"And pigs might fly," Rose said.

But she did as Vanessa asked, and packed up the precious ration book. She also bought her several of her favourite comic papers and film-star magazines and told her she hoped she would enjoy them; and if ever she wanted to come back, she was to write to them direct, and not go through the billeting people again.

"You must be mad," Bert said, when she told him what she had done. "She's never been the easiest of children, and you're more soft-hearted than you like to admit, aren't you, Rosie?"

"Oh well, I doubt that we'll ever hear from her again, but I just wanted her to know that she's always welcome."

"I suppose she was one of the family for a good few months, and they can't all be little angels," he agreed. "And you've still got the other three to fuss over."

"Four," she reminded him. "Daisy's not too old to enjoy a bit of fussing."

"Thank you, ma'am," Daisy said with a grin and a genteel bob.

But Rose knew there was something bothering Daisy lately. She had an exuberant nature and was never happier than when she was busy. Her nursing career certainly saw to that, and when she was off duty she was still enough of a tomboy to enjoy a rough and tumble with the boys.

But in Daisy's quieter moments, Rose often thought she glimpsed a strange look in her brown eyes that was hard to define. It wasn't exactly fear; it was almost a resigned look, a look of waiting for something to happen; and if it didn't happen soon, Rose wondered if she was going to explode with apprehension.

If she had been able or willing to put it into words, Daisy could have told her aunt precisely what was wrong. But putting it into words meant bringing the fear out into the open, giving it shape and form as if it was some living, evil thing. Hanging over her like a death knell – which was exactly what it was, of course.

But not *her* death knell, nor even that of the poor wounded servicemen who were brought to the hospital by nearly every train now, until they were almost full to capacity, and couldn't take many more. War wasn't yet defiling the beautiful, burgeoning spring of the English countryside, but it was so near, almost within touching distance across the English Channel in France and the countries of Europe. And it was here in Weston General, where every time Daisy tended a wounded soldier or airman, and heard his halting, whispered words as she wrote a letter to his family on his behalf, she thought of another hospital, another sick bed, and of her friend Lucy Luckwell.

Some days her restlessness was worse than others. She wrote regularly to Lucy, but the replies were sketchy now, simply because Lucy had so little to say about the dullness of her life in the sanatorium. She had once been so full of life, so eager to excel at her riding skills and become an equestrian star, and now she had nothing at all to look forward to. Only the endless weeks and months to endure until this foul disease killed her.

At least the wounded servicemen in Weston General had had the chance to do something worthy in their lives, thought Daisy. Something that gave them dignity and a feeling of a job well done. Something for their country. Something to die for and to make their families proud of them.

"I'm going to the Luckwell farm," she said suddenly to her aunt. "I need to see Lucy's mother and find out how she is."

"Do you want me to come with you?" Rose said.

"No. If you don't mind, I'd rather go alone."

She didn't know why she felt the way she did. How did you explain a sense of foreboding, a premonition, a need to share pain? Unless it was because she felt that need so often on the wards and, young as she was, she knew she embraced it – absorbed it even – and was somehow able to give comfort.

*A born nurse*, some of the older ones called her, but she knew it wasn't just that. It was the legacy her sensitive, beautiful mother had given her. Frances had transmitted a rare sense of emotional giving from the stage, while Daisy used it to the best of her ability when holding a dying man's hand or smoothing his brow. Right now, she knew she needed to be with Lucy Luckwell's mother.

The farmer's wife met her at the door of the farmhouse, her eyes red and swollen with crying.

"I was going to phone you as soon as I felt able, and now you're here. I always said you must be one of them thought-readers, Daisy."

She held out her arms, and Daisy went straight into them, each of them holding on tight, each supporting the other – the slender young girl and the buxom country-woman. Behind her, Daisy glimpsed the shadowy figures of the men: Lucy's brother Ben, and her father, helpless as all grown men seemed to be at times of great emotion.

There was no sign of the evacuee children, but since it was halfway through the morning, Daisy remembered that they would be at school. It was odd how things became disconnected in the brain at times like these. The sun still shone, the grass grew, schoolchildren attended their classes, and somewhere in Europe a bitter war was raging. And none of it was as important as this moment in time, when she knew without being told that her friend was dead.

"It's happened then," Daisy said, in a voice as wooden as if it was carved out of oak.

Mrs Luckwell nodded, releasing her. "The people at the sanatorium phoned to tell us an hour ago. It was peaceful, they said. She just slipped away in her sleep. We have to be thankful for that, don't we, Daisy?"

Her eyes pleaded with Daisy to agree, not to strain these moments still more by being angry, and railing against a God who could let a vivacious young girl die like this, far from home, and without the chance to say goodbye to those who loved her most. Daisy bit back the bitter words she felt like saying, knowing she must keep them until later, and not distress this family still further.

But as she drank the endless cups of tea that Mrs Luckwell pressed on her, and listened to the awkwardness of the men's conversation, it dawned on her how doubly tragic it was that this was a family who couldn't truly reach one another when they needed one another most. They were all suffering, and they had all loved Lucy; but they found it impossible to express it in words. And it shouldn't be like that. The patients in the wards who faced death found it easier to speak of their fears to the nurses and, young as she was, she listened, sympathised, and held their hands. Who had held Lucy's hand, she wondered? Or had she died all alone, as her mother implied? If so, Daisy didn't want to know about it.

"You'll have arrangements to make," she said awkwardly, when the stilted conversation dwindled to silence. "I know my aunt will want to come and see you, Mrs Luckwell. May I tell her? And is there anything else I can do? Anyone I can inform?"

Lucy's mother shook herself. "Oh no, my dear. Ben will see to all that, and the family doctor's coming soon, and he'll tell us what to do. We want Lucy brought home, of course, and we'll tell you when… when – well, anyway – yes, tell your auntie I'll be glad to see her whenever she can come."

As her voice became more disjointed, Daisy swallowed hard.

"Would you like us to take the children off your hands for a few days?"

"Lord bless you, no! Their little lives have been disrupted enough, and they need us. I'll be meeting them from school, just like always."

Privately, Daisy thought it was the Luckwells needing the evacuee children now, and she pedalled back home with tears blinding her eyes, to throw herself in her aunt's arms and sob her heart out.

# Chapter Five

Two weeks later, the trauma and sadness of the funeral was all over. Lucy had been laid to rest in the town she loved, and to Daisy it seemed that her family was being remarkably strong. It sometimes seemed as if she was the only one still trying to make sense of it all. Why her? Why Lucy?

Anyone with a brain in their head knew there would be casualties in a war. You read about them in the newspapers every day. You heard the reports on the wireless, and if you were a nurse, you had to be prepared to deal with injuries that in peacetime would never have been within the scope of your abilities. Nursing was not the gentle activity of simply putting a cup of tea to a wounded soldier's lips – if it ever had been.

Daisy knew that only too well. War brought injuries and death. You had to steel yourself to deal with whatever the next trainload of wounded servicemen brought in. You did it because you were trained, and because they were strangers. Compassion and efficiency went hand in hand. But you weren't trained to deal with the death of a friend, who had done nothing worse than just get progressively sicker. You weren't trained to deal with your feelings in that situation. You didn't know how to handle them...

She read the words she had written in an impassioned letter to Cal Monks. Baring her soul, she thought dramatically, because she had vowed that between friends and lovers there should be no secrets festering away inside like a cancer. He was her dearest friend, her best friend in all the world now that Lucy was dead. She had to keep saying it to believe it. Even though she hadn't seen Lucy for months, she had still been her best friend and confidante.

She would dearly have liked to share her feelings with her sisters, but it wasn't fair to burden Elsie with her misery, and Imogen seemed to be having quite a good time with her Captain Beckett too. By all accounts she was driving him here, there and everywhere, Daisy thought, in a small fit of jealousy, and making new friends. If she didn't get out of the bedroom that was stifling her, she was going to go quietly mad, and what good was that going to do Lucy or anyone?

She screwed up the letter to Cal and threw it in the waste-paper basket. It wouldn't be fair to him to write as emotionally as she had, when he would assuredly be having his own battles to fight. She had heard from him at last, and he seemed to be having a good time as well, from his wild descriptions of dogfights and zooming in and out of the sun. The letter was heavily censored, but although she could sense his enthusiasm, it made her feel more detached from him than ever. His obsession for the sheer exhilaration of soaring into the sky in a silver machine was comparable to her brother's about the sea.

Drying her eyes that seemed to be perpetually damp now, Daisy took a few deep breaths and told herself it was time to pull herself together. Life went on. She went downstairs and called out to the three boys messing about in the garden that she would race them down to the beach.

Meeting her Aunt Rose's approving eyes, she knew she had already turned a corner, however tiny it felt.

–

Baz Caldwell's confidence was growing. From the day he had enjoyed ferrying passengers across the River Avon with old Enoch Bray, to his recklessness in running off to join the fishing fleet, he'd known he would never be happy doing anything else but going to sea. It was all he'd ever wanted, and after the first sticky moments with his father when he'd tried to explain how much it meant to him, he knew he had found his destiny. By now, life behind the counter of his father's shop seemed as if it belonged to another world. He had never been cut out for it. It was women's work, and even his sisters had eventually agreed to that. Of course, the war had changed everything. He wasn't surprised that his sister Elsie was already expecting a baby after her marriage to Joe Preston. They obviously *did* it, he thought, with the familiar stirring in his young loins. But he still marvelled that his older sister Imogen had been so keen to join up, and as for Daisy being a nurse – well, that was a turn up for the books and no mistake.

"What are you grinning at, Bazzer? Dreaming of some pretty little miss you've been toying with?" his mate asked him in the waterside pub that evening. Baz wasn't old enough to drink in pubs, but because of his hefty size and the company of his seafaring mates, few ever questioned his age.

The third man sniggered. "Give the lad a chance, Duggie. He's still wet behind the ears. Don't know what he's got it for yet, do you, Caldwell?"

Baz snorted. "Maybe I do and maybe I don't. In any case I ain't spreading it around like you two buggers and risking a dose," he added daringly.

The others laughed. "Quite right, kid," Duggie said. "You leave it to the experts. There's time enough for you to find out what's what. You do what you've got to do beneath the blankets."

Baz felt his face flame now. Bastards, he thought furiously. He was the youngest on the trawler and their baiting didn't normally bother him, but tension was never far from the surface these days, and the North Sea waters where they fished weren't getting any warmer, despite the fact that it was springtime now. They weren't the safest place to be, either, what with the German U-boats a constant, stealthy underwater menace.

The three of them were weaving their unsteady way back along the waterfront towards their digs late that evening, all somewhat the worse for drink, when Duggie stopped suddenly, pointing dramatically out to sea.

"Look out there, kid. Iceberg ahead!"

As Baz's heart leapt, he gave a loud gasp, and Duggie chortled again.

"Oh sorry, my mistake – it's just a wave. Christ, you'd think we were on the *Titanic*, the way he reacted, wouldn't you, Harry? Here, kid, take another swig to calm your nerves."

He handed over a half-drunk bottle of beer. Booze was officially forbidden on the boat, but once on shore they took advantage of the watered-down ale the pubs provided, and sneaked more than a few bottles on board, since no one took much notice of regulations when the temperature was freezing, and they were wrapped up to the gills in heavy gear.

Baz felt Duggie sling his arm around his tense shoulders.

"Cheer up, boy; there's worse things at sea, ain't there? And are you sure you want to join the bloody Navy?" he slurred.

"If it means getting away from you buggers, I'm sure all right," Baz snarled, wondering for a moment what his father would say if he could see him now, rolling along a waterfront with a pair of rogues for company, to sleep the sleep of the unjust in a seedy seamen's boarding house until they put to sea in the morning.

He found himself grinning as his two mates began telling bawdy stories to liven up the rest of the evening, and he felt the usual surge of excitement at their risqué jokes. To hell with what his father thought. This was what he'd always wanted, and if it wasn't exactly adventure on the grand scale, it was adventure such as he had never dreamed of; and who knew what the future held?

–

By the end of April it was clear that it was going to be an exceptionally warm spring. If anything was designed to cheer the spirits, despite the food rationing and miserable reports of Hitler's relentless march through Europe, at least the weather was fine, Rose Painter told her niece, with typical British optimism.

"And it's time you spent more time in the fresh air, stopped moping around and thinking about people who are worse off than yourself."

"How can I?" Daisy said. "I see them every day on the wards!"

"You don't live at that hospital, Daisy. You're young and healthy, and Lucy wouldn't thank you for turning yourself into a nun on her account. You're still allowed to have fun, you know."

Daisy's first reaction – to snap that she didn't know what she was talking about – was tempered by her aunt's look of understanding.

"I know that," she said slowly. "It just seems wrong, that's all."

"It's not wrong, darling. Look at those boys in the garden now. Teddy's adapted well to living here because we're his family; but even though the other two are far from home and missing their mother, they're having a wonderful time now with Bert and his chickens."

Daisy looked and nodded. "It was the best thing Uncle Bert ever did, buying some chickens and letting everyone name their own."

"*And* providing us with eggs for breakfast when they condescend to lay them," Rose said. "I swear they have minds of their own, though, and prefer waking us up at the crack of dawn to doing what nature intended them to do."

Daisy was laughing now. "Oh, Aunt Rose, you always did me good!"

"So do as I say, my love. Go out and have some fun."

Daisy knew she was right, but before she did anything about it, she was going to do what she always did on Friday evenings, and that was to go and talk to Lucy. It didn't feel weird to crouch down by her grave and put some flowers in the little pot she'd bought especially – checking first with the Luckwells to see that they didn't object – and talk things over with Lucy.

"Aunt Rose thinks I should go out and have some fun," she said, as she removed the dead flowers from last week and replaced them with daffodils.

Most of the garden at home was thriving with young cabbage plants and sprouting potatoes and the feathery tufts of carrot tops now, but they still kept the front and side garden bright with flowers. And these were special, for Lucy.

"I wouldn't go anywhere if you thought I shouldn't," Daisy went on. "Your parents are still having the annual gymkhana at the farm, and they say there's going to be a special prize in your memory this year, Lucy; but I couldn't bear to be there. You understand that, don't you?"

Her heart gave a stab as she remembered last year's event, when they had both been so excited and happy at performing, and Lucy had excelled in everything she did. Such a short time ago, and yet it seemed like a lifetime.

No, she definitely couldn't go this year. Maybe next year... she was sure Mrs Luckwell would understand.

"Is that you, Daisy?" she heard a voice call out. Her head jerked around at this intrusion into her private time with Lucy. Across the fragrant-smelling churchyard, she saw one of the other nurses from the hospital walking towards her.

"I thought it was you! Come to visit your friend, have you?"

Daisy had only ever spoken to this girl once or twice and didn't particularly want to speak to her now. She couldn't even remember her name for a few moments. It was Alice something-or-other. Alice Godfrey – that was it. She muttered that yes, she was visiting her friend, feeling rather absurd to be saying the words out loud, as if this was a social call for afternoon tea...

"I'm visiting my brother," Alice said. "It's about the only time he can't answer me back. I never thought I'd miss it so much. Daft, isn't it?"

"I didn't know you had a brother," Daisy said, for want of something to say.

Alice shrugged her narrow shoulders. "He was older than me, nearly twenty-two. He was in the RAF, and he bought it over France."

Daisy's heart jumped again. "Oh – how awful – how long ago was it?"

"More than six months now. Long enough for us to get used to it, and even be glad in a funny way that he's not coming back in the circumstances. He'd always been so good-looking in a Robert Donat sort of way, but he'd had half his face burned away in the crash," she said, almost matter-of-factly. "They brought him home after he died, and my dad and me went to see him, but my mum couldn't face it. I'm glad she didn't; then she doesn't have to keep remembering it."

"But you do."

"'Fraid so," Alice said. "But you have to get on with things, don't you? I make it my business to be extra gentle with those boys who come into the hospital with burns, though, I can tell you."

She took a deep breath. "Anyway, I didn't mean to depress you still more. You'll be missing your friend, I daresay. I heard something about it and I'm sorry. Young, wasn't she?"

"Seventeen," Daisy said, her head drooping. It still seemed cruel and unbelievable to even put it into words, but at least Lucy had died peacefully, and didn't have half her face burned away...

"Look, Daisy, we all have to face up to these things. We don't have much choice, do we?" Alice said, with twenty-year-old wisdom. And then she perked up.

"I'll tell you what: there's a dance at the Methodist Church Hall to raise funds for servicemen tomorrow night, so why don't we go? A group of the other nurses were talking about it, and there's always safety in numbers, isn't there?"

As Daisy hesitated, she grinned. "Oh, do say yes. There's sure to be a lot of young chaps keen to dance with a couple of smashers like us. There'll probably be quite a few from RAF Locking. What do you say?"

For a minute Daisy couldn't say anything at all. Locking Camp was so near to the Luckwell farm. It was also the place where Cal had done his training, and she missed him and Lucy so much… and this girl's words were bringing it all back to her. It was on the tip of her tongue to say she couldn't possibly go dancing, even if Aunt Rose permitted it… and then she remembered that Alice's family had gone through a terrible bereavement too, and they all had to get over it in the best way they could.

"I'll have to see if it's all right with my family first," she said lamely.

"Well, I'll wait for you outside the Hall at half past seven then. Try and come, Daisy. It does help, believe me. And remember that it's all in a good cause."

–

That's what she told Aunt Rose, half-hoping that her aunt would forbid it, and half-hoping that she wouldn't. It was Aunt Rose who had said she should have some fun, and that you couldn't let Adolph spoil everything. And she was

71

sure Lucy wouldn't have objected. If Lucy had been here, she would have been eager to go too. But Daisy hadn't been at all sure it was what *she* really wanted, until she saw the doubt in her aunt's eyes.

"I'm not sure about this, Daisy. Dancing with young men – strangers…"

"Oh, Aunt Rose, I'm not a child! I do know how to behave, and I attend strangers every day, remember! And don't tell me you and Uncle Bert never tripped the light fantastic, or the black bottom, or whatever you called it!"

"We certainly did not dance the black bottom! I must admit we had our moments, but we were courting then, of course," she added hastily. "Young girls didn't go to dances unaccompanied in our day."

"I won't be unaccompanied. I'll be with Alice Godfrey."

"Do her parents own one of those small hotels on the seafront?"

"I don't know. Why? Do you know some people by that name?"

"There's a Mrs Godfrey who's just joined our knitting circle. I did hear that she had a son who'd been killed," Rose said vaguely.

"There you are then. It's all perfectly respectable!" Daisy said, glossing over that bit of information. "Oh Aunt Rose, please say I can go! You know how I used to love to dance when Mother was alive. Remember how I used to try to copy her footsteps when I was little, before Teddy was born? And Daddy used to stand me on his slippers and try to waltz me around the room with his two left feet and made us all laugh…"

She caught her breath, filled with the bittersweet memories of times past, and the imagery of her mother, still young and beautiful, at the height of her success, and of her family who adored her. How long ago it all seemed, and yet the imagery was as vivid in her mind as if it was only yesterday. The yearning to dance was as strong a passion in her now as it had been then. Dancing was like living in a dreamworld, floating on air, swaying to the music and blotting out the terrible things that were happening in the world today; and it was in her blood.

"I suppose you had better go and see if you've remembered anything your mother taught you, then," Rose said, her eyes suspiciously moist. "But your uncle will take you and he'll fetch you at ten thirty sharp."

"Oh but—"

"No buts, Daisy. If you want to go dancing, you have to go on my terms."

From the steely tone in her voice now, Daisy knew there was nothing more to be said; so her thoughts turned instead on what to wear. She had nothing remotely suitable, of course. She had never been to a grown-up dance before, and anticipation quickly turned to panic as she riffled through her wardrobe.

In the end she chose her Sunday-best pink-and-cream floral frock and her cream-coloured shoes with the smallest of heels, washed her hair and gave it a vinegar rinse to make it shine, and brushed it out to a shimmering sheen. She couldn't tame the shock of natural curls, but why should she? she thought defiantly. Her hair was her crowning glory, or so they said; and even though Cal wouldn't be there to see her, she wanted to look her best.

The rest of the family assessed her as she came into the parlour for their approval on Saturday evening, still nervous, but brimful of an excitement she couldn't deny. She was seventeen and she was going dancing...

"Cor, you look just like one of them film stars, Daisy!" Norman said, and Ronnie nodded in brotherly agreement, struck dumb for once.

She smiled on them benevolently.

"She don't look like a film star," Teddy snapped. "She just looks like our Daisy done up like a dog's dinner."

"Well, thank you, Teddy dear," Daisy snapped back. "When I need approval from a baby I'll ask for it!"

"I'm not a baby! I'm nearly eight!"

"Oh yes, I was forgetting. You'll be joining up next, won't you?"

Rose intervened before the squabbling got serious.

"Daisy, if you don't stop scowling your face will stay like it, and you'll be cracking that make-up before you even reach the Methodist Church Hall," she said meaningly, assuring Daisy that she knew very well she was wearing a touch of rouge and face powder and that her lips were several shades redder than usual.

"Anyway, I think she looks a real treat," Bert said heartily. "And a credit to her mother."

"Thank you, Uncle Bert," Daisy said with a lump in her throat, because it was the nicest compliment anyone could have paid her.

"So if you're ready, my lady, your chariot awaits you," he went on grandly, holding out his arm to her.

She crooked her arm through his, feeling like a princess as they swept out of the house, even though the old Morris car took a bit of cranking to start and rather took the edge off it all as it wheezed down the hill towards the brightly lit church hall.

People were already going inside or waiting for friends to arrive and, with a feeling of relief, Daisy caught sight of Alice Godfrey as Bert stopped the car and pressed her hand for a moment.

"You have a good time, my love, and don't go fretting over your aunt's fussing. She cares for you, and it's just her way of showing it."

"I know," Daisy said. "And you know I'd never let either of you down."

She leaned forward and kissed him on the cheek before she got mopey again and ruined her spanking new look. She desperately hoped she had managed to wash all the vinegar out of her hair and cover the smell with a splash of eau de cologne so that it didn't waft into his nostrils, or those of any dance partner.

"You look lovely, Daisy," Alice Godfrey said enviously, as if she had never seen her before. Nor had she, except in her nurse's uniform, and the cardigan she had worn over it at the churchyard on Friday evening.

"So do you," Daisy said, realising that the cut of her new friend's clothes was far superior to her own. It took a haberdasher's daughter to know that, she thought, to cover any thought of embarrassment.

Alice pulled a face. "Oh, I'm no beauty, and I know it. You are though. You could wear a sack and look nice. And your hair is such a gorgeous colour," she added with a sigh.

Daisy started to laugh as they went inside the hall. "Stop it, for goodness' sake. You'll make me swollen-headed. Anyway, my brothers and sisters have all got the same colour hair, so I'm used to being called a ginger-nut!"

"I would never call you anything so beastly," Alice declared. "But it makes me realise I don't know anything about you, Daisy. I didn't even know you had a big family.

We must get to know one another properly if we're going to be friends. And I think we are – aren't we?"

Daisy realised they had linked arms as if to give each other courage as they went into the hall where the band was playing on a raised dais. Couples were already dancing, and there was a fair sprinkling of servicemen among the young girls and chaperones. There was also a large banner proclaiming that this evening's event was for fund-raising purposes for our brave boys in uniform.

For a moment Daisy thought wistfully how Lucy would have loved this if she'd ever had the chance to be here. But then her heart gave a lift. She knew she would never forget her, but Lucy wasn't here anymore, and now there was someone new, if she wanted to give friendship a chance. It seemed more than coincidental that they had met in the churchyard where Lucy was buried, so near to the spot where Alice's brother lay too. It seemed like fate, and Daisy wasn't one to sneer at fate.

She smiled at Alice now. "I think we could be very good friends," she said.


She wrote in her diary that evening that today had been another turning-point in her life. She had a new friend, and she had danced with a boy called Jed.

Her fingers poised over her pencil as she wrote his name, seeing him in her mind's eye as she did so: tall and gangly in the army uniform that seemed far too big for his slight frame; remembering how he had asked her to dance – clumsily, awkwardly, almost apologising for being alive at all.

"You won't find me much good, I'm afraid," he'd said. "I've got a gammy leg from a shrapnel wound, but if you're willing to take a chance, we could always hop around slowly. Mind you, I don't know the steps either—"

"Oh, for pity's sake," Daisy said, starting to laugh. "Are you sure you want to do this?"

"Quite sure. I spotted you the minute you came in, and I've been plucking up courage to come over and ask you ever since."

"Good heavens, have you?" Daisy said. "Am I that frightening?"

"Not frightening at all. Just very pretty." As he spoke, he went red with embarrassment. "But if you don't want to dance with me, I'll understand…"

"I do," she said, standing up at once. "Of course I do. And don't worry if you don't know the steps. I can teach you."

She held out her hand and, as he took it, he drew her on to the dance floor to mingle with all the other couples in a slow waltz.

Much later, when she had related all that she was going to about the evening to Aunt Rose and Uncle Bert, and she was out of her finery and snuggled up in bed, she continued writing in her diary that it was just like the romantic novelettes told you it would be.

A kind of electric shock had tingled through her the moment their fingers touched. It had almost made her faint for a moment, because she had been so certain she could never be attracted to anyone else but Cal. *He* was her young man, the one she had decided dreamily that she was going to marry one day – not this soldier with the intense brown eyes and the rather haunted expression on his face.

He wasn't even good-looking – not in a film-starry way, anyway – and in any case he was hoping to go back to France soon, once his leg healed. He clearly had plans of his own. He wasn't a patient at Weston General, but in a convalescent home nearby, which was why Daisy had never seen him before. But before the evening had ended, he'd said he wanted to see her again, and she didn't know what to do about it.

## Chapter Six

On her next day off, Daisy took the train to Bristol, and walked to Vicarage Street from Temple Meads. She needed to talk to Elsie. Though quite what she was going to say to her, she didn't know. They had talked over many things in the past, but never anything as personal as how you knew if you were really in love. But Elsie was a married woman now and must know some of the answers.

She saw Elsie watching out for her from the window of the upstairs flat she now occupied in the family home, and she waved wildly. It felt good to be home. She loved Aunt Rose and Uncle Bert, but this was where she really belonged, she thought with a surge of guilt for having decamped there so readily. Then she forgot any of it as her sister greeted her at the door with open arms, and the only thing Daisy could think of to say was:

"Good Lord, Elsie, what have you got beneath that pinny? A whale?"

Elsie laughed, pulling her inside. "Well, I can see your education has advanced in more ways than one since you've been nursing, Daisy dear. Is everyone so frank about such things now?"

"Cripes, I'm sorry – I didn't mean to be rude…"

"It's all right, you goose; I'm just teasing. It's rather refreshing, actually. Father studiously ignores it when he can, but I have to admit that it's quite a bump for less than four months, isn't it?" she said, patting her stomach affectionately. "I keep telling him if he doesn't stop growing at this rate, we won't be able to get through the front door by the time he's ready to be born."

"You're sure it's going to be a boy then," Daisy said, noting the cosiness of the rooms with their unmistakable mark of Elsie's tidiness and attention to detail.

"No, but I have to call him something, don't I? I can't think of him as just an *it*. There's a real little person growing in there, Daisy, and it's one of life's major miracles."

Daisy forbore mentioning one of the cruder nurse's comments that anyone could do the necessary to produce a kid, and it was a bloody sight harder not to get caught. But anyone seeing the bloom on her sister now, and the glow in her eyes when she talked about her baby, could surely only think of it as the major miracle that she did.

"So let's have some tea and then you can tell me all the news," Elsie said. "Is everyone well? I told you about Immy driving an officer around, didn't I?"

"Yes. I wonder what James Church thinks about that."

Elsie's face sobered. "Oh Daisy, she had such a terrible letter from him recently. His tank regiment was involved in action, and one of them was blown up. Everyone inside it was blown to pieces too. James described it in graphic detail to Immy, which was a bit unfair, to upset her like that, I thought. I mean, she must realise it was something that could happen to James too."

Daisy was shaking her head. "It might seem unfair to you, Elsie, but they have to do that. They have to tell someone, or they would burst with the anguish of it all. It helps them to talk and to get it out of their systems.

Believe me, I've heard plenty of harrowing tales on the wards, and if Daddy knew half of them – some gruesome, some downright intimate…"

She half-grinned, to take the seriousness out of her words, and Elsie paused in the little kitchen area, studying her sister thoughtfully.

"Is this really my flippant little sister talking? You've certainly grown up a bit, Daisy."

"Well, for goodness' sake, I am almost eighteen, even though Aunt Rose seems to forget that sometimes. And that's rather what I wanted to talk to you about, in a roundabout kind of way."

Now that the moment was here, she found herself floundering; but as Elsie put the tray of tea on the table and poured them both a cup, her sister looked at her with more concern.

"There's no trouble between you, is there? You know Aunt Rose means well, Daisy. Remember how Mother always used to say we should put that on her headstone someday?"

"And we never thought Mother would be the first one to have a headstone, did we?" Daisy murmured. "The Luckwells are going to get one made for Lucy soon, but apparently the ground has to settle first."

She bit her lip, not wanting to be discussing headstones and churchyards and all that went with them, and not really knowing how the conversation had veered that way.

"Well, this is turning out to be a jolly day, isn't it?" Elsie said briskly. "If you've got something dire to tell me, Daisy, let's get it over and done with; otherwise let's talk about something more cheerful, shall we?"

Daisy took a long drink of tea, weaker than they used to have it, because they all knew tea would be one of the next things to be rationed. Tea was precious now, and what was already in the store cupboard had to be hoarded and couldn't be wasted. She took a deep breath.

"It's nothing dire at all. It's probably a silly question, anyway, and I can feel myself getting all hot and bothered at even asking it. It's – well – it's how do you know if you're really in love, Elsie?" she finished in a rush.

"Is that all?" Elsie said in some relief. "Oh, I'm sorry, darling; I can see this is important to you, and it's not silly at all. But how can anyone answer such a question? You just *know*."

"Well, that's no answer at all," Daisy said crossly. "How did you know for certain that you were in love with Joe – or is that too personal a question?"

Elsie gave a long sigh, her eyes faraway with remembering. "It's not too personal, since it obviously means so much to you – and we'll get around to just *why* in a moment or two. I knew, because my heart began to pound every time I saw him, and even the anticipation that we were going to be together could start it racing. I knew, because I couldn't imagine being without him ever again. I couldn't even bear the thought of it. Does that make sense?"

"I think so." It made it all the more emotive, because Elsie had always been quieter and more reserved than Immy or Daisy, and she had never opened her heart to her so frankly before.

"So come clean, little sister" – Elsie was more assertive now – "who is this paragon of virtue you think you're in love with? He *is* a paragon of virtue, I hope? And I think you know what I mean."

"Don't worry, I'm not about to besmirch the family honour, Elsie. But I really did think I was falling in love with Cal. I told you about him, didn't I? And then Aunt Rose let me go to a dance last Saturday, and I met someone called Jed, and I'm not sure about anything anymore."

"Aunt Rose let you go to a dance on your own?"

"Of course not. I went with another nurse, and it was for fund-raising purposes, so it was all very proper, and Uncle Bert took me there and back – and just telling you all that makes me feel about six years old," she added crossly.

"You rather look like it, sitting there with your arms folded and that mutinous expression on your face. So who is this Jed?"

"He's a soldier on convalescent leave, and I really *liked* him, Elsie, and he says he'd like to see me again – and to write to me when he rejoins his unit. So do you think it would be disloyal to Cal if I agreed to it?"

Elsie leaned across and kissed her cheek. "I think it would be a lovely thing to do to write to a soldier and give him news of home. I know how Joe appreciates my letters. And where's the harm in being friendly to two young men? Providing you keep them both as friends, of course."

It wasn't what Daisy had once had in mind regarding Cal, but that wasn't something she wanted to keep reminding her family of, least of all Elsie, who had only ever had eyes for one man. She wasn't so sure about Immy. Her oldest sister had always thought her too young and scatty to confide in, and Daisy had never known about any young man in her life before she had fallen in love with James Church. They always seemed such a perfect couple, and it was so romantic to realise that someone you had known all your life was someone so special…

They heard the outer door open downstairs, and to the relief of both, the time for confidences was over. The next minute Quentin Caldwell had knocked on the door of his daughter's flat and poked his head inside.

"Well, this is a rare treat," he said heartily. "Two beautiful daughters at one fell swoop. We only need Imogen to surprise us and we'd have the full set."

Daisy laughed, giving him a quick kiss. "How are you, Daddy? And how's the fire-fighting? Adolph's not sending anything to keep you busy yet, is he?"

"Don't be too complacent, my dear. Being prepared is not only the Boy Scouts' motto, and we'll be ready for whatever comes our way."

"Nothing, I hope," Elsie said quickly, crossing her fingers.

"Don't you believe it, my love." Then he turned to Daisy as he saw Elsie's face pucker. "Has your uncle got around to building that air-raid shelter yet?"

"Not yet. He doesn't think any bombs will come our way. He calls Weston a soft target, whatever that means. Probably all that mud and sand," she added.

Quentin shook his head. "What he really means is that it doesn't have the same risk as Bristol has, darling. No docks or aircraft factories."

"Well, how do the Germans know about that?"

"Of course they know it, just as we know which cities to target when we send our aircraft over there. Warfare has become far more sophisticated these days, and they'll know where and when to strike, believe me."

Daisy shivered, and she couldn't help seeing how this conversation was upsetting Elsie. Men saw war on a different level from women, she thought shrewdly. They only saw the need to fight, and to win at all costs, while women saw the pain that war inflicted.

"If the danger of bombing is so much worse in Bristol, then why don't you both come down to Weston with the rest of us, Daddy?" she said impulsively. "There's still plenty of room in that old house of Aunt Rose's, and I know she'd love to have you both, and Teddy would adore it…"

They answered simultaneously.

"I can't do that, Daisy. I'm still the manager of Preston's Emporium, and with so many young men away in the services, it would be like deserting a sinking ship. I have my AFS work to think about too…"

And Elsie: "I'm not leaving here! Joe and I have made this our home for the duration, and he'll want to be sure he has me to come back to…"

"Gosh, I'm sorry I spoke!" Daisy said.

"Actually, Joe keeps suggesting I should go north to stay with his family," Elsie went on. "But I only met them once, when we had a few brief days there on his Christmas leave, as you know. I'll want to get to know them properly someday, of course – and they'll want to see their grandchild. But Immy made an even dafter suggestion. You remember that housing agent she used to work for, who got stage fright even before the war began and left Bristol in a blue funk?"

"Mr Harris – yes," Daisy said. "I thought he was a rather sweet old boy, in a roly-poly sort of way."

"Not so much of the old boy, if you please, Daisy," her father said with a laugh. "He was younger than me!"

"Anyway," Elsie put in, "Immy keeps in touch with him for some strange reason that I can't fathom. He went to Cornwall to live with his brother who has a market garden somewhere near Penzance. Only now they've gone into partnership with a small boarding house as well."

"Is this conversation getting anywhere?" Daisy enquired.

Her sister smiled at her impatience. "Yes. Apparently, Kenneth Harris says that any time any of Immy's family feel they should get away from Bristol, he would make room for us at his boarding house. Immy told me to think about it, but why on earth would I want to move so far away from my family?"

Daisy agreed. The family had been to Cornwall years ago, and it was quaint and pretty, full of old tin-mine chimneys and china-clay workings – and miles from anywhere. The beaches were lovely, though, she remembered in an unexpected burst of recollection. There were such tales of smuggling and magic and mystery that had enchanted them as children. But you wouldn't want to *live* there!

Quentin cleared his throat, as if he too had been remembering the past.

"I'm sure Imogen meant it for the best, Elsie, and it was certainly a nice gesture from Harris. But we all have to do things in our own way. Now, how about some tea for your father, or am I already being rationed?"

–

Daisy was almost glad to get on the crowded train back to Weston. Her visit hadn't really solved anything, except that she'd decided she owed it to Cal to write and let him know that one of her patients had asked her to write to him as a friendly gesture. It wasn't *quite* the truth but putting it like that didn't make it sound too bad – or too personal. That was what she would do.

There was one thing that scared her, though. All the time Elsie was talking about Joe, it was clear that she was seeing his face in her mind. She had been with him very recently, Daisy reminded herself, and it was how it should be... but she sometimes found it hard to visualise Cal, and not only Cal. Sometimes she couldn't even visualise Lucy's face either. She didn't want to lose the image or the memory of either of them, but it was happening, and she couldn't seem to stop it.

Now there was Jed, who was very nice, but who didn't make her heart pound the way Elsie's heart pounded whenever she thought of Joe. He didn't make her starry-eyed at the thought of seeing him again, and that scared her too. Maybe she wasn't destined to fall deeply in love with anyone... or maybe she simply hadn't met the right one yet after all.

When she arrived at the Weston house in the early evening, it was to find them all in an uproar. Teddy was covered in spots, and the other two boys were scratching themselves in sympathy, with Aunt Rose trying vainly to plaster them all in calamine lotion and ignoring their squeals at the coldness of it.

"Chickenpox," Rose announced to Daisy. "Teddy's quite bad with it, and I'm sure the others are going down with it too. Have you had it, Daisy?"

"Yes. I think we all did when we were little, and it's beastly."

"They'll have to stay away from school, of course, and you'd better see what the position is at the hospital, Daisy. It's very infectious and you can't risk giving it to the patients. We must keep to ourselves until all risk of infection has gone."

"I'll telephone right away," Daisy said with a groan, thinking that the infection had probably spread already. But with three fractious little boys in her care, Aunt Rose would need all the help she could get.

There was another sneaking little thought in her mind too. Fate had a strange way of sorting things out sometimes. She obviously couldn't see Jed now. She must also telephone the convalescent home and get a message passed on to him. It was the only decent thing to do before he tried to get in touch with her.

But half an hour later, when she had made the calls, including one to Elsie, who assured her that she also had had chickenpox, she had heard the matron of the convalescent home give her the news that Private Jed Williams had already been sent home to make room for more patients. Without even contacting her, thought Daisy. So much for romantic dreams that meant nothing…

A week later she received a letter from him, sent to her via the hospital.

> Dear Daisy,
>
> I thought I was going to be in Weston for a few more weeks, but all in a rush they bundled me off to convalesce at home with no time to let you know. So I'm back in Folkestone with my parents until I'm fit. It's not the best place to be, as we can hear the bombing from the other side of the Channel and the air seems to be constantly full of searchlights looking out for enemy aircraft, but, so far, we haven't seen any. I'll be glad to get back in the thick of things myself. Still, it could be worse, and I've got hardly a limp now.

*I just wanted to say I'm sorry we didn't meet again but if you'd like to start writing to me, I'd love to hear from you sometime.*

*I thought you were a really smashing girl, and maybe one of these days I'll get the chance to say "save the last dance for me", if you don't think that's being too forward.*

*Yours sincerely,*
*Jed*

Daisy sat back and read the letter all over again. It could hardly be called a love letter, but she liked him all the more for that. He was nice. A nice young man. One that her father would approve of. And even though he didn't say as much, the town where he lived was obviously so much more dangerous a place than here.

All the same she knew she shouldn't let sympathy cloud her judgement. She would definitely write to him, but Cal was still her young man, and she would do as she intended and let him know about Jed. It would salve her conscience.

–

It was tedious being at home all the time for the next couple of weeks and attending to the ever more demanding needs of three bored children. Daisy found herself hoping Elsie knew what she was in for, but presumably one little baby wouldn't cause as much disruption as these three. She also found herself reading the newspapers and listening to the wireless more avidly than before, and as April slid into May, everyone anticipated the sound of air-raid sirens, even if nothing seemed to be happening yet.

But the awful reports of what the European countries were suffering brought the reality of war in this lovely spring ever nearer. It wasn't only buildings that were being destroyed, it was thousands of people too; and Hitler's boast of invading England was no longer to be dismissed as the dreams of a madman, but a real possibility. Every wireless bulletin made it sound graver.

"It looks very bad," Uncle Bert told his wife and niece, after listening intently to the latest one. "I fear for all of us, my dears, and this ineffectual government is doing nothing to relieve the situation. Chamberlain will have to go."

"There's no doubt about that," Rose said, "and the sooner the better. The poor little countries in Europe stand no chance against a dictator like Hitler, and if he has his way, we'll be next."

"Of course we will. Britain is his goal, and he has to overrun all the others before he can get to us."

"Do you really think it will happen?" Daisy said fearfully. "I don't want to have to think of myself as a German. I'm English!"

"We'll always be English, my love," her aunt told her stoutly. "He may rule our country, but he'll never rule our hearts and minds. I'm sure the people in those other countries all feel the same."

"He'll never rule our country, Rose, so get that notion out of your head. We'll win in the end because we have right on our side."

Daisy wasn't so sure any more – she wasn't sure of anything – and when the news came through that Hitler's army had taken Holland and Belgium, it looked as if the whole world was teetering on the brink of a massive Nazi triumph. Only France stood in the way of the invasion of

Britain. If that fell, Germany's long-range aircraft would be able to bomb every corner of Britain.

But what looked like the beginning of the end took a dramatic twist. As Hitler's relentless march proceeded, the Prime Minister resigned at the end of a disastrous reign in parliament, and by the Whitsun weekend of May the tenth, Winston Churchill was ready to form a new coalition government. It seemed as if the whole country breathed a collective sigh of relief.

"It doesn't change the fact that our boys are still being sent to France, and many of them are coming home maimed or worse," Bert said grimly. "Elsie must feel constant anxiety over her husband, and the Good Lord only knows where young Baz is nowadays."

Daisy could have added that Immy would be full of anxiety about James Church too, just as *she* was about Cal – and Jed.

She found it a relief to be finally back at work after the stress of caring for the three bored little boys, and the enforced insularity of home life. But when she came home from her first day back at the hospital, she had news of her own to impart. She took a deep breath.

"Please take a look at this leaflet, Aunt Rose. They're asking for volunteers to join a special unit of nurses for the hospital ships bringing the wounded home from France, and I need you to persuade Daddy to let me go. I know he'll say I'm too young, but I'll be eighteen next month, and people younger than me are risking their lives every day, so please support me," she finished quickly.

"Oh no, Daisy; France is such a dangerous place these days…"

"It's no more dangerous than London, or Kent, or Sussex will be very soon," Daisy said, dragging up her knowledge of the south-east counties. "And even Bristol, if what you've all been surmising is correct. I really want to do this, Aunt Rose. You do see that, don't you? If Mother were here, I'm sure she'd understand."

She didn't often use her mother's name to gain a point, and she wasn't even sure that Frances *would* have sanctioned her joining the special unit or agreed with her need to do something. But it was more than a growing need now. The restlessness inside her was stronger than the need to stay in safe surroundings, even doing such a vital and necessary job in Weston General.

"What about your fellow nurses? I doubt whether many of them have this sudden urge to be in the midst of such danger," Rose said, not rising to the bait of being no more than a surrogate mother to the Caldwell progeny.

"At least four that I know of as yet, and one of them is Alice Godfrey. You remember – the nurse I went to the dance with. You said you knew her mother."

"And is Alice Godfrey's mother willing for her to join this special unit?"

"Yes, she is. In any case, Alice is twenty, and very sensible, Aunt Rose. I'd like you to meet her."

"I think I should, since she seems to have such influence over you," Rose said decisively. "You had better invite her to tea on Sunday afternoon."

"And you'll think about what I've said – about persuading Daddy that I really do need to do this?" she persisted.

"Perhaps. But first of all I'll have to persuade myself that I don't think it's the maddest idea you've ever had," Rose said drily.

–

"She'll do it," Daisy told Alice confidently next morning when they were having a welcome break in their shift. "We always relied on Aunt Rose to get around Daddy when we wanted anything. My mother used to say she was as immovable as the Rock of Gibraltar. She's Daddy's older sister and she always had influence over him, but in a very sensible and logical way."

"She sounds pretty formidable to me! My mother said so after meeting her at their knitting circle afternoons, but she seems to like her."

"And so will you. She can be tough, but she's also the sanest and kindest person you ever met. So please say you'll come to tea and further our cause."

Alice looked at her curiously. "You really are set on this, aren't you, Daisy? I keep having second and even third thoughts, although I know I'll do it in the end. But you're different. It might sound sugary and pathetic, but I'd say you have a real burning light in your eyes. You're not a descendent of old Florrie, by any chance?"

Daisy laughed. "Not that I'm aware of, but thanks for the compliment – if it *is* a compliment. Or are you just implying that I'm jumping in with both feet because I'm still a juvenile?"

"You're anything but that, sweetie," Alice said lightly. "I think you're someone to be admired, if you must know – and at such a tender age too," she added teasingly.

## Chapter Seven

Quentin Caldwell's voice was loud enough to make his sister hold the telephone well away from her ear.

"Of course I object. The girl's far too young, Rose, and I expect you to make her see that!"

"And what if she simply joins this special unit, anyway?"

"How can she, without my permission?"

Rose sighed, knowing this was going to be a sticky conversation. But she had been in the habit of getting her own way for far too long to be beaten now. Contrary to what Daisy had expected, she now admired the girl for being determined to follow her heart, if not her head.

"Quentin, I'm not at all sure that she *will* need your permission. You agreed she could train to be a nurse, and if she's required to do a certain job, I think she's obliged to do it."

She didn't quite believe it, but she hoped he would. But when he didn't answer immediately, she plunged on before he remembered that this was a voluntary unit.

"You have to let them go, Quentin," she said gently. "Daisy's a young woman now, and you should be proud of her."

"I am proud of her, woman. You don't need to tell me to be proud of my own children."

"Frances would be proud of the way she's grown into a responsible young woman too."

She heard him sigh heavily and knew she had won.

"Then tell her she has my blessing," he said, before he put down the phone, then went on to report this latest development to Elsie, the only one of his children he still had at home.

Even she didn't belong to him anymore, but to Joe Preston.

In his heart Quentin still felt it wasn't right for women and children to go to war. It was against the nature of things. Man was traditionally the hunter and woman the homemaker, however old-fashioned the idea was nowadays. In the last war they had lost thousands of their young people, and it looked poised to happen all over again. Logically, it *must* happen again, because no war ever ended without casualties and tragedies.

In fact, for all the preparations, which sometimes seemed as unreal and ineffectual as some of Frances's old stage sets, he felt uneasily that Bristol itself was holding its breath. Like many cities, it was merely awaiting the inevitable. Once France fell – *if* it fell – *when* it fell – there would be no stopping the enemy.

Elsie could see at once that he was troubled. He told her of Daisy's plans and saw the matching mixture of worry and pride in her eyes. He cherished Elsie's placid company in the family home, but he knew he finally had to say what was simmering away in his mind. It had to be said.

"Elsie, my love, I've been thinking about that sugges-tion of Immy's for you to go to Penzance and stay at Kenneth Harris's boarding house for a while. And before you start objecting, just hear me out."

"He agreed to let me go without any fuss?" Daisy said in astonishment, when her aunt relayed most of the conversation with her father. "I always said you were a marvel, Aunt Rose!"

"I wouldn't say that, nor am I entirely convinced I did the right thing, even now; but I know your heart is set on it."

"You've always known the right things to say to Daddy, though," Daisy said, her mind already winging ahead with all that it meant.

"I've always known how to get around my brother, you mean. So what's the next move?"

As if only just realising how much she was going to miss her niece and also just what she was giving her blessing to, she cleared her throat awkwardly. Daisy put her arms around her and kissed her.

"I have to sign up for the special unit, and then we just await orders. Alice has already done it. We're going to stick together, so each of us will take care of the other. You don't need to worry."

"You can be sure of that, can you?"

"I just believe it, that's all," Daisy said candidly, refusing to be dampened by her aunt's genuine unease now that the deed was done. "Of course, I shall expect you to say an extra prayer at church on Sundays from now on to keep the whole unit safe."

"You can rely on that," Rose said. "And I hope you're a good sailor."

Alice Godfrey said the same thing when Daisy told her in delight that she had put her name down for the new venture. Alice's father had a small boat and Alice had been used to the choppiness of the Bristol Channel from an early age. Daisy had only had a few trips on a Bristol pleasure boat or on the river ferry when her brother Baz showed her his ferrying skills, but she wasn't going to let a little thing like boating inexperience put her off. What was there to worry about, anyway?

Two weeks later she had rather different thoughts. They left Folkestone on what had once been a cross-Channel ferry, now painted white with a large red cross on it to identify it as a hospital ship. She had been excited to find they would be based at Folkestone, and had tried to contact Jed immediately, only to find that he had already returned to his regiment. If he had tried to let her know, the letter must have crossed with her coming here.

But right now, with the boat heaving up and down in the heavy swell of the English Channel, and her stomach trying hard to mimic it, Jed was the last thing on her mind.

"Keep your eyes on the horizon, Daisy," Alice advised her. "Actually, this is reasonably calm, so you'll soon get used to it. Don't look at the water whatever you do."

"I'm trying not to," she gasped.

"And don't turn your face into the wind," a less sympathetic nurse remarked alongside her.

Daisy made a superhuman effort to keep the contents of her stomach intact and failed. You didn't need food rationing to streamline your figure, she thought wildly. All you needed to do was step on a boat and let the elements do it for you.

She realised Alice was holding her tightly while she dispatched the rest of her breakfast to the fishes.

"You'll feel better now," she was told. "And once you get your sea-legs it won't bother you at all, however rough it gets."

"Tell that to the fairies," Daisy muttered. "My brother said one of his mates was always seasick, and he'd been at sea for years on a North Sea trawler."

"Oh well, I daresay the North Sea's different," Alice said, dismissing it. "But you'll be as right as rain soon, Daisy. You'd better be, otherwise we'll be putting you in a bunk alongside the patients."

"Maybe that's what she's got in mind. Is that it, Caldwell?" the other nurse said with a knowing smirk.

Alice turned on her. "If you haven't got anything else to do, Nichols, go and see if they've got any ginger in the galley. Chewing on that can help. Or a drink of ginger cordial."

"Am I her nursemaid now?" Nurse Nichols said at once.

"Oh, just *do* it, for pity's sake, and don't be a grouch all your life!"

The girl marched off, and Daisy grinned, feeling marginally better now.

"She doesn't like being told what to do, Alice."

"She'd better get used to it then, because none of us really knows what we're in for. It's not going to be as cosy as dealing with patients on the wards, with all the proper equipment at our disposal. In desperate situations, we'll probably have to improvise."

"Like hacking off a leg with a kitchen knife?" Daisy said, without thinking.

"Something like that," Alice said solemnly, at which Daisy heaved violently again and spent the next ten minutes leaning over the side, while the waves and spume sped by below her.

When she finally raised her head, to find a glass of ginger cordial thrust in her hand from the uncompromising Nurse Nichols, she saw the coastline of France in the distance. As she saw it, still grey and hazy beneath a dull sky, they all realised they could hear the sound of distant gunfire, and the bile in her mouth turned to the first real taste of fear.

"Alice," she said hesitantly.

"I know. I'm scared too. But we're here to do a job, and we're bloody well going to do it, aren't we?"

Daisy hadn't heard her swear before, though she was well used to hearing cuss-words and blasphemy from the hospital patients. Who could blame them, when it was the only way to relieve their feelings? It never bothered her. It didn't bother her to hear Alice swear so calmly now, because it all seemed to fit in with the determined mood they were feeling.

They were here to bring their boys home, to patch them up as best they could and send them back to fight again... and they were bloody well going to do it, she thought daringly.

"You're right," she said. "We're bloody well going to do it."

As Alice laughed and squeezed her hand, she suddenly felt weirdly calmer. Not that she thought she was never going to throw up again – she was sure she would – but it wasn't going to bloody well stop her doing her job. And that was enough, she told herself severely. Aunt Rose would have a fit if she could read her thoughts. So it was a b— jolly good job she couldn't!

The job of the hospital ships was to act as shuttle ferries, the administrator had told them officiously. They all had to think of the ship they were on as an extension of their base hospital. The nurses wouldn't be expected to set foot on French soil except in emergencies. The stretcher-bearers and orderlies would bring the wounded on board, where they would be quickly assessed and sent to various sections of the ship. It would all be done with quiet efficiency, just as if the nurses were working on the wards at Weston General and other hospitals from which the nurses had been recruited.

Daisy remembered those words when the ship eased into the dockside of the strange French town and the first wave of patients was brought on board. There was nothing of the quiet efficiency they had been led to expect. A dark cloud of uniforms seemed to rise up at their approach – those who could stand at all – and the rush to get on board would have seemed an ungodly scramble, had it not been for the distress of the majority, and the uninhibited screams of those who could no longer hold them in.

There was complete chaos for an hour while they were all admitted on board; but the initial helplessness at not knowing what to do was overtaken by swift realisation that the really helpless ones were these once strong young men who seemed so pitiful now, and who needed help from the even younger, stronger, but so-called weaker female sex.

Daisy found strengths she didn't know she had as she helped to ease patients tenderly from stretcher to bunk or was advised to simply leave them where they were, as their needs were quickly affirmed. There wasn't time to blanch at open, gaping wounds as the call for bandages rang out time and again, bleeding was staunched, and doctors snapped for assistance in minor stitching operations and morphine injections.

But fumbling fingers became more efficient as they began the reverse journey back to Folkestone. Eyes and ears were sharper in the intensity of patient care. There was no time to think. All Daisy's concentration was on the patient she was tending at the moment… and then the next one… and the next.

In some cases the wounded had travelled miles on foot and farm carts, and any other way they could. It was raw, instant nursing, creating a bond between the members of the voluntary unit like none of them had experienced before.

"You did well, Caldwell," Daisy heard a voice say as she straightened up her back from holding together the ragged pieces of a soldier's arm while the surgeon sewed it together temporarily. He had moved on now, but the older nurse beside her gave her shoulder a pat.

"Thanks," Daisy muttered, not sure whether or not to risk saying more, in case it resulted in her spewing all over the patient, now that reaction was setting in.

"She did, didn't she?" the husky voice whispered from the bunk. "What's your name, girlie? Just so I can tell my old woman it weren't really no angel who helped me. And t'other one as well."

"Daisy," she murmured.

"And I'm June. June Nichols," the voice beside her went on.

Daisy hadn't even noticed who had been working beside her so efficiently, but now she saw that it was the nurse neither she nor Alice had cared for very much. She didn't look so severe now, and she certainly wasn't crowing over Daisy's seasickness any more. All of them were dishevelled, their uniforms spattered with blood, and in some cases drenched with it; but they had all worked together as a team, respecting each other without the need to say as much.

"Come on," June said brusquely. "We've got more patients to see to. We'll come back and see you again in a while, soldier."

"I'll be here," he said hoarsely. "And the name's Tom. How about a date?"

"Oh yes, and what's your old woman going to say about that?" June said cheekily. They heard him chuckling weakly as the nurses moved away.

"It doesn't hurt to humour them," June said. "Poor devil probably isn't going to get much more use out of that arm when he gets back to Blighty, even if they save it."

"Do you think it's that bad?" Daisy said, shocked. "I thought not, since the surgeon had patched it up…"

June shrugged. "It'll do for now, but my guess is he'll be invalided out soon. Don't let it get you down, kid. You'll see plenty more like that on these trips; but if we keep smiling, so will they."

"Have you done this before then? I know you're not from the same hospital as my group…"

"I've been on it for a couple of weeks, and due for a few days off soon, thank God. You can't go on for ever, so when you get the chance, take my tip and have some fun, Daisy Caldwell. Remember: you're a long time dead."

Daisy shivered, and then had to forget Nurse Nichols's advice, as they were needed urgently. She may be a cynic, Daisy thought, but she had plenty of compassion too, and she respected her more by the time they had done a second trip that day. By the time she almost fell into their assigned billet in Folkestone late that evening, she was more tired than she had ever been in her life before.

"I lost sight of you hours ago," Alice said, when they were both stretched out in their beds, tenderly flexing muscles they hardly knew they'd had. "Were you working with the dreadful Nichols?"

"I was, and she's not so dreadful once you get to know her."

"That's good," Alice murmured, too tired to discuss it.

"She says we should have some fun on our days off, because we're a long time dead."

"Is she a philosopher or something?"

"No, but I think she's right. Maybe we can find a local dance or the flicks, Alice. What do you say? There's no Aunt Rose around to tell me not to go!"

Alice was wider awake now. "Why, Daisy Caldwell, I'm surprised at you," she teased. "But I'm all for it. I heard there's a Canadian Air Force unit based near here. How do you fancy dancing with a Mountie? They're supposed to always get their man – or woman!"

When Daisy didn't answer, she half sat up.

"What's up now?"

"Can you tell me if this billet is moving about or am I still on that bloody ship?" she said weakly.

"It happens when you've been at sea for a while. Breathe deeply and try to sleep and it'll pass. We have to do it all over again tomorrow, remember."

"Oh, I remember," Daisy muttered.

–

They were to be given one day off every week; and remembering what June Nichols had recommended, on the following Saturday they sought out the nearest dance hall, if only to get the smell and sight of blood and bodies out of their memories for a little while. The stories some of the soldiers told were too horrific to keep in mind for more than a few minutes, or they might have been in danger of losing their nerve completely and asking to be transferred back to Weston General on the next train. There were also rumours of a huge retreat in the offing, in which case the little town of Dunkirk would be even more chaotic.

It wasn't only Daisy who was affected by seasickness. Alice was often greener by the end of a mercy voyage than she was at the beginning. But on that Saturday evening they scrubbed their hands with carbolic soap, washed their hair and set it with Amami setting lotion to make it smell sweeter, dabbed eau de cologne profusely behind their ears, and donned their prettiest summer dresses.

Alice said daringly that if she knew what a brothel smelled like, they must smell just like one by now. Daisy laughed, adding jokingly that she had no wish to know what a brothel smelled like anyway!

Like all the streets and buildings in the town, the dance hall was all in darkness because of blackout regulations, but once they were inside the double inner doors, it was so brilliantly lit, it hurt their eyes for a few moments.

Alice linked her arm inside Daisy's. "There's nobody to tell us what to do now except the dragon sister-in-charge, and she's not likely to pop up and tell us how to spend our evening off, so let's enjoy it."

"Right-oh," Daisy said, aware that she was having more freedom right now than she had ever had before.

She might be almost eighteen years old, but she was still cosseted to a degree and treated as one of the children by Aunt Rose and Uncle Bert. She had never been away from home like this before, and while the nurses had been more or less chaperoned and regimented on the hospital ship, with a serious job to do, now they could let their hair down.

The release of tension was suddenly enormous. Almost at once she realised the grip on her arm was lessening too, as a young sailor headed straight for Alice and asked her to dance.

"You don't mind, do you, Daisy?" Alice murmured.

"Of course not..." she began, but she was talking to thin air, as the sailor whisked Alice away and on to the crowded dance floor.

Daisy stood uncertainly for a moment or two, and then edged towards a vacant chair, vainly trying to recall how her sister Imogen's friend, Helen Church, had a remedy for feeling at a loss.

Helen was far more sophisticated than any of the Caldwell girls, what with her parents being so well off, and her father a solicitor and everything. Helen said you should always behave like royalty: never fiddle with your hands or your hair, always think serene thoughts and try to be calm and composed at all times. If you feel confident, you'll look confident...

"May I have this dance, ma'am?" she heard a voice say, while she was still deciding to tell Helen Church a thing or two about trying to feel calm and composed when everyone else seemed to be having a good time, and you felt suddenly abandoned by your only friend...

She jerked up her head. A tall young man in an Air Force uniform was standing in front of her, leaning towards her so that his features were momentarily shadowed. He held out his hand, and she automatically put hers into his as he drew her to her feet.

"I'm sorry. I know you people prefer to have the introductions made first, but there didn't seem anyone around to do it. So allow me. Flight-Officer Glenn Fraser, originally from Toronto, now attached to the RAF, and recently deployed to somewhere in the south-east, as they say, at your service," he finished with a small bow.

"Oh!" Daisy said. "Well, uh, how do you do, Flight-Officer Fraser…"

"It's Glenn, please. And you are?"

"Daisy Caldwell. Nurse. Originally from Bristol and Weston-super-Mare, currently attached to one of the hospital ships based in Folkestone."

The lengthy introductions suddenly seemed ridiculously formal when everyone around them was blatantly determined to have a good time. The war seemed a million miles away, and without warning they laughed simultaneously.

"So shall we dance, Daisy Caldwell? Or are we going to stand here looking at one another all evening? Not that I have any objection to that, either."

"I'd love to dance," she said, more breathless than she meant to be.

His smile was warm and admiring, and Daisy felt her heartbeats quicken. She liked his voice, and she liked his style and his politeness, and as he guided her on to the dance floor and she went into his arms, she reminded herself that she would probably never see him again – that Mounties may always get their man, but it didn't necessarily apply to women too.

"You're amazingly light on your feet, Daisy," he told her, when they had circled the floor several times, adroitly missing the clumsier dancers. "Were you training to be a dancer before you became a nurse?"

"No, but my mother was a dancer, and it always came easily to me. My sisters aren't bad, either," she added.

"You mean there's more than one of you? I can't believe it."

"What can't you believe?" she asked, smiling at him more provocatively than usual, because she felt safe in this atmosphere where people were desperate to make the most of evenings like these – while they lasted. And because she already liked him a lot.

"I can't believe any man could be fortunate enough to have more than one daughter with the looks of an angel," he said, the pressure of his hand on the small of her back increasing slightly. Just enough to make her skin tingle at his closeness. The floor was packed, so it might have been just an involuntary movement. They were already pressed close together, and she could sense every part of him, and she knew it must be the same for him. Before she knew it, she took fright.

"You're the second person to say that to me lately, but he was half-delirious at the time and I didn't believe him either." She spoke lightly to cover her nervousness, since the atmosphere between them had suddenly become rather too intimate, too soon.

He laughed softly, just as if could read her mind, and he leaned forward so that his cheek touched hers for a moment.

"Not everyone's just throwing you a line, Daisy, though you must hear plenty of them in your business. Some of us are actually sincere."

"I'm sorry," she said, embarrassed now that she might have offended him. "But you're right. Some of the patients do say the daftest things, and it would be silly to believe all of them, wouldn't it?"

"It surely would. You need to be selective."

The band finished playing the tune, and reluctantly they broke apart.

"Thank you," he said gravely. "Perhaps we can have another dance later."

"Possibly. But I have to find my friend now. It was very nice meeting you," she said, and rushed away from him.

Now he would think her a complete idiot, she thought, fuming, as she found her way to the ladies' cloakroom for a breather, away from too many prying eyes on her blazing cheeks. But the cloakroom was so crowded that she couldn't hide away, and Alice was already there, dabbing powder on her cheeks.

"Good Lord, Daisy, you look like a whirling dervish. I saw you dancing with that good-looking fellow. Lucky you! I got stuck with a boring rating. So how did you get on? Did he ask you for a date?"

Daisy looked at her dumbly. No, he hadn't asked her for a date, because she hadn't stayed around long enough for him to make such a move. And if he had, what would she have said? That she couldn't go out with strangers because her Aunt Rose wouldn't approve? That she wasn't sure when her next day off was?

Or that she already had a young man in the RAF who never wrote to her, and there was another boy on the horizon whom she couldn't contact?

"No," she said crossly. "But he's asked me for another dance, so that's something, isn't it? I think."

"Well, don't bite my head off. I thought he looked smashing, so why are you so jumpy? He didn't make a pass at you, did he? You know what I mean, I suppose," she said, lowering her voice.

To Daisy, the delicacy of the question implied that Alice suspected she didn't know what was what.

"He was very nice and very polite. And if he does ask me for a date, I shall probably say yes."

"Well, he's not going to ask you if you stay in here all evening, is he? So we'd better go back to the fray – unless you've got cold feet."

# Chapter Eight

By the end of May the general complacency that still lingered, to some degree, gave way to total panic as the threat of invasion became very real. As the Germans overran Belgium and parts of France, newspaper and wireless reports couldn't hide the news that the British Expeditionary Force, which had fought such valiant battles in France, was being inexorably herded into a corner on the twenty-mile stretch of beach in and around Dunkirk. The Germans were surrounding them on all sides, and there was no way out except by sea or surrender.

Bert Painter, self-styled eyes and ears for the family now, with his addictive attention to whatever the newspapers and wireless announcers had to say, reported the latest facts to his wife once the boys had gone to bed.

"It looks bloody grim, Rose," he said, "and our Daisy's in the thick of it. We should never have let her go on those hospital ships."

"We couldn't have stopped her," Rose retorted, knowing she had played her part in Daisy's departure, but knowing too that her niece had too much self-will not to have gone anyway. "But it's too late for second thoughts now. She's doing her bit as she always wanted, and we can be proud of her."

"I am proud of her, woman, but it doesn't stop me worrying about her."

"And you think I don't?"

She stared at him in resentment, wondering why they were bickering like this, when by all accounts there was an army of men waiting to be evacuated from somewhere called Dunkirk, which to Rose was no more than a dot on a map on the northern part of France.

"So what do the papers say will happen next?" she went on less aggressively.

"Whatever it is, they won't give us the full facts," Bert said. "Churchill's got a hell of a lot to deal with after only three weeks in office, so let's hope he's got the guts for it. And you'd better say a few extra prayers at church on Sunday."

The fact that he didn't set as much store by such things as Rose did made his words all the more ominous, and she found herself wishing she had a crystal ball to see just how her niece was faring; and just as instantly, she was guiltily glad that she didn't.

–

Daisy was terrified. It was like a nightmare. Theirs was only one hospital ship among many large craft waiting offshore, and what seemed to be hundreds of smaller craft of all descriptions – fishing boats, pleasure steamers, trawlers – all ferrying men out to the bigger ships to take them home to England. The hospital ships had been doing a necessary job of work before, receiving the wounded off the French beaches. Now, it seemed as if the whole world was trying to cram into the fleet of ships awaiting them.

The town of Dunkirk itself was burning and a pall of smoke hung over the port, enhanced by the sickly smell of rotting corpses of horses and men. The beaches had quickly become choked with the swelling numbers of starving, weary soldiers, and word had quickly gone out from Whitehall that any ship that could float was to be sent to the French coast to get the men out. A vast flotilla of little boats of all descriptions had set to sea at once.

As the men were rescued, the harrowing tales they told were of burning lorries, abandoned vehicles, and men and horses mown down by German bombers and left dying and stinking by the roadside. Some had walked for days to reach the coast without food or water and were literally starving.

The bigger ships, including the hospital ships, were obliged to stay away from the beaches near the breakwater known as East Mole, while the smaller ships made day and night rescue sorties and brought the men out to them in batches. And all the time they were being bombed by German aeroplanes, intercepted by the swooping RAF Spitfires, so that the air was filled with noise and the bitter smell of burning oil and white-hot metal. Nearby a huge fire was raging in a refinery, adding to the chaos and sending clouds of acrid smoke over the entire area.

"It's like something out of hell," Daisy Caldwell whispered to her friend Alice, both of them white-faced, their hearts pumping as the whine of enemy aeroplanes and screaming shells split the air.

They held each other's hand tightly, wondering if their own distinctive hospital ship was going to be defence enough against an enemy who cared little for human life. And Daisy, aware of the incongruousness of the little ships moving like a tidal wave in and out of the beaches with their precious cargo, wondered desperately if her brother Baz was among them.

The two girls strained their eyes in the gloom of evening, but all they could see in the light of the German flares were the thousands of black dots that were men, trying to reach a boat that would bring them nearer home. Some of them never made it at all. Some were trampled by their companions; some overfilled the small boats and were lost in the stampede; some found themselves in a small boat that took a direct hit from a German bomb. Larger vessels had already been sunk by German U-boats, including the destroyers *Wakeful* and *Grafton*. Even though there was a cordon of British submarines guarding the evacuation ships, the might of the German forces seemed invincible as word filtered through that the two destroyers were only two among the many British ships that had been sunk.

"You two nurses – stop gawping and see to these men!" they heard someone bellow behind them. They jerked backwards, aware that they had been so awestruck and horrified by what they were seeing that they had momentarily forgotten what they were here to do.

Half-sobbing with fear and nerves, Daisy and Alice rushed to do the medical officer's bidding as several small boats coasted near to them, and the men were hauled aboard, ragged and hollow-eyed after trekking for miles on foot to reach the coast.

"Let's pray for bad weather tomorrow so the German planes can't fly," Alice said grimly, as she and Daisy both tried to staunch a soldier's badly wounded leg, both being horribly sprayed by the bubbling, sweet-smelling blood of an artery.

"Oh God, I can't stand it," Daisy babbled in a sudden panic, knowing that it was hopeless, completely hopeless. He was so obviously about to die. To her horror, the soldier suddenly looked her straight in the eyes and gave a weird smile.

"That makes two of us, girlie," he said, before he choked on his vomit and slumped backwards.

"Leave him," they heard an officer say behind them. "He's beyond help, but there are others who need you nurses. Now *move!*"

Like automatons they leapt to obey him, thankful for the orders, for without them they knew they would probably slink away into a corner like terrified animals. There were always others to be helped, others to be bandaged and given a cigarette or drink of water, or held tightly as a surgeon performed an impromptu operation, while desperately trying to be oblivious to their screams…

Joe Preston had lost sight of his unit hours ago. He'd lost his rifle and all his ammunition, and his boots as well. God knew where they had gone, but the pain in his feet now was so bad he didn't know where it began or ended. He couldn't even be sure if he had caught a bullet in one of them; he only knew that if he didn't keep moving towards the beaches of Dunkirk he'd be trampled underfoot by the crawling army of men pushing him forward.

But by now he was so exhausted and so disorientated he knew he had to stumble out of the ragged column and sit by the dusty roadside for a while to gather his senses. He fell over an arm that had once held a rifle and was now separated from the rest of its owner, and almost gagged with the horror of it all. He was a strong man, but men had never been born to deal with this, nor to be reduced to unmanly weeping. The taste of dust and death was in his mouth and the sight seared his eyes; he staggered farther into the fields and lay there panting to get some strength back before going on.

In desperation he tried to think of home, of his parents, and especially of his sweet Elsie and their coming baby, because if he had to die here, then it was Elsie's image he wanted to take with him to his Maker.

It was hard to think of anything but the stink in his nostrils and the steady drone of the German bombers overhead. He was light-headed from lack of food, and he carefully raised his head, dream-like, as he saw the column of men ahead of him scatter in an almost beautiful slow-motion formation when one of the enemy bombers bore down on them, screaming death from the skies. The next minute the group of men were no more than corpses as the bomb made a direct hit. And but for his need to breathe clean air for a few moments, Joe would have been one of them.

As it was, his senses were shattered, his hearing blasted. The shame of not being one of his dead travelling companions was a tormenting pain in his mind, and he staggered forward again, sobbing, shouting, unable to hear his own voice, except in his head, raging at a God who could let this happen. He hadn't known those men, but they were all his brothers, and he hadn't been man enough to share their final moments. And then, with an almost fiendish need for survival, the next thought in his head was that maybe somewhere among the corpses he might find a pair of boots that would fit him, allowing him to go on...

He didn't hear the sound of a vehicle right behind him as he staggered back on to the road. He couldn't hear the driver shouting at him. He hardly felt the pair of arms that lifted him into the field ambulance and laid him on a stretcher, although he was aware that there were people surrounding him who were still alive, still breathing. He was conscious of the fact that at least he was not going to die alone, and the last thing he saw before he closed his gritty, bloodshot eyes and let it happen, was the sight of the sand dunes in the distance.

—

As if the gods were taking pity on the evacuation forces, there was a thick sea fog on May the thirtieth, making it impossible for the German bombers to take to the skies, and on that day thousands of men were transported to the ships. One of them was Joe Preston, courtesy of the field ambulance that had miraculously found him wandering about half-crazed the night before.

"Here's another batch for you ladies," the driver said cheerfully to the nurses on the hospital ship waiting to receive the wounded. "It'll do their poor eyes good to see a few pretty faces, so give 'em a smile. This unlucky bastard's in danger of losing a foot – pardon my language – and needs a surgeon pretty damn quick…"

"Joe? *Joe?*" Daisy stuttered, finding it hard to recognise the emaciated man with the blackened face on the stretcher, muttering and pulling at the covering blanket incessantly. "It is you?"

"Do you know this one?" said the stretcher-bearer. "You won't get any sense out of him. He can't hear you. Shell-shocked, I reckon, and hasn't said a word since we picked him up. Just keeps mumbling Elsie, or Esther, or some such name. That's not you, is it?"

"No. It's Elsie. My sister. Joe's her husband. Oh my God, *Joe*…"

As her voice threatened to rise hysterically, she was pushed out of the way by a medical orderly.

"You're no use to me here, Caldwell," he snapped. "Go and pull yourself together and send me someone who isn't going to fall to pieces at the sight of a gangrenous foot."

"I'm sorry," she stammered again, humiliated. "But he's my brother-in-law – and you don't really mean it about his foot, do you?"

Her pity for Joe overcame her panic for a few seconds, but then she realised he was trying to say something, and she bent low over him in order to hear the mumbled words.

"Caldwell… Elsie…"

"He must have heard my name," Daisy said, but the orderly shook his head as Joe's eyes resumed their wild look.

"I doubt that. Probably read my lips. Now do as you're told and get out of here. There are others who need you, and this one's going straight to the theatre."

Daisy scuttled away, knowing that the theatre was a grand name for the cabin they used as a makeshift operating room. She prayed that Joe's foot would be saved, even though she had the guilty feeling that if it wasn't, then at least Elsie would have him home. Joe's war would be over.

There was nothing she could do for him now, but when they returned to base for a few hours off she must telephone home at once to let Elsie know that Joe was safe. She wouldn't give any more details, since he would assuredly be sent to a British hospital as soon as they landed, no matter what happened here.

The orderly was right. There were others who needed her. By the time the ship reached Folkestone, to the usual accompanying cheers and placards of what seemed like hundreds of onlookers at all the south-east ports, waiting to welcome their boys back home, no matter what the hour, it began to look more hopeful that Joe wasn't going to lose his foot. The bullet had gone straight through, but the infection hadn't turned gangrenous after all and was responding to treatment. He was still in dire need of nourishment, but although his hearing hadn't yet returned, he was conscious enough to recognise Daisy.

"Who'd have thought... Elsie's little sister... would turn out to be... such an efficient nurse?" he said haltingly.

"Not so efficient," she murmured, knowing he couldn't hear, but not wanting to let him know how awful she had felt at letting him down. She wasn't much of a nurse after all, she thought, if she couldn't even help her own brother-in-law. The shame of it didn't escape her as Joe squeezed her hand. She mouthed the words at him slowly so that he could read her lips.

"I'll let Elsie know you're safe, Joe, but I don't know where they'll be sending you yet."

He nodded, and then closed his eyes in weariness, so there was no point in saying any more. But if she knew him, then once his foot had healed, his war wouldn't be over at all. With a fervour she hadn't felt in weeks, Daisy wished that hers was. She wished she could go back to being what she was before – scatty Daisy Caldwell, not putting her mind to anything serious, just enjoying being who she was, with an indulgent family all around her; and for the first time in ages, she felt a sob tear at her throat, knowing that nothing could ever be like that again.

–

The evacuation went on for several more days and was pronounced a huge success. The enormousness of the numbers filtering through to the newspapers had civilians reeling. Thousands upon thousands of British and French troops had been rescued in little over four days. Returning soldiers with little or nothing to write on had thrown slips of paper out of lorry and train windows taking them to British hospitals, and the cheering crowds had promised to send them on to waiting wives and sweethearts. Quentin Caldwell had received one such note from his son.

"My God, has the boy gone completely mad?" he roared to his daughter Elsie, his leonine expression belying the emotion he felt.

By now Elsie knew that Joe was safe, and in a military hospital somewhere in Essex. But this small scrap of paper inside an envelope from Baz, sent from Dover, was something his father had never expected.

> *What a lark, Father, ferrying our boys back and*
> *forth from France.*
> > *Hope to see you soon.*
> > *Your loving son, Baz.*

Quentin's mouth worked as he finished reading it out to Elsie. As if it wasn't enough that his eldest daughter Immy was God-knew-where, and his youngest was doing dangerous work on the hospital ship. Now this. Did God mean to test him by sending all his children to war? Thank God Teddy was far too young ever to be involved, and Elsie too pregnant.

"You should be proud of him, Daddy," he heard her say softly. "It was a pretty fair bet that when Mr Churchill asked for anything that could float to take to sea, Baz and his mates wouldn't hesitate."

"Of course I'm proud of him. I just don't want to lose him," he said abruptly.

"I'm sure you won't. He's like a bad penny. He'll always turn up just when you least expect him."

But she said it with a smile because she didn't think Baz was a bad penny at all, and she was enormously proud of what both he and Daisy were doing. For Daisy to have actually been on the hospital ship that brought Joe home was a good omen that she was doggedly not going to ignore.

"You're a good girl, Elsie."

"No, I'm not. I'm a useless one. All I can do is sit around waiting for my baby to be born while everyone else is being brave and useful," she said, frustrated all over again at her inability to do anything for the war effort. She had tentatively offered to go to the shop for a few hours each day, since most of the young men had enlisted now; but Quentin wouldn't hear of it in her condition. It simply wasn't done. So she sat at home and knitted comforts for the troops, feeling as matronly as her Aunt Rose and her knitting circle.

"Elsie, I think you should think seriously now about going to Cornwall to stay at the boarding house run by Immy's old boss," Quentin said next, glad to have something else to think about besides his son's reckless behaviour.

"Why now? And why on earth should I, when Joe's back home and likely to get convalescent leave?" she exclaimed.

"Because, my darling," her father said carefully, "I think the threat of invasion is becoming imminent, and I would rather know you were safely out of harm's way when Hitler decides to start bombing us. Now that he has no opposing army standing in his way, his bombers will be able to reach every part of Britain."

Elsie stared at him, her stomach gnawing at his words. For so long now, they had believed Bristol's docks and aircraft factories would be a prime target for bombing, but the planes had never reached here. Already, town and city signposts were being removed, so that if the invasion came, the Germans wouldn't know where they were. It all seemed so farcical, since why on earth would the victors care which town they overran?

"I won't leave here, Daddy," Elsie said stubbornly. "Not unless Joe insists on it."

"Or Hitler does," her father said.

–

On June the fourth Winston Churchill's speech to the House of Commons was later broadcast to the nation. By then, Daisy and Alice and their companions were crowded around the wireless set in their billet, listening to the measured words of the orator. He pronounced the evacuation a resounding success, praising everyone who had taken part, from the nurses and medical staff to civilians who had welcomed the brave soldiers back home; and above all Churchill praised the RAF for their part in the proceedings. He emphasised that without them casualties would have been far higher than they were, and that no one should underestimate the skill and devotion of our airmen.

"I wonder if your dashing Canadian's listening," Alice whispered to Daisy. And Cal, thought Daisy, with a catch in her throat. And Cal...

But Alice was shushed at once as Churchill's voice continued. His final words made them all fall silent, with emotions running high.

"We shall go on to the end; we shall fight in France, we shall fight on the seas and oceans, we shall fight with growing confidence and growing strength in the air, we shall defend our island, whatever the cost may be; we shall fight on the beaches, we shall fight on the landing grounds, we shall fight in the fields and in the streets, we shall fight in the hills; we shall never surrender."

"Well," said Alice, when the broadcast was finished. "I'll say this for him: he has a way with words, if nothing else."

"I thought it was perfectly thrilling," Daisy said, choked. "If anyone can lift the nation's morale, it's him."

"So now we've heard him, and we're all feeling better for it," one of the other girls said practically. "So what do we do now that we've got a few days off? I say let's go into town and see if there's a dance anywhere. After dealing with so many half-deads all this time, a bit of live, red-blooded male to whisk me around the dance floor is just what I need."

At any other time it might have sounded callous and heartless, but they were all weary, and longing to get the lingering smell of blood from their skin and clothes, and they were all in full agreement. What possible harm could it do to enjoy themselves? It was hardly going to stop the war effort.

"We'd better check with the CO first," Alice said.

But as expected, there was no objection, and an hour later, when they had somehow all managed a bath in the regulation five inches of water, scrubbed every inch of themselves and changed out of uniform into something more feminine and sweet-smelling, they marched in a small convoy with their arms linked, down to the centre of town, looking for anything to wash away the memories of the last few days, for a little while at least.

It was almost a replica of another night that wasn't so long ago in reality, and yet that seemed like a lifetime ago in many respects. The dance hall was open and crowded with girls and servicemen, and the music was in full swing when they entered. There was no RAF contingent from Biggin Hill that night, but there were plenty of willing partners for six reckless young ladies intent on enjoying themselves.

They didn't talk too much about where they had been. They were conscious of careless talk costing lives, as the posters put it, in case there were German spies among the friendliest and most admiring of young men; and now, with talk of invasion more glibly on everyone's lips than before, the danger of careless words seemed even more of a threat. Daisy didn't quite know how it could be, but she stuck to the rules anyway.

The evening did something to settle the nerves that were still very much in evidence in all of them. Earlier, Daisy had managed to phone her father to tell him she was safe and heard the news about Baz. She was very proud of her little brother and could just imagine how his adventurous soul had relished the chance of beating the Germans at their own game, and fishing soldiers out of the sea right under their dive-bombing noses.

She thought of it in Baz's terms, and found herself grinning at the melodrama of it all, though she was careful not to make too much of it to her father, and just said how thankful she was that they had both come out of it unscathed – was able to reassure him about Joe too.

"I should think he'll be in hospital for quite some time, but with any luck they'll transfer him somewhere nearer home," she told a tearful Elsie, when she too came on the line. "But I'm sure he'll be writing to you as soon as he can."

She had crossed her fingers when she said it, because when she had last seen him he hadn't seemed capable of holding a pen, let alone writing a sensible letter. But there were always nurses willing to write letters for soldiers who couldn't do it for themselves. She had done it enough times. But she had also seen what shell-shock did to people. It went deeper than anyone realised, and she only prayed that Joe would be restored to full health again, for her sister's sake as well as his own.

"Wake up, Daisy; it's time to go back to base unless you want to get a rollicking," Alice urged her at the end of her evening, as her thoughts wandered.

"Sorry, I was dreaming," she said hastily.

Alice grinned. "I know. You were wishing your Canadian had been here instead of that sweaty-palmed sailor who was jigging you about."

"Something like that," Daisy told her, wondering why Alice persisted in mentioning Glenn at all. It was hardly likely she would ever meet him again.

That was another thing about war. You met, you fell in love – or not – and then you were parted for ever. Unless, by some miracle, something happened like Joe Preston being brought to her hospital ship. That was a coincidence, if you like. But coincidences did happen, and she had the proof of that, even if she didn't care to think about her own behaviour too often. She had simply gone to pieces at seeing someone close to her, and that was something she *wasn't* proud of.

The next morning, as they idly awaited orders for their next assignment, the daily batch of mail brought a letter addressed to her. She didn't recognise the handwriting, and the original postmark was blotted out. She took it back to the billet, empty for once, and for a moment her heart leapt, wondering if it could possibly be from Glenn, knowing she hadn't forgotten him at all, despite her airy-fairy reactions whenever Alice mentioned him.

Her heart began to beat faster, instantly recalling the deeply attractive Canadian voice. Then she realised that it couldn't possibly be from Glenn, since the overwritten address on the letter told her it had been forwarded from Weston General Hospital, and her heartbeats became more sickeningly agitated now as she tore open the envelope and took out the single sheet of paper.

For a few seconds she stared disbelievingly at the tortured words, unable to take in the sense of them immediately as they danced in front of her eyes. *Unwilling* to take them in at all, as she let her gaze slip down to the end of the letter and the scrawled signature at the end.

Sheilagh Monks. Cal's mother.

# Chapter Nine

Alice had some news. She found Daisy alone in the billet, hunched over a screwed-up letter in her hand. It was obvious that something was very wrong.

"What's happened?" she asked at once, sitting beside Daisy on her bed, and taking her cold hand in hers.

Daisy looked at her vacantly.

"I wish you had known my mother," she said finally. "Did I ever tell you she was quite a famous dancer? She had the voice of an angel too. We all loved to watch her perform on the stage."

"I know. You told me," Alice said, trying not to show her alarm at this apparent retreat into the past.

Daisy took a deep breath. "It's all right; I'm not going mad. I'm just trying to put into practice some of the things she told me, and it's difficult."

Her mouth trembled before she went on. "I even told the problem child Vanessa how my mother got me over my fear of clouds by saying they were castles in the sky when I thought they were monsters. What kind of a blithering idiot would think clouds were monsters anyway?"

"I suppose some might," Alice murmured, not having the faintest idea who Vanessa was. "Is that what's troubling you now?"

"Of course not. But she also said that if there was something bad – really bad – in your life, then sometimes it helped to try putting it aside for a little while and coming back to it later. Think of something pleasant, she always said – if only for a few moments – but it doesn't work, does it? Because all I can think of is… is…"

Alice put her arms around her, seriously alarmed now.

"Is it something to do with that letter?" she asked, knowing it had to be. A family thing, perhaps. One of her sisters was expecting a baby, and it was her husband they had just brought back from France. Surely they hadn't had to amputate his foot after all… The letter fell to the floor, and Alice picked it up.

"Read it," Daisy said in a choked voice. "Read it out loud, then perhaps I'll start to believe it."

Alice uncreased the crumpled letter, which Daisy had presumably screwed up in order to deny its existence. But she couldn't deny it for ever, and Alice started to read it aloud, slowly and deliberately, as if reading to a child.

> *Dear Miss Daisy Caldwell,*
>
> *I'm sorry to have to write to you since I don't know you at all, but I thought my Callum would want me to. The telegram came three weeks and two days ago, and a parcel of Callum's belongings was sent home a little later.*

Alice swallowed. The preciseness of the timing was heart-breaking, as if the letter-writer was counting every day since the telegram came. She knew that feeling. And everyone knew what telegrams meant these days.

> *The telegram said my Callum had been killed in action. A letter came from his squadron-leader a*

*week ago, saying that he had died heroically in the course of duty, so that was a comfort.*

*Your name and the address of the hospital where you worked was in Callum's notebook, so I thought you would want to know the news. I'm very sorry to be the bearer of bad tidings, Miss Caldwell.*

*Yours truly,*
*Sheilagh Monks (Mrs)*

"Oh Daisy, I'm so sorry! This was the young man you met in Weston doing his Air Force training, wasn't it?"

Daisy's voice was clipped now. "Yes. Cal. I thought I was going to marry him one day. But it's all a waste of time, isn't it?"

"What is?"

"Falling in love. Getting to know someone. Thinking you might have a future together. It's all a waste of time and energy, because if the TB doesn't get you, then bloody Hitler will. We all lose people in the end."

For a minute Alice didn't connect the two, and then she remembered Daisy's friend Lucy, who had died in a TB sanatorium far from home; and seeing how Daisy was shivering uncontrollably now, she knew she had to say something positive to shake her out of her depression.

"How can you say that? Was it a waste of time knowing Cal? Would you have missed one second of the time you shared with him? And your friend Lucy too. Wasn't she your very first best friend – and the one you shared your very first secrets with, I'll bet? Of course we lose people in the end, Daisy, because that's how life is, and we can't stop it or change it. I lost my brother too, but no one can take away my memories of him, and you'll think the same way about Cal when you've had time to adjust to losing him."

"Oh really. And will I adjust to my guilt over not being so sure I loved him after all? And thinking about writing to Jed – and dancing with Glenn…"

"For pity's sake, Daisy, you're making me really angry now. Grow up and stop being so self-centred. Think about how Cal's mother is grieving. Her loss is far greater than yours. I know how my mother felt when we heard about Roy, and Cal was still his mother's baby, however much of a hero he was."

She didn't say what they all suspected: that the glib remarks about every one of them dying a hero were no more than words to soften the blow and give the bereaved a semblance of pride – and the deceased some dignity.

Daisy didn't say anything for a few minutes, but her face began to show a little more colour. She finally replied slowly, as if it was a great effort.

"Oh, I know you're right. And I know I'll have to write back to Mrs Monks, though I can't think what on earth to say. It won't help me, but I suppose it might help her, and I can hardly ignore her letter. It would seem as if I didn't care."

"That's my girl," Alice said, giving her shoulder a squeeze. "And it *will* help you, believe me. And I didn't come in here just to pry…"

"You didn't pry. I don't know what I'd have done without you."

"You'd have coped. You're stronger than you look, Daisy Caldwell," Alice told her with a glimmer of a smile. "Anyway, let me say what I came to tell you. We're being disbanded."

"What?" Daisy frowned, unable to switch her thoughts so quickly after the enormity of the letter.

"Well, not all the hospital ships, of course. But the special units – which means us, my sweet – are being sent home for a week's leave now that the evacuation's over, and then we have to report back to our own hospitals again."

"Just when I was getting used to my sea-legs," Daisy replied, with the first *almost* hint at a joke she had made since hearing from Cal's mother.

Alice found herself breathing a small sigh of relief. Daisy was one of the resilient kind, thank God, though they were all going to find it strange to be back on the wards again after the excitement – if that was the word – of being at the sharp end, as they called it.

—

"You're not to fuss over Daisy when she comes home," Aunt Rose told the three small boys sternly. "She'll be feeling very tired, and she's coming home for a rest before she goes back to work at the hospital again."

"Ain't she going to tell us about her boat, and all the operations she did, and the *blood*?" Norman said at once.

"She won't want to talk about any of that, so you just keep your gory little thoughts to yourself," Rose said sharply.

She hesitated but decided not to mention the letter that Daisy had told her about on the telephone the previous night. It was obvious by the way she had said it and then gone on all in a rush to say what time she expected to be home that she didn't want any questions about Cal either. Not yet, anyway.

Although, in Rose's opinion, the sooner you spoke about such things, the sooner you came to terms with them, she knew Daisy had to deal with her young man's death in her own way.

It was more than likely that she would want to spend a few days at home in Bristol too. Her father would want to see for himself that his youngest girl was all right, and Elsie would want to hear about her husband at first hand.

"Our Daisy's coming home! Our Daisy's coming home!" Teddy began chanting. "Will she be bringing presents?"

"Of course she won't, you loony," Norman honked at him. "She's been fixing up army blokes with broken bones and legs hanging off. She won't have been buying presents for babies…"

"I'm not a baby," Teddy howled, red-faced, throwing a cushion at him, and getting it hurled right back.

Rose ignored their usual antics, more concerned with how Norman's younger brother had paled. Ronnie was not the robust character his brother was, and the chickenpox had hit him far harder than any of the others. He had a persistent cough that reminded her all too well of Lucy, though the family doctor had assured her that it was nothing remotely like consumption, and that Ronnie was merely a more delicate child than some.

Being a foster-mother was not always the easiest of occupations, thought Rose, wondering for the umpteenth time how Vanessa was getting on these days. They had heard nothing since that one letter, but she supposed it was to be expected. As Bert constantly reminded her, the children were only borrowed. One day they would all go home, and there would be just the two of them again.

It was only right and proper, she thought stalwartly, but it would be a wrench all the same. She was being a selfish and wicked old woman, because when they all went home again, it would mean the war was over, and nobody could deny how they would all rejoice at that.

"Who's going to help me get Daisy's room ready for her then?" she asked and was predictably talking to thin air as the boys all scuttled out of the house to feed their chickens.

For Daisy, it felt weird to be going home again. Everything seemed to be happening at a slower pace and a far lower level than in the furious days of Dunkirk. It was strange to see people going about their everyday lives, queueing for food, discussing the weather, gossiping with neighbours about the price of fish or the latest on who had done what with whom… If it hadn't been for the glaring newspaper reports, it would have been just as if Dunkirk had never happened at all.

Daisy found it hard to deal with. She had been in the thick of something more horrendous than in her worst nightmares, and now there was nothing to do but spend time at home and wait for the days to pass before she reported back to Weston General. It was an awful anti-climax, and a shameful one too, because it implied that she had *wanted* the trauma to go on – that she had *enjoyed* being thought of as some poor wretch's guardian angel, his little Miss Nightingale – and she knew such feelings weren't worthy of her.

"There's to be a special service at church on Sunday, to give thanks for all the soldiers who were brought home safely," Aunt Rose told her when she had been listless and uncommunicative for two days. "You'll come with us, of course."

"Must I?"

"Certainly you must. I'm sure Alice Godfrey and her family will be there as well, and Teddy's very proud of you, you know."

"Oh well, *Teddy*," Daisy said, dismissing him. "He's just a baby. What does he know about anything?"

"He knows you did a very brave thing, and he doesn't understand why you won't talk to him. And he's not a baby; he's an intelligent child, if only you'd give him half a chance. In fact, all the boys are dying to hear about your experiences whenever you feel ready to tell them, and we can't creep about the house for ever for fear of upsetting you. Don't shut us all out, Daisy."

It was the first time Rose had come near to criticising her.

"Is that what I'm doing?"

"Well, isn't it?"

Daisy spoke abruptly. "I'll think about it. Right now I need some fresh air, Aunt Rose. I'm going to see Alice. Is that all right?"

"Darling, whatever you want to do is all right with me," Rose said gently. "You know that."

Sometime soon Daisy knew she would have to talk about Cal. That was something else she had kept bottled up inside. Only with Alice could she seem to talk freely about anything these days, and half an hour later the two girls were walking along the wide stretch of sands, watching the rippling tide wash it clean.

"Will they put barbed wire along our beach, do you think?" Daisy said dully. "Spoiling everything."

"I doubt it. I can't imagine the Germans will bother coming ashore in the Bristol Channel when they've got the whole of the south coast to invade," Alice said cheerfully.

Daisy scuffed at the sand with the toe of her shoe, resentful that Alice seemed to be coping with the aftermath of Dunkirk far better than she was. Even *thinking* about the Germans invading England was enough to send cold shivers down Daisy's spine, let alone talking about it so calmly.

"Doesn't it bother you?"

"Don't be stupid, Daisy. Of course it bothers me, but I'm not going to let it take over my life, and nor should you. We just have to get on with things, like Mr Churchill said." She hesitated. "Have you written to Mrs Monks yet?"

"No. I don't know what to say."

"Say how you feel. Say what's in your heart."

"That's a bit difficult, since there's nothing there at all any more. It's just a great big empty void."

Alice stepped right in front of Daisy, stopping her in her tracks, and shaking her by the arms.

"You've got to stop this, Daisy. You're not the only one to have lost someone, you know. You're not the first and you won't be the last, and a fine sort of nurse you're going to be if you can't cope with the fact that people are going to die in a war. If you're thinking of reporting to the hospital with that attitude and that gloomy face next week, you'd do better to stay away."

"Well, thank you for that! You don't understand how I feel—"

"Yes, I *do*. I understand very well, but Daisy darling, we all have to go on. Would Cal want you to fall apart because he was killed? Wouldn't he want you to go on helping others with your lovely smile and your chirpy nature that cheers everybody up? You know darned well he would."

Daisy didn't say anything for a while, and they automatically resumed walking again while she digested her friend's words. She wished she could hate her for saying them, but, in her heart, she knew it was the best piece of common sense she'd heard yet.

"We met just about here," she said slowly. "Me and Cal, I mean. I was just as miserable then – and I had every right to be, because Lucy had just told me about her TB. Cal cheered me up with his nonsense." She felt herself give a half-smile, remembering.

"There you are then," Alice said. "Isn't that just what I told you? Think about the good times you had and be glad of them."

"I'll try," Daisy said, taking a long breath. "I really will."

Even when they heard a squadron of aeroplanes flying low overhead, she wouldn't let the pain rush in. If Alice could bear it, so could she; and although she felt a mite better by the time she got back to the house, her new resolve was immediately tested as Norman and Ronnie came hurtling in from the garden.

"Norman says your boy was prob'ly flying one of them planes," Ronnie shrieked, "and I said he wouldn't still be here, cos he'd be shooting down Jerries by now, wouldn't he, Daisy?"

She heard Aunt Rose draw in her breath and start to scold the pair of them, shooing them out of the room; but Daisy stopped her.

"No, don't be cross with them, Aunt Rose. I can't hide it for ever."

It was sad that little boys had to hear of death and destruction and come to terms with it, as they all did. Taking away their innocence, because of a madman. But she didn't know how to tell them without breaking down. Then, like a bolt from the blue, she tried to imagine how her mother would have handled this, and somehow, she found the words.

"Sit down, boys, and Teddy, come here too," she said, seeing him in his usual corner, curled up with George. "Remember all those pictures in your comics with the aeroplanes and their brave pilots zooming about the skies?"

"Yeah," said Norman, his eyes lighting up. "That's what I'm going to be when I grow up too."

"Are you?" Daisy said, momentarily diverted, but glad of the small lead. "It can be quite dangerous, you know. You know how the comic pictures show some of the planes going down in flames, don't you?"

"Oh yeah, but they're not our planes," Norman said confidently.

"It's not only the enemy planes that get shot down, Norman. It's our planes as well, and sometimes it's our pilots and our airmen who get killed."

Ronnie started to snivel, while Teddy continued to clutch George until he whimpered in protest. But Norman, with uncanny insight, stared into her eyes, reminding her of Vanessa, who had had that kind of directness too.

"Has that happened to your boy?"

"I'm afraid so, Norman. Cal's mother wrote to tell me. She said he was a hero, and she especially wanted me to know that."

Ronnie rushed out of the room with Teddy following. Norman continued to stare at Daisy, while she desperately tried to remain unblinking and dry-eyed.

"That's good, isn't it?" he said at last. "That he was a hero, I mean."

She gave him a weak smile.

"I think it's the finest thing any man could have said about him, Norman. My Cal was a hero, and we must always remember that and try not to be too sad about it. Now, if you don't mind, I'm just going to change my shoes before Aunt Rose tells me off for bringing all this sand indoors."

She just managed to get out of the room with her head held high, seeing the small nod of approval in her aunt's eyes before she rushed upstairs, kicked off her shoes and threw herself on to her bed to sob her heart out for Cal, with healing, wrenching tears.

–

"Well, what do you think of our Daisy?" Imogen asked Helen.

They had managed to get a forty-eight-hour pass together at last and had decided to spend it in London rather than going home. What the folks didn't know about wouldn't hurt them – and there might not be too many more chances like this once Hitler started bombing them.

There was a feeling of recklessness about them as they checked into the small hotel that weekend, shared with most other people intent on having a good time while it lasted.

"I think she's marvellous," Helen said. "And young Baz too."

"Oh, *Baz*," Immy said, finding it easy to push her daredevil brother out of her mind. "It was always on the cards that he'd be in at the deep end, pardon the pun. But I never expected Daisy to end up such a dedicated nurse, *nor* go to sea."

"You never did give her credit for knowing her own mind, did you, darling?" Helen said airily, as they unpacked their small suitcases and hung up their frocks in the minuscule wardrobe. *Real* civvy summer frocks, she thought with satisfaction, not the beastly uniforms that had become almost a second skin now.

Immy laughed. "That's because she so rarely *did* know her own mind, and you know it. I must admit, though, I feel rather proud of her."

"And so you should. But don't let's spend all weekend thinking about Daisy or anything to do with the war. It's such gorgeous weather, and there are plenty of young men around, so let's just concentrate on having *fun*, Immy."

"All right. Just as long as you remember I'm practically engaged to your brother, so I've got no intention of doing anything awful!"

"And you think I have?" Helen said innocently.

"Given half a chance, yes! Though not too awful. Just a little bit daring to liven up our dull lives."

Helen sighed. "I must say the war's not giving us anything spectacular to do so far, is it? I'm stuck in the catering corps, and my mother seems to think the experience will be terribly useful for when I marry and give dinner parties – though she should visit the army canteen before she says that!"

"And I'm not going to set the world on fire, either!" Immy said, before going on casually: "By the way, have I told you we're moving to London shortly? Captain

Beckett's being transferred to the War Office, and he's requested that I go with him as his official driver, promoted to lance-corporal."

Helen squealed. "You lucky stiff. You'll be right in the thick of all the excitement here and I'll still be stuck in Bedfordshire."

"You might not think I'm so lucky when the bombs start falling."

"And what about your Captain Beckett?" Helen said, ignoring that. "He's not falling for you, is he, Immy?"

"Good Lord, no. He's got a wife and three children."

"What difference did that ever make to anything?"

Immy laughed. "None, I suppose, except that he's very much a family man, and I'm in love with James."

Her face was pink as she whirled around in her floral cotton dress and fluffed up her distinctive red hair.

"So what do you think? Will I do for this stroll in the park we're going to take this afternoon if you can *ever* make up your mind what to wear!"

"All right. Providing we go looking for somewhere to go dancing tonight. I'm sure James would have no objection to your making some far-from-home soldier happy for a few minutes while you trip the light fantastic with him."

*Probably not*, Immy thought, *but, in my dreams, it will still be James's arms I'm dancing in… and I miss him so much…*

"Helen, there's something I haven't told you," she said more soberly.

"Good God, don't tell me your Captain Beckett really *has* made a pass at you? I was joking, Immy!"

"Of course he hasn't, and please be serious for a minute. It's about Daisy. You remember the young airman she was mad about?"

139

"Go on. What about him?"

"He was shot down. You know the form – killed in action."

"Oh Lord, I'm so sorry. Poor boy – and poor Daisy." She shuddered. "It makes me glad I'm not attached to anyone. How's she taking it?"

"How do you think? I haven't spoken to her myself, and I know I must, but it's hard to know what to say, isn't it? I had a letter from Aunt Rose a few days ago, and Daisy's shocked and grieving, naturally. Cal's mother wrote and told her the news just before she went back to Weston on leave, so I gather the poor darling's still pretty numb from everything."

She looked at Helen, wishing she hadn't had to say anything to mar their few days off, but unable to keep it to herself for this entire weekend. Besides, what affected one of the Caldwell girls affected them all, and she grieved for Daisy too. But since Helen clearly didn't quite know how to handle this situation, she squeezed her arm and managed to put a bright smile on her face.

"Oh, let's cheer up. Are we going out to paint this town, or aren't we? We'll find a dance hall this evening, raise a glass or two of lemonade in Cal's memory and be extra nice to some other baby-faced Air Force erks. What do you say?"

"I say Daisy's damn lucky to have a sister like you," Helen said with a catch in her throat.

"What rot you do talk sometimes, Helen!"

But she felt a deal of pleasure at the words all the same.

# Chapter Ten

After half a dozen stilted attempts, Daisy wrote a short letter to Cal's mother, saying how very sorry she was to hear the news, and that she would always remember Cal with love. It seemed little enough to say, but she simply couldn't eulogise about him. She remembered his bright and breezy personality, and still couldn't come to terms with the fact that he no longer existed.

It was one of the horrible things you learned when you were a nurse. One minute you were there, and the next you weren't. It seemed inevitable when people were old and had lived a long life and died peacefully in their sleep. You could deal with that because it was a dignified and expected ending. But being blown out of the sky as if you were of no more importance than a fly being swatted out of existence was something else.

She didn't tell anybody about the night sweats when she awoke in terror, imagining the scream of the German plane homing in on Cal's; trying not to imagine the terrifying moment when the crew knew the inevitable, split seconds before they were hit; wondering if Cal, with his Irish Catholic background had had time to make whatever peace those people did, before the agonising burning began, and his skin shrivelled and fried...

Daisy wished desperately that she could blot it out of her mind. For a nurse in wartime, who had already experienced more that most girls her age, there was the added dread of going back on the wards and seeing those broken young men who would remind her all too vividly of Cal.

She was called into Matron's office on her second day back.

"I've been hearing reports about you, Nurse Caldwell."

Daisy flinched at the shrewd look in the older woman's eyes.

"You're not doing too well, are you?" she went on briskly.

"I'm sorry, Matron," Daisy murmured.

"I'm sure you are, but being sorry's not really enough, is it? There's no place in my hospital for nurses with only half their minds on their work."

Daisy felt a surge of fright at her words.

"I don't want to leave! Please don't make me!"

"Sit down, Daisy," Matron said. "Please don't think I don't understand. I know that being involved in the Dunkirk evacuation must make our routine work seem very tame…"

"I would never say such a thing, nor think it."

She didn't think of the work as tame. She just seemed to be in some kind of never-never land, going about her tasks like an automaton…

"I also know that you've had some personal bad news recently, and in view of this, I'm going to suggest that you take a little more time to adjust. Two more weeks won't go amiss."

Daisy was aghast. "But I won't know what to do with myself. Please, Matron, I'd far rather come to work."

"And I would far rather have a nurse who gives herself wholly to her patients, and right now you're not doing that, are you? Think of these two weeks as a temporary reprieve, and we'll assess you again when you return."

Daisy's mouth trembled, and she swallowed hard. But she wouldn't break down. Her chin lifted. To be thrown out of the job she loved would be shaming and terrible, and if she had to see this as a temporary reprieve then, somehow, she would come back well and strong, even if she didn't know how…

–

"So what do you plan to do with yourself?" Aunt Rose asked, when she had reported home with the news, thankful that the boys were all at school and couldn't see how upset she was.

"I don't know. What do you suggest? Not join your knitting circle, I hope," Daisy said dully.

"I wouldn't dream of suggesting it. We have some very lively afternoons, and we certainly wouldn't want a gloomy face putting a damper on our gossip."

Daisy gave a wan smile. "I know what you're trying to do, Aunt Rose, and it won't work. I'd put a damper on everyone right now."

"Then go home for a few days. You may not have noticed, but the boys are creeping about the house, afraid to say a word for fear of you snapping at them. You're not being fair to them, Daisy."

"Oh, thank you! And they have such gigantic problems to deal with compared with mine, don't they!"

Rose looked at her thoughtfully before she spoke again. "Well, I suppose you can discount Teddy's trauma of seeing his mother fall over a cliff to her death, which is why he clings so tightly to George for security. And

Norman and Ronnie are far from home and still being tormented about the way they talk by the local school-children. Added to which, they don't even know if they'll have a home to go back to if Hitler starts dropping his bombs on London. And Elsie's husband is shell-shocked and still having treatment for his injured foot. This isn't just your war, Daisy. Other people have a few little problems, wouldn't you say?"

"I'm going to my room," Daisy said abruptly, flouncing off in a way that would have done credit to Vanessa.

"A good idea. It will give you time to think."

They so rarely quarrelled, and Rose watched her go, grieving for her insecurity, when she had always been so strong. But she was still very young, and young girls weren't meant to see the things they did nowadays. She turned thankfully to Bert as he came stumping in from the garden, for once ignoring the mess he brought in with him.

"I know now why I was never meant to be a mother," she stated.

Astonished at such an announcement, Bert put his arms around her. He smelled of earth and the freshness of the outdoors, solid and dependable, always her rock. As the words slipped into her mind, she felt a weird sense of premonition, because nothing was solid and dependable in these dark days.

"What's up, old girl? And why are you shivering on this lovely warm day?" Bert said gently.

"A goose walking over my grave, perhaps," she replied. And then: "I always wonder why people say that. Did you ever see geese walking over graves?"

"Come and sit down and tell me what's happened," Bert said, knowing this prevarication hid the real problem.

"It's Daisy, I suppose. You didn't expect her to get over the news about her young man so quickly, did you?"

"I didn't expect her to be given two weeks' extra leave from the hospital because she's not pulling her weight, either."

"Ah. Is she here?"

"Don't *ah* me like that," Rose said with an irritated gesture, slipping into the usual format for one of their spats. "She's in her room and I don't know if what I said to her has done any good or not. Probably made it worse."

"And all this is why you don't think you were cut out to be a mother?"

"Yes. No. Oh, I don't know. You can't change what the Good Lord intended for you, anyway, so what do you want for your dinner?"

Bert chuckled, well used to her quick-fire change of tactics. "Anything you want to serve up, my love – even a bit of tongue pie, since it will tell me you're back on form. Meanwhile, I'll go and have a word with Daisy."

"It won't do any good…"

But he had already gone, padding through the house in his socks now, and she didn't have the heart to scold him for not finding his slippers. George probably had them anyway…

Half an hour later Bert and Daisy came downstairs together. Daisy was red-eyed by now, and she flung her arms around her aunt.

"I'm sorry for being so beastly to everyone," she whispered.

"Daisy, my love, you couldn't be beastly if you tried. Now then, are you hungry? It's only toast and spam, I'm afraid."

"I love spam. And Aunt Rose, I think I'll do what you said – go home, I mean. Just for a few days. I think I need a bit of space to think about things. Providing you don't think I'm not grateful for being here."

"Don't be silly; of course I don't think that. Sometimes we need to go back to our roots to find out who we really are – and that's enough of me being the amateur philosopher for one day, so let's eat, and afterwards you can phone your father and tell him to meet you from the train."

–

"I'm really glad you're here," Elsie told her, when they had hugged one another, and Daisy had exclaimed again at her sister's blossoming shape. "At least I will be as long as you don't keep making disparaging remarks about my infant!"

"You know I'm only teasing, don't you?" Daisy said. "I didn't mean anything by it, Elsie, truly."

"I know that – and since when did you take every remark so seriously?"

"Since Cal died," she said simply.

Elsie folded her arms over her bump, seeing the misery in her sister's eyes, and she felt a huge burst of sympathy for her. It wasn't right that any of them had to go through these things, she thought fiercely. It wasn't right, and it wasn't fair. What had ordinary people done to deserve being maimed and killed?

"Oh Daisy, I was so sorry to hear about Cal. I never knew him, but I felt as though I did, and I know he meant a lot to you."

Daisy looked down at her hands, held tightly together in her lap. "Maybe not as much as I thought he did, and that's the awful thing about it. I did love him, Elsie, but I know it wasn't the kind of love you and Joe have. And he died believing it *was* that kind of love, while I was out dancing with other people and having fun…"

"It didn't sound much like fun being on that hospital ship, darling!"

Daisy shrugged. "Well, of course not. It was like something out of hell when we were taking the men off the beaches. But in between times…"

"In between times, you have to have some fun, or you would go mad. There's no shame in that, Daisy. Do you think Cal never had any fun when he couldn't see you? Didn't he ever go out for a few drinks with his mates, or chat to some other pretty girl? I'm sure he did, unless he was a saint, and it didn't mean he thought any less of you."

"I never thought of any such thing!"

"Well, think of it now. How does it make you feel? Better, or worse?"

"Jealous," Daisy said spontaneously.

Without warning, they were both laughing, until Elsie clutched at her side where the baby was starting to press uncomfortably against her. At six months now, it was certainly making its presence felt.

"Are you all right?" Daisy asked her.

"I'm fine. And so will you be. That was the first touch of the old fiery Daisy I've heard in a long time. Don't lose it, darling. Remember Cal with loving affection and let him go, the way we had to let Mother go."

It was so rare for any of them to speak about their mother nowadays that Daisy felt her heart jump.

"Do you think about her, Elsie?"

"Quite often, actually, and especially at night when this babe won't let me sleep, and I wish she was here to give me advice. Not that she could have told me anything sensible in her last years, of course. But I remember her before Teddy was born and the illness began. I could have gone to her with any problem then."

Daisy felt an unreasoning jealousy that her older sisters had known their mother for longer than she had – that they had had those extra years with her.

That was the second stab of jealousy in five minutes, she found herself thinking. The second real feeling inside her numbed body in ages.

"What do you want to do while you're here?" she heard Elsie ask more briskly. "Father's still busy at the shop, of course, so we'll be left to ourselves during the daytime; but he's terribly glad you've come home, Daisy."

"Is he?"

"Well, of course he is! He doesn't show his feelings, and never did, except to Mother, but he misses you all. That's one of the reasons I won't leave him, even though Joe still wants me to go and stay with his parents in Yorkshire for the duration, or at least until the baby's born. But how can I? I hardly know them."

Daisy only heard the things she wanted to hear. "Elsie, you can't stay with Daddy just because he misses the rest of us. That's piling the guilt on to us. And besides, don't you owe it to Joe to go along with his wishes? You must have said as much at your wedding, with all that love, honouring and obeying rot."

"My goodness, you really are getting back on form, aren't you, sweetie? And of course I want to do as Joe wishes, but I'm not leaving Bristol and that's flat. If I did, I'd rather go to Cornwall, anyway."

She looked at Daisy, her eyes lighting up. "That's an idea! Why don't we both go there for a few days, and take a look at this boarding house Immy's old boss has taken over? Just the two of us, Daisy – well, three if you count my bump, and he's not big enough to argue yet."

"I think I've done enough travelling lately…"

"Oh, nonsense. Anyway, I'm supposed to be the stop-at-home, not you! For someone who once wanted to follow in Mother's footsteps, I don't know why you're hesitating. She wouldn't have hesitated for a minute. You know how she always loved Cornwall, and so did we, remember?"

"Of course I remember," Daisy said, cross at being considered such a stick-in-the-mud. "But what about Daddy? Didn't you say he was glad I was here?"

"Daisy, you're really making me angry now, and it's not good for my blood pressure," Elsie said, to take the sting out of her words. "He wouldn't object for a few days, and I'm sure Mother wouldn't. Let's talk it over with her."

Daisy's heart jolted. It was one thing to talk to Lucy in the privacy of the small Weston churchyard, but it was something you had to do alone; and she had never associated Elsie with such a thing. But perhaps everyone did. Perhaps she wasn't as unique – or as crazy – as she had thought. Alice talked things over with her brother too, she remembered.

"I'm not mad, Daisy. I sometimes like to walk over the Downs and stand at the place where Mother fell, that's all. I remember the picnic we had on that perfect day, and how happy we all were. And I remember Mother in one of the lovely, floaty dresses she always wore, and how she almost danced towards the edge of the cliff, still happy, not knowing what was facing her—"

"Stop it! I don't want to hear this."

"Well, you should. It was a lovely day for all of us, and when I go there and think about her, it gives me a kind of peace. It would do the same for you."

Daisy didn't believe it, but, in the end, she agreed to leave the house and walk to the Downs on this lovely June day. The grass was sweet and young, and the trees were in full leaf. People were sitting in the sun and enjoying picnics; others were walking their dogs as usual and, apart from the many uniforms in evidence, it was easy to forget that somewhere in Europe the war was raging, and people were dying. And if the news was to be believed, since so much of France was occupied now, that war was coming ever nearer to themselves.

Daisy hadn't come to the Downs since her mother had died, unable to bear being reminded so painfully. But until now, it hadn't occurred to her that she had shunned this place where the Caldwell family and their friends used to come so often. The thought flashed into her mind that there was more than one kind of war. There was the one that threatened so much of the world now, and there was the inner war within a person. Daisy's war.

"Let's walk towards the edge," Elsie said. "There's nothing here to hurt us."

"I'm not sure if I can…"

Elsie linked her arm through her sister's. "Darling, you've already proved that you can do anything you want to. I'm proud of you, and she would be too."

They walked slowly and deliberately across the springy grass to where the Avon Gorge plunged down to the silvery ribbon of river far below. It looked beautiful today with sunlight glinting on it, and no hint of the many tragedies it had witnessed over the years, both on the graceful span of the Clifton suspension bridge – that favourite haunt of suicides – and at the jagged cliff edge that Frances Caldwell had seemed to float towards, her arms outstretched as if in some kind of slow-motion embrace, mistakenly thinking that a straying child was her own darling Teddy.

Daisy shuddered, remembering as clearly as if it was happening now. It was cruel of Elsie to bring her here, and yet she knew in her heart that it was something everyone had to do. She had felt she same way over saying goodbye to Lucy, with the sense of needing to finalise something. Perhaps wise old Aunt Rose had meant exactly this in saying that Daisy needed to go back to her roots.

"It sounds silly, but I wish I had some of Mother's favourite roses to throw over the edge right now," she said slowly. "She loved them so much, didn't she?"

"They would last longer if we put them on her grave, darling. We can go there tomorrow if you're up to it." Her eyes challenged Daisy's, knowing her sister had only visited their mother's grave a very few times.

"Perhaps. And *then* perhaps – *perhaps* – I'll think about Cornwall."

Their heads jerked round as they both heard the cheerful shout at once.

"The Caldwell girls, by all that's wonderful! Two out of three isn't bad, though naturally I'd have preferred the third one, if you don't mind my saying so."

They saw the tall young man in the army uniform striding towards them, and they broke into relieved smiles, both glad to be free of the unbearable tension of the last few minutes.

"James!" Daisy said in genuine delight. "How lovely to see you. And if you didn't prefer Immy to either of us, we'd have thought there was something seriously wrong with you. How is she, by the way? I presume you've heard from her since we have?"

James Church laughed easily. "The last I heard, she and Helen were taking a weekend's leave, living it up in London—"

"*What?* Instead of coming home?" Elsie said at once.

"And you don't mind?" Daisy broke in.

"Of course not. Our leaves didn't coincide, anyway. War's not much fun, Daisy, whether you're driving a tank in the thick of the action or chauffeuring some pompous officer about. As for poor old Helen stuck with the catering corps, I should think she's bored witless. I don't begrudge them a few hours' fun, and besides, I'm sure they'll keep one another in order."

It seemed to underline what Elsie had told her, thought Daisy. War wasn't fun for anyone, and providing you remembered where your loyalties lay, what did it matter if you let your hair down now and then? The fact that James and Immy obviously trusted one another implicitly made her momentarily ashamed. But she knew she was thinking more of herself than Immy right then. She had never physically let Cal down, and if she had toyed with writing to Jed, and danced with Glenn, it hadn't fundamentally changed her feelings for Cal.

"I heard your news, Daisy, and I'm sorry," James said more soberly.

"Thanks."

"But I gather you're something of a Dunkirk heroine now," he went on. "Who would ever have thought it of our young carrot-top?"

"Oh, stop it, for pity's sake," she said, starting to grin at the teasing look in his eyes. "I only did what I was asked to do."

"Well, there speaks a real heroine; but I won't embarrass you anymore. And since it's rare for me to have two pretty girls to escort, how about if I buy you both a sticky bun at the Whiteladies Tea Rooms? Or even two sticky buns for Elsie, if that's not an indelicate remark to make."

"If you weren't my sometime-in-the-future brother-in-law, I'd take offence at that," she said, laughing. "But since I'm sure Daisy and I could both manage two sticky buns, I won't."

"Come on then."

They crooked their arms through his and set off across the Downs with far lighter hearts than when they had arrived there. The sun shone brilliantly in a clear blue sky, and somewhere high above a lone seabird wheeled and dived with all the grace and fluency of a dancer, as protective as a guardian angel. As the thought soared into her head, Daisy felt extraordinarily uplifted.

Afterwards, she couldn't have said what had changed her. It might have been simply Elsie's ever-calm influence and sensible approach to life. Or her insistence on retracing their footsteps to the Downs and facing their dragon, which was how Daisy had always viewed the scene of her mother's death.

Or maybe it was James Church and his teasing, friendly manner, treating Daisy as the little sister she would be when he and Immy were married, and the fact that he restored a continuity to their lives that had been missing for so long.

Whatever it was, she began to think of that day as a turning point in her life. It was the day she rediscovered her roots and knew that some things were constant after all. The following day she and Elsie picked a bouquet of their own garden roses and placed them on Frances's grave.

"So have you decided, Daisy?" Elsie asked her quietly in that peaceful place. "Do we go to Cornwall for a few days and see what Immy's Mr Harris is doing with his life?"

Daisy looked at the inscription on the headstone for a long moment. Apart from the date they would never forget, it said simply:

FRANCES CALDWELL
BELOVED WIFE AND MOTHER
SAFE IN THE ARMS OF JESUS

Daisy nodded slowly. "I think Mother would approve, don't you?"

Elsie put her arm around her and hugged her close. "I'm sure she would, darling. So we'll break the news to Father tonight."

"And then we'll have to get in touch with this Mr Harris and see if he's got room for us," she said more practically, when they were walking back to Vicarage Street. "It would be too bad if the boarding house was filled up after we'd started making our plans."

"It won't be. Immy said he'd always make room for the Caldwell family," Daisy said, with the ultimate confidence of youth.

Elsie blessed her intuition that had led them to the Downs that day, and in particular she blessed James Church's healthy male optimism. No wonder Immy loved him. Not that he could hold a candle to her Joe, of course, she thought at once. Not in *her* heart, anyway.

As if her thoughts were in tune with Elsie's, as they so often were when they were together, Daisy asked if she had had any recent news of Joe, knowing guiltily that she should have asked long before this if she hadn't been so consumed with her own misery.

"They're keeping him in that military hospital in Essex for the time being. The shell-shock has affected his hearing, but they hope it will only be temporary," Elsie told her. "Thank goodness his foot is responding to treatment, and I know Joe. Once it's completely healed, he'll be eager to get back to his regiment."

She gave a half-smile and her words couldn't disguise her pride in her husband. "You'd never have thought a mild-mannered shop manager would be so aggressively patriotic, would you?"

"I never thought Joe was mild-mannered – not in a soppy way, anyway. He must have been pretty persuasive to get you to elope and get married without Father's consent."

"Oh, I didn't need much persuading, darling," Elsie said softly, remembering. "I knew Joe was going to enlist the moment war was declared, and I simply couldn't bear to live without him."

"But isn't that just what you're having to do now?"

Elsie pressed her hand lightly over the mound of her belly. "Not while I have this little one to keep me company. Nor while I have the memories of all that we've been to one another. And that's quite enough intimate information for an unmarried young lady to be told," she added teasingly.

"Oh pooh," Daisy retorted. "You forget that I'm a nurse. We have privileged information about lots of intimate things."

"Well, not *my* intimate life you don't!"

Daisy laughed, hugging her arm as they approached the tall house in Vicarage Street that had seen all the Caldwell children born. Solid and welcoming, as always; the flowers in the front garden were in full bloom now, scenting the air with Frances's favourite roses and bringing her presence very close for one breath taking, ethereal moment. As if she only had to turn around and her mother would be there, dancing in the wonderful, legendary way that had entranced everyone who saw her, her feet hardly seeming to touch the ground, her delicate features making everyone adore her. Daisy gave a small, secret smile as she heard the soft sigh of the breeze rustle through the trees, as sweet and tremulous as her mother's voice, and felt more at ease with herself than she had felt for a very long time.

The feeling wouldn't last, and Daisy knew it; but for now, it was enough.

# Chapter Eleven

The trains travelling to the south-west from Paddington disgorged hundreds of servicemen returning from France at Stapleton Road and Temple Meads stations, where willing hands were ready to receive them and despatch them in trucks to the various hospitals and reception centres.

Most of them had nothing but what they stood up in, and there was now a tented inner city for the able-bodied, while they were assessed. The Red Cross, WVS and other organisations were in the forefront now, as well as ordinary civilians, ready to help where they could.

"I've offered to take in several soldiers while you girls are away," Quentin Caldwell told his daughters. "There's plenty of room here, and they'll be more comfortable than sleeping in a tent until further orders. Mrs Meakin, our old housekeeper, is coming in to supervise and make our meals. Her son was killed in France, so she thinks it's the least she can do to help some other mothers' sons."

"I think that's very brave of her," said Elsie.

"And it will help her too," Daisy said more practically.

"So now there's nothing to stop you two enjoying your few days in Cornwall," Quentin went on. "I've spoken to Kenneth Harris on the telephone, and there's a room all ready prepared for you. You can stay for a week, if you like, and you're not to worry about paying him, because it's all been taken care of."

"Father, that wasn't necessary!" Elsie said at once.

"Maybe not, but it's done."

"Thank you, Daddy," Daisy said. She kissed his cheek, her instinct telling her more than Elsie's did how much he wanted to do this for them. As if by sending his girls to Cornwall, to the place where the whole family had always been so happy in days gone by, he too could recapture some small sense of those halcyon times.

"Yes, well," he said now, reverting to his usual brusqueness, "just enjoy yourselves, and remember to send me a postcard. Nothing too saucy, mind!"

"We'll telephone you the minute we get there," Elsie promised.

"And you're sure the midwife said it's all right for you to travel?"

Elsie laughed. "For the tenth time, *yes*! And you're the one who's been urging me to get away from Bristol all this time! Providing we're not too squashed up in the train, I'm sure I shall be perfectly all right."

The kind of leisurely ride to Cornwall they used to enjoy was very unlikely. With fewer private motor cars on the roads owing to the precious hoarding of petrol, every train was hot and crowded. But with a panache that took Daisy by surprise, Elsie blatantly flaunted her pregnancy, which got them seats all the way to Marazion station, near the much larger resort of Penzance. The last couple of miles excited them as always, as the line meandered along the beach, reminding them that they were actually there at last.

They finally emerged on to the platform, stiff and exhausted from the long journey, immediately assaulted by the smell of sea and sand and the screech of seagulls as the one ancient remaining taxi took them to Kenneth Harris's seaside boarding house in Marazion.

They smiled at one another. Frances had always said that if her heart had had a spiritual home, this was the place. Neither of them said it today, but Daisy knew they were both remembering it.

"We did right to come here, didn't we?" she said softly.

Before Elsie could answer, the green-painted front door opened, and a portly, middle-aged man emerged to greet them, arms outstretched.

"Oh Lord, he's not going to kiss us, is he?" Daisy whispered in alarm.

"My dear young ladies, how good it is to see you," Kenneth Harris said, beaming. "And you both grow more like my dear Imogen every day. Come in, come in do, and have some tea. You must be parched after that ghastly journey."

He was as quaintly fussy as ever, and when had her sister ever been his "dear Imogen"? Daisy thought darkly. Immy had only been his assistant in his housing agency, for heaven's sake; but perhaps he had had delusions of making her more than that. She stifled a giggle, unable to imagine her beautiful older sister in the arms of the rotund and slightly perspiring Kenneth.

All the same, the bizarre image settled her stomach, which she hadn't realised until now was churning ever so slightly at the end of this long train journey. Elsie, too, looked paler than usual, and needed to get indoors and relax. Her training took over.

"We'd love a cup of tea, Mr Harris, but I think we would appreciate seeing our room first and having a short rest," she said firmly. "Perhaps we could come down for the tea in about half an hour."

"Of course, my dear; but there's no need for that. For my honoured guests, tea shall be brought to your room on this occasion."

He spoke with all the pomposity of the overlord of his domain, and Daisy didn't dare glance at Elsie, sure that the two of them would burst out laughing. They managed to contain themselves until they reached their room and were alone.

"Isn't he priceless?" Elsie gasped, tears streaming down her face. "How on earth did Immy work with him every day without falling apart?"

"Lord knows. He's straight out of Charles Dickens. Mr Micawber?"

They convulsed again, until Elsie held her side and begged Daisy to stop, because it wasn't doing the baby any good at all.

"Yes, it is," Daisy told her positively. "At least he'll come out smiling!"

She flopped down on the second bed while they roared with laughter again.

"We'd better stop this, or Mr Harris will think he's got two hooligans in here," Elsie said finally, wiping her eyes.

"Agreed. So why don't you lie down for ten minutes, and I'll go and see if I can telephone Daddy to tell him we've arrived safely," Daisy said. "He'll only fret himself silly until we do."

It wasn't a bad idea to separate for a short while either, she thought, as she went downstairs to enquire about the telephone, since the minute they looked at one another now they started laughing. But it felt so good to laugh again. Daisy felt better than she had in ages, being able to laugh at inconsequential things – to feel young and scatty again and forget all their worries for a little while.

She knew they were already absorbing some of their mother's delight in this corner of the world that Frances had always said was full of Merlin and mystery, and where she had instilled a love of all things fey and magical in her children, and none of the fear.

The boarding house overlooked the long stretch of sands known as Mount's Bay on the outskirts of the village. The fairy-tale castle of St Michael's Mount soared into the sky, as breathtakingly beautiful as they remembered it as children, and whether by accident or design, they had been given a room facing the sea, with a perfect view of the bay and its castle. A narrow causeway separated the mainland from the castle and its island, which could be reached on foot at low tide.

"What absolute bliss," Daisy said later, kicking off her shoes and standing by the window looking out. By then she had telephoned her father, and Kenneth Harris had personally brought them a tray of tea and biscuits. "Do you think it was fate that dear old Kenny decided to settle here, just so the Caldwell girls could renew their acquaintance with Mother's favourite haunts?"

"Probably," Elsie said lazily. "Mother was a great believer in fate."

"She was, wasn't she?" Daisy said with a feeling that was more than satisfaction, and more like a glorious sense of continuity. "Do you remember the tales she used to tell us? I liked the one about Joseph of Arimathea coming here. Oh, and the lost land of Lyonesse, stretching from Penzance all the way to the Scilly Isles. Oh, and Dozmary Pool, and Merlin's sword…"

Elsie was laughing at her again. "You're such a romantic, Daisy! And we always thought you were such a scatterbrain; but you really think deeply about things, don't you?"

"You have to when you're a nurse," Daisy said, her face clouding over for just a moment.

"Well, you're not a nurse for the next week, and I don't need nursing," Elsie told her firmly. "We're going to enjoy ourselves and spend every morning walking on the beach looking for fossils and pebbles."

"Just like we always did," Daisy said happily. Finding their roots. Being children again – providing you could disregard the bump beneath Elsie's dress – and forgetting that a war existed.

Not that Elsie could forget it for very long, and almost the first thing she did was to write a letter to Joe. She sat in the window seat, describing the view to him, wishing he was here to share it with her, wishing she could stay here for ever.

She drew in her breath as the thought entered her head. Because, of course, she could. Or at least, for the duration. Her father was always urging her to do so for her own safety – but how could she desert him?

They joined the other residents in the dining room that evening, mostly elderly folk, some of whom were permanent boarders, and a few holidaymakers. Kenneth had told them he didn't advertise too much, because there was always a select clientele happy to enjoy the quiet life he offered.

"It's strange to find somewhere so peaceful, isn't it?" Daisy commented the next morning as they took their first walk along the sands. Without warning, she reflected that Cal was at peace too. No more fighting. No more

162

war. Thoughts of him were usually painful, but, in that instant, she realised she had begun to accept his death, and come to terms with it, as she had to.

"I think it's perfectly lovely," Elsie said. "It relaxes the mind and gives you time to think – and the best thing is, there's no overwhelming talk of war in the dining room. I suspect Kenneth has banned it."

Daisy took her seriously. "He can't do that, and Cornishmen have joined up the same as everybody else. There are plenty of servicemen about."

"I know that, Daisy, and I was just teasing. Cornwall does give you a lovely sense of peace, though, doesn't it? And did I tell you that Kenneth's promised to take us to have a look at his brother's market garden one evening after supper?"

"Oh joy! What excitement!"

Elsie laughed. "It's enough excitement for me and the babe, Daisy. I don't want to go rushing around for the next few months, nor dancing the night away."

"You want to stay, don't you?" Daisy asked her baldly.

"Good Lord, no! I couldn't leave Father on his own, could I?"

But she didn't meet Daisy's eyes as she spoke, and she should have known that her sister was shrewd enough to have noticed it.

"You know it's what Daddy wants for you, Elsie. And Joe too, since you've brushed off his offer of spending time with his parents."

"I haven't brushed it off, as you so charmingly put it. I just wouldn't want to be there without him. There's a difference."

"Oh well, don't let's quarrel about it. I'd race you to the causeway if it wasn't a foregone conclusion that I'd win," she said airily.

She knew the mild and gentle air was having the desired effect, though it wasn't the way a lively seventeen-year-old expected to feel for very long. And she would be *eighteen* in a couple of weeks, she reminded herself, realising that she had almost forgotten her birthday with all that had been going on lately.

Uncannily, Elsie tuned in. "So what delights do you want for your birthday, little sister?" she asked.

*Cal*, Daisy thought instantly. *Lucy*. And to be rid of her guilt at knowing she had danced and flirted with Jed and Glenn while she was still in love with Cal. For everything to be the way it used to be. No more war, no irritating little evacuees getting under everyone's feet, and her mother. Most of all, her mother.

"I daresay Aunt Rose will manage to make me a cake if the rations run to it," she said, swallowing the futility of her thoughts. "The infants will expect it, though I'm not sure I want to blow out eighteen candles!"

"Of course not. It's so *old*, isn't it?" Elsie said with a grin.

Daisy playfully scuffed sand at her feet and got a shoeful back. Right then she felt about six years old, and it was a good feeling. She knew she would miss Elsie dreadfully if she did decide to stay.

"You and Daddy will come down to Weston for my birthday, won't you? Unless you've taken up residence here, of course."

"Darling, it's not going to happen," Elsie said slowly. "This is an interlude, no more. It's a place to come back to, the way we always have in the past, but not to stay; so let's say no more about it, please. In any case, of course we'll be in Weston for your birthday, and I don't think I care to be travelling up and down the country too many times in my condition!"

Daisy knew she had come to a momentous decision, without really knowing why. She guessed it must have something to do with feeling even farther away from Joe in this isolated corner of England. Whatever the reason, it was their business, and for once she held her tongue, and didn't ask.

—

They arrived back in Bristol on June the fourteenth, two days before Daisy's birthday and four days after the news broke that Italy, having joined forces with Germany, had declared war on Britain and France. The little Italian restaurant that had been part of the row of shops including Preston's Emporium, where Quentin was manager, had been closed at once, and the owners immediately interned.

"How awful!" Daisy exclaimed, when they had been welcomed back to Vicarage Street and their father had told them the news. "You mean that nice Mr Bertorelli and both his sons are in prison? And his wife too?"

"All of them, I'm afraid, since they're now officially our enemies. All Italians in this country will have suffered the same fate."

There were many Italian families in business in the south-west, and it seemed barbaric to round them all up as if they had suddenly become the enemy overnight. But that was what they were now, Daisy realised.

"I can't believe it. Mrs Bertorelli was such a nice lady, and they had lived here for years. How can they be considered a threat to anyone?"

"Such things are under government control, Daisy, and it would be the same for British citizens living in Italy or Germany, and in any of the occupied countries. They would want to get out as soon as possible, or risk imprisonment."

"Well, I think it stinks," she said, not having appreciated this angle of war until now. Going back and forth to Dunkirk on the hospital ship had been a daring adventure, despite all they had had to see and do; but this was an insidious way of taking away people's liberty, and it frightened her.

"That's not the worst of it," Quentin went on grimly. "Anti-Italian riots have broken out in London, according to the newspapers. Windows have been smashed and Italian shopkeepers threatened with violence. So far there haven't been any reports of it here, but swift internment is the best answer, for their own safety."

"Daisy, there's nothing we can do about it, however much we sympathise with the Bertorelli family," she heard Elsie say. "Come and help me unpack my things, and then we'll tell Father what we did in Cornwall, and how Kenneth Harris is lording it over his residents."

Daisy knew she was right, but it didn't stop her disgust that people she knew were being imprisoned in their own adopted country, just for where they had come from.

"I suppose we'll be allowed to send them things; or will they be put in the condemned cell?"

"You're getting this all out of proportion, Daisy," her father said sharply. "Elsie's right. There's nothing we can do about it, and if we raise our voices in favour of the

Italian immigrants, we risk being vilified ourselves. You would do well to remember that."

"So we just sit back and let it happen, do we?"

"That is exactly what we do, because we can't do anything else." Knowing better than to continue the futile argument with her father, she marched out of the sitting room and upstairs to Elsie's flat ahead of her sister. Elsie took a little longer to climb the stairs, but when she had closed the door behind her, she turned on Daisy.

"You're being very short-sighted, you know, and Father's right: internment is for the Italians' own safety as much as anything else."

"I know," Daisy said miserably. "I just feel so sorry for them, that's all. It's hardly their war, any more than it's yours or mine; but we all have to pay in one way or another, don't we?"

"If you've realised that, then you've grown up a lot, darling."

"You have to grow up when you're faced with death every day and your young man's been blown to bits, wouldn't you say? Oh Lord, I'm sorry, Elsie; I know you've got your own worries over Joe, and I shouldn't be making you feel unhappy when we've just had such a lovely time, but it never goes away does it? You can't really escape from what's happening in the world, because there's nowhere far enough."

Elsie spoke calmly. "So let's just concentrate on doing something very ordinary instead of trying to sort out the world's problems. And if you want to do something *really* ordinary, I'll show you the baby's layette and you can coo over the thought of becoming an auntie."

Daisy gave her a reluctant smile and tried to put the shock of what her father had told her out of her mind.

The crazy temptation to march through the streets waving banners and announcing their friendly neighbourhood Italians' innocence in all this madness, as if she was some latter-day suffragette, flitted into her head and disappeared as quickly as it had come. As her father said, it would no good, and such stupidity would only bring the wrath of warring Bristolians down on their heads. He was right. There was nothing they could do.

"Auntie Daisy! Now that does make me feel old!" she said instead. "All right, let's get unpacked, and then I'll put up with being shown this wonderful layette for the most wonderful superbabe yet to be born."

"Was there ever any doubt about that?"

"So Elsie wasn't tempted to move down to Cornwall for the duration, and she's staying in Bristol, just as I always thought she would," Rose told Bert, putting down the telephone.

Daisy had just let them know that they'd had a lovely time, and they would be with them on Sunday, Daisy's birthday. Since there were no trains on that day, they were to use the car, with the petrol Quentin had been hoarding for just such an important occasion. You couldn't let a daughter's eighteenth birthday go by without travelling in style.

Teddy began jumping up and down with excitement.

"Our Daisy's coming home on Sunday," he chanted, repeating everything for confirmation as usual; and then he frowned. "I can't always remember what our Elsie looks like, though."

"Well, you goose, she looks just like Daisy, only older," Bert reminded him. "Your sisters were always like three peas in a pod."

He had only been a little one when his mother died, and he and Rose had taken him in, Bert remembered. Teddy hadn't seen much of any of the others since, except Daisy, and the war had separated all of them, the way it had separated so many families. It sometimes made him a little uneasy to think how he and Rose had absorbed two of the Caldwell children into their lives, when they still had their own home, and their father, and siblings of their own. As he reminded Rose now and then, all these children were only borrowed, and that went for Teddy and Daisy as well as the evacuees. He didn't care to look too far ahead and think how it would affect her when they all went home again.

"What are you looking so gloomy about, Bert?" she scolded him.

"Nothing that need concern you, my love. But if I'm going to get that bookcase finished for Daisy's birthday present, I'd better get on with it."

"And Teddy and I are going to make Daisy's cake, aren't we, love?" she asked him brightly, seeing the puckered look still on his face as he tried to remember what the rest of his family looked like. Rose resolved to get out the old family photo albums soon.

–

Bert deliberately avoided mentioning the Italian situation. It was bad enough that all the newspaper headlines were black and heavy, predicting the worst, now that Mussolini's navy was at Hitler's disposal. *Newspaper reporters*, Bert thought, with a scowl. Scandalmongers, most of 'em, and what they didn't know, they invented. Right now they were inventing all kinds of things about the most innocent of folk.

One of Rose's knitting circle was the wife of a small restaurant–owner on the seafront, and neither of them had been seen or heard of for several days. Everyone knew what must have happened but putting it into words made it seem a hundred times worse, and speculation never helped anyone.

Besides, he and Rose had three young boys to care for, and every new mention of the war's progress had Ronnie wetting his bed, while Norman became ever more angry and wanted to go home. It was for their sakes that Bert tried to keep everything as normal as possible. Daisy's birthday, and the small family party that would bring most of them together again for a short while, was the best boost any of them could have right now.

"You boys can come and help me," he called out to Norman and Ronnie as he went down to the shed at the bottom of his garden. The bookcase was no more than three open shelves, but he knew she would welcome it for all her nursing manuals. He was staining the shelves this afternoon, and it should be thoroughly dry by the time she arrived home on Sunday.

"Our Mum don't believe in birthday presents," Norman said with a sniff. "She says she ain't got no money for daft stuff nobody wants."

"It's always better to give people something they want," he agreed. "Now that I've got into my stride with the woodworking, I might make you and Ronnie a box with a lift-up lid next, to keep your comics in. What do you think of that?"

Norman shrugged. "'S all right, I daresay."

"I think you're nice," Ronnie said suddenly.

"Well, thank you, Ronnie. I think you're nice too," Bert said.

"'Cept when he pees himself," Norman hooted.

Bert ignored that, concentrating instead on the fair job he'd made of Daisy's bookcase. He was pleased with it, and he hoped she would be too. Teddy would be up to his elbows in flour now, he guessed, helping Rose make the cake for Daisy's birthday tea, and these two were engrossed in watching him stain the old wood to a deep gloss.

If they were able to ignore the occasional sounds of planes going off in formation from RAF Locking, they could almost think this was an ordinary summer's day with nothing sinister to threaten their world.

"Did you finish your drawings for Daisy's birthday?" he asked the boys. Norman was no mean artist when he tried, and Ronnie had an eye for colour.

"Course we did," Norman said. "Ronnie can get them and show you."

He glared as his brother started to protest, and then gave in as he usually did. They would never get on, Bert thought, but presumably that was the way brothers close in age behaved. Give them a real problem to cope with, and they stuck together, close as clams.

Ronnie came back five minutes later with their birthday drawings. Ronnie's was a crayon sketch of Daisy, her bright hair tumbling around a smiling face. Norman's was a picture of the house seen from the front, where there were still borders of flowers in the garden. It was bright and cheerful, and seeing it through a child's eyes brought a daft lump to Bert's throat.

"I know Daisy will love them both," he told them. "Take them back inside now, Ronnie, and put them somewhere safe until tomorrow."

"Can I show them to Aunt Rose first?" he said.

"Of course you can."

He wasn't really a clinging child, but he had become attached to Rose, which sometimes caused friction between him and Teddy, since Teddy considered Rose his property, she being his real aunt and not just a pretend one. He sighed, glad that Rose understood them better than he did, even without having had children of her own. It was the female instinct, he supposed, and then gave up thinking about anything at all except the more pressing need to get his handiwork done.

## Chapter Twelve

Being eighteen years old was quite a milestone, Daisy thought, and although it would have been perfect if her mother and Lucy had been here to share it, she was determined to let nothing cloud this beautiful day. She wasn't so grand that she couldn't be as excited as a child again, wondering what gifts she was going to receive when her father joined his daughters for breakfast.

Elsie had made her a silk scarf from a piece of material Daisy had admired for a long time in her sister's box of fabrics, which she'd once thought was like an Aladdin's Cave; and Quentin presented her with a small silver locket that opened. Inside was a tiny photo of Daisy's mother.

"You always liked that particular photo, and I thought you might like to have it as a keepsake," he said gruffly.

"It's the most perfect gift you could have given me," Daisy said, finding it hard not to cry, but determined to resist, for all their sakes.

"So now let's have our toast and porridge, and then we'll get started," Quentin said briskly. "Elsie and I will want to get back here in good time this evening, so we'll want to spend as much of the day in Weston as we can."

The soldiers who had been given temporary accommodation in the Caldwell house had been efficiently moved on before the girls arrived home from Cornwall, much to their relief. Neither of them had relished the thought of having to make conversation with strangers, while hearing about their experiences would have revived too many memories of Dunkirk for Daisy, and of Joe's injuries for Elsie.

So once they were ready they set off in the big old Rover, determined to feel as carefree as anyone could in the middle of a war. Rose had already telephoned to wish Daisy a happy birthday, and to let them know she was making a rabbit-and-vegetable pie for their dinner, so she hoped they would all have good appetites. Daisy managed not to groan out loud until she had heard Teddy's excited squeals at the other end and had put down the phone to report.

"She'd have you all looking as well fed as me," Elsie laughed, patting her stomach. "But she shouldn't go to so much trouble, nor try to stretch the rations."

"Oh, you'll never stop your aunt trying to feed the five thousand, no matter how meagre the rations; and I daresay those farming friends of hers supplied the rabbit, so there's no need to feel guilty," Quentin said complacently. "Now, who's for a song to speed us on our way?"

It was what they had always done when they set out in the car on a family occasion. They sang until they were hoarse, and then they played I-Spy, leaving Daisy with the feeling that she should be eight years old again, not eighteen. If she had been, Frances would have been sitting in the front seat, Immy and Baz would have been here with them, and Teddy wouldn't even have been born yet...

"A penny for them, Daisy," Quentin said suddenly, noting her silence.

She drew in her breath, but she wouldn't cast a shadow over this lovely day by making them aware of a small sad moment. She spoke cheerfully.

"I was just thinking how lucky we are to have each other, that's all."

"Well, we all know that," Elsie said, giving her hand a squeeze. "So let's have another song now that we've all got our breath back."

It certainly helped to make the journey go faster, and when they drew up outside Rose and Bert's house in Weston, Daisy looked at it with real affection, knowing with a little shock that this was more truly her home now than the one in Vicarage Street, and Aunt Rose had been the one to make it so.

Then she couldn't think of anything else but the three small boys rushing out of the front door to greet them, followed by the adults. Teddy flung himself into his father's arms, and as the evacuee boys hopped up and down from one foot to the other, Daisy thought briefly that she hoped this didn't presage an accident on Ronnie's part. Then everyone was talking at once.

"We've got presents for you, Daisy," Teddy shrieked.

"We made them ourselves," Norman shouted, eyeing Elsie's bump somewhat suspiciously, but deciding to ignore it for the moment.

"How wonderful!" Daisy said.

"And Elsie, my love, you're really looking in the pink," Bert said, beaming.

"Thank you, Uncle Bert, and it's marvellous to see you all again," Elsie said, as she was embraced by her aunt and uncle in a great bear hug.

"And you had a lovely holiday? You both look very well!" Rose said.

"They do, don't they?" Quentin put in, the proud father, with Teddy in his arms now, and valiantly resisting the urge to scoop the excitedly yapping George away from his feet. "The Cornish air was just what they needed."

"So let's all go inside, shall we?" Rose said more practically. "We'll have the neighbours wondering what's going on, and I'm sure they already think of us as a completely mad household."

But she was smiling as she spoke, since nothing gave Rose more pleasure than to be surrounded by children and family. For now, all thoughts of whatever else was going on in the world could be put aside, especially the news that Alice Godfrey's mother had passed on to her that week.

They had a mutual friend, an American lady by the glamorous name of Gloria Feinstein, who had owned a dress shop in Weston for many years. But now, with the tragic events in France and wide concern by America and the neutral countries over Italy's involvement, the American government was urging all its citizens to leave Britain at the first opportunity.

So with her typical impulsiveness, Gloria had done exactly as her government advised and had already left Weston, leaving her affairs in the hands of her solicitors until further notice, Mrs Godfrey had told Rose tearfully. It was as if the American government had already decided there was no hope for Britain, and that invasion was imminent. It had taken a long while and quite a few cups of tea for Rose to calm her down, and another long chat with Bert that night to calm herself down.

If Daisy hadn't been enjoying a well-earned holiday in Cornwall at the time, Rose knew she would have spilled it all out to her long before now. But not today. This was Daisy's day.

"Come and see what I made for you," Teddy was shrieking wildly now.

"And me!" yelled Norman, echoed by Ronnie.

"Now come on, boys; let's all calm down a little and get our breath back," Rose ordered. "We'll go inside and have some lemonade, and then we'll all give Daisy our presents, one by one. Youngest first," she added, before they could clamour over who was to get priority.

They all knew that Teddy would have yelled that he had to go first anyway, since Daisy was his real sister, and only a tacked-on one for the other two; but Rose's words saved any argument, and Daisy was delighted with the primrose plant Teddy had dug up from his own patch of garden and put into a pot for her bedroom, tied with a scrap of yellow ribbon.

"It's lovely" she told him. "Just what I wanted."

The pictures Norman and Ronnie had done were produced next, which Daisy admired and promised would go on her bedroom wall. Then it was Bert's turn. He was no more than an amateur carpenter, but the bookcase had been made with love, and was truly just what Daisy needed. She threw her arms around him, hugging him close.

"I love you," she whispered in his ear so that only he could hear.

"I love you too," he whispered back.

"And if you two can tear yourselves apart, there's one more present to come," Rose said, unexpectedly touched by the sight of them. If she'd ever been lucky enough to have a daughter, she would have wanted one just like Daisy, she found herself thinking...

She went to the sideboard and produced an envelope. She could see by the boys' faces that they didn't think it looked like much and hoped Daisy wouldn't think the same.

"Gloria Feinstein has gone back to America, Daisy," she said. "All the stock at her dress shop is being sold off at bargain prices, and since you always loved her fancy supply of clothes, I thought you should have your pick of it. So there's a little money to make the shopping expedition worthwhile. At my age I've got plenty of clothes to see me out."

Daisy opened the envelope and gasped at the crisp notes inside it. It was a totally unexpected gift, and she felt a rush of tears in her eyes, thinking how dear her aunt was, and how her occasional brusqueness hid a genuinely kind heart.

It was Rose's turn to get a huge hug now, and stammering thanks that Rose quickly brushed aside.

"You can thank me best of all by doing justice to your dinner and putting on a bit of weight. You don't want to follow those film stars and end up looking like a stick. Oh, and I nearly forgot – there's a letter for you on the mantelpiece. It looks like Immy's writing."

There was no reason for Daisy's heart to jump, thinking it might have been from someone else. Not from Cal, of course... unlikely to be from Jed, since he seemed to have forgotten all about her... and not from Glenn, who didn't know her address. She tore open the envelope, thankful that her family couldn't see how her thoughts had immediately gone to three young men. But why not? She was young and healthy and...

"Oh! Immy's sent me some money for my birthday too!" she exclaimed, fingering the two crisp pound notes inside the letter and card. "She says I'm to do what I like with it, within reason." She started to laugh. "What does she think I'll do? Book my passage to America!"

She immediately wished she hadn't said that, remembering Aunt Rose's friend who had taken fright and gone home when she had thought Britain was about to be invaded; but Aunt Rose was busy in the kitchen by now and hadn't heard.

"Our Daisy's rich now," Teddy chanted.

"Well, hardly! But it was very nice of her, wasn't it, Daddy?"

"Very thoughtful," he said, touched that his oldest girl had taken over the role of Daisy's mother in that instance, whether or not it was intentional. Eighteen was definitely a milestone, and Frances would certainly have thought so too.

"What does Immy say in her letter?" he asked.

Daisy skimmed it. "Just that she and Helen had an enjoyable weekend in London recently, and now she and her Captain Beckett are based there, so she doubts she'll be seeing Helen too often. But the good news is that James is due for a forty-eight-hour pass soon, and he plans to stay in London so they can see one another."

She folded up the letter carefully, her head full of dreams, imagining what it must be like to be sharing a clandestine weekend far away from home and family with the man you were going to marry. It might not be clandestine at all, of course, she thought hastily, but then again, it might… and the dreams took shape so swiftly she was almost scared that the others might see them in her eyes.

But the boys were squabbling on the hearthrug as usual, fighting over who was going to hug George, until the poor dog squealed and yapped in protest at such devotion.

Her father and uncle were already deep in quiet conversation about the progress of the war, and Aunt Rose was producing the most glorious smell of cooking that was making her mouth water... Even though it was the middle of a lovely summer's day, Daisy was somewhere in dreamland, in the arms of an unknown lover whose kisses were sweeter than wine, and who was telling her passionately that he adored her...

"Who's for rabbit pie then?" Aunt Rose announced. "Go and wash your hands, boys, and then come and sit at the table, all of you, before it gets cold."

If anything was designed to bring a dreamer down to earth, that was it.

–

They had heard nothing from Baz, though Daisy had hardly expected to. Younger brothers were not in the business of remembering birthdays without a mother to remind them. In any case Baz was too busily involved in saving his skin to be thinking of such trivial matters. The ageing fishing trawler had finally been put out of action in the Dunkirk evacuation and he had parted company with his mates. Somehow, he had found himself stranded on the French side of the Channel, and in the general confusion everywhere he had decided that he might as well become the adventurer he had always wanted to be.

While most of the BEF was struggling to make its way to the coast, in the next few days Baz was scrabbling about through fields and hedgerows and making his way west. His aim was to get back home, and he reasoned that there had to be other British ships in the vicinity ready to pick up servicemen. There were plenty of others doing the same as himself, but in his flight from Dunkirk he had somehow found himself alone.

Being an adventurer, living on his wits and what he could find to eat, wasn't as exciting as he had once imagined. He quickly became disorientated as he kept his head down and dug himself in every time he heard the whine and roar of enemy planes overhead, and the spatter of machine-gun fire.

A week later he was filthy and starving when he lifted his head cautiously from a ditch where he had been cramming down what he hoped were edible purple berries and met the eyes of a young girl gazing down at him.

"Where am I?" he croaked.

She didn't answer but continued with that cold wide stare. He wished he'd bothered to learn a few words of French, but there had never seemed the need, for a Bristol ferryman or a fisherman. In desperation he pointed to his mouth, making a gesture that he was hungry and thirsty too, since the berries seemed to have dried up the inside of his lips. He suddenly panicked, wondering if he had been poisoned by them.

The girl continued to stare, and then they both heard a shout, and she turned and fled, screaming out something that he couldn't understand but which certainly seemed to indicate that the best thing he could do was to run. And run like hell.

Weren't the French supposed to be their allies...? Before he could even move, he was suddenly hauled to his feet by a large and aggressive farmer with a pitchfork in his hand. My God, he was going to be stabbed to death here and now, Baz thought in a wild panic. Maybe the farmer thought he was German. He had dodged several columns of German soldiers marching this way, and the rumble of tanks had frequently shaken the ground. He had no idea where he was, and he bellowed out the first thing that came into his head.

"I'm English!" He shouted, the way people did when speaking to foreigners. "*English*. You understand? I need to find a ship. A boat."

The man spoke rapidly to the girl, who sped away from him towards the farmhouse Baz could now see across the fields. He'd obviously wandered inland well away from the coast – and that was that, then. The farmer didn't understand him, and he either thought he was a thief or a runaway, and he was going to turn him in.

"You want food?" the farmer said.

Baz felt his legs turn to water and, in his relief, he had a job not to let the hot gush of piss fill his pants.

"Thank God. You speak English," he gasped.

The man shrugged. "And you want a boat."

"No. Well, *yes*," Baz said. Of course he bloody well wanted a boat. He wanted to get home. He had never wanted it more. They were slightly at cross purposes, but the end result was the same.

He grabbed a handful of the berries he had eaten, feeling their purple juice squeeze through his fingers. Now that he realised he wasn't going to die by the pitchfork, his belly clenched with the thought that he might have poisoned himself.

"Are these good?" he stuttered, gesturing towards his mouth again.

Without answering, the farmed picked another handful, put them in his own mouth, and began to chuckle.

"*Oui*. Good, eh?" he asked. The grin faded. "You know what happens?"

"What happens?" Baz croaked. Whatever it was, he didn't want to know. Couldn't the bastard see that he needed something solid in his guts before he passed out completely?

"France has surrendered," the man snarled. "The German pigs" – he turned and spat on the ground – "they our masters now."

Baz stared at him in cold horror. His head seemed to float on his shoulders from the lack of food, but his brain was still active enough to tell him that this wasn't a game anymore. He was in occupied France, in what was virtual enemy territory, and while these people had no choice but to put up with the invaders, he knew *he* would be considered the enemy if he was caught.

He would be shot. And he would also be putting this farmer and his family in danger if they were seen to be helping him. He knew that too.

"The coast," he said urgently. "Which way?"

He swayed as he spoke, and the farmer gripped his arm. "You go nowhere. You come to farm and eat, and then we think about boat."

Baz could have wept then as he almost dragged himself along beside the farmer. It wasn't far across the fields, but with the sore and bleeding blisters on his feet that he'd hardly noticed until now, it seemed like a mountain to climb before they were safely inside the stone-flagged farmhouse. And he still didn't know the details of France's collapse. The farmer's wife didn't speak English, and the daughter was either too young or too frightened to try.

But from the way they gabbled to each other in French, with many arm-wavings and glares his way, it was painfully clear that the woman wanted to get him away from there as quickly as possible, and he couldn't blame her for that. He wanted it too. But eventually the farmer made it obvious to her that Baz needed food, and he greedily ate the bowl of stew she finally slapped down in front of him, and downed several glasses of water, before he felt in any way human again.

"You rest now," the farmer ordered.

More alert now, Baz looked at him suspiciously. How did he know he could trust any of these people? The farmer had seemed affable enough, but his wife was decidedly unfriendly. They could easily turn him in to win favour with the Germans, and for the first time he knew how it felt to be hunted, and to trust no one. He started to protest, but the farmer spoke again, pointing to the stairs.

"You rest here for one hour."

"I'm grateful, but I think I should leave right away," Baz said uneasily. "You may be in danger if I stay."

The man shook his head vigorously. "We leave after dark. Now, you rest!"

The aggression had returned, and Baz knew he had little option. He was so tired he was almost collapsing where he stood, and he winced as he put one foot in front of the other on the creaking wooden staircase. He was shown into a white-painted boxroom with a narrow bed and various Catholic artefacts on the small chest of drawers. He couldn't be sure, but as he sank on to the bed and heard the door close, he thought he also heard a key turn in the lock. But he was too weary to care anymore, and the last thing he saw before his eyes closed was the face of the Virgin Mary on a painting above him.

The creaking on the stairs woke him with a start of fear. He had no idea how long he had been asleep, but he was sure it had been more than an hour. It had still been daylight when he reached the farm, and through the tiny square of window he could see the dark blue of the night sky, dotted with stars. He heard the key turn in the lock and knew his earlier thought had been right. They had locked him in, and now he was about to learn his fate.

His heart drummed sickeningly, and he stared hard at the door, wondering if it was about to be kicked in by jackboots, and if a machine gun would spray him with bullets. It would be a bloody shame to splatter this nice, clinically white room with blood, he found himself thinking incoherently.

For some wild reason he found himself thinking it must be how his sister Daisy felt in her nice, clinically white hospital ward: defiling all the nice, clinically white wards with blood – he couldn't seem to get the bastard words out of his head now.

He was very tempted to scream that he was willing to surrender, even though he knew it was the coward's way out, but his mouth and throat were so dry he couldn't utter a sound. The walls seemed to be revolving, and he knew he must be hallucinating, so the farmer's wife had probably slipped something into his stew to make sure he remained docile until the Germans came...

The door opened, and two men came inside as he cowered in terror on the narrow bed. His only hope was that if they were going to kill him they would do it quickly. He wasn't cut out to be a hero, and his only consolation was that when he met his sweet mother in heaven – if he went to heaven – she would understand and forgive him the way she always had.

"We go now," the farmer said.

Baz blinked in the patch of light showing through the door.

"Go?" he croaked. "Go where?"

"To boat. This man takes you."

He swung his legs off the bed, forcing himself not to vomit with relief that he wasn't about to be killed, and feeling a surge of shame at his momentary willingness to surrender. It would never happen again, he vowed. But he was finding it hard to walk, and he knew he was in no state to go anywhere.

"I can't," he said finally. "My feet are too swollen."

The other man spoke rapidly in French, and the farmer nodded.

"You not walk. You ride in cart. Please – go now."

Baz swallowed, sensing that the wife's fears had been transmitted to her husband. He hobbled to the door and down the stairs as carefully as he could. There was no sign of the wife and daughter, and he tried to thank the farmer as he went outside into the cool of the evening and saw the horse and cart outside. He had nothing to give the family, but he scribbled his name and address on a piece of paper, just in case they should ever need help.

Then he was bundled inside the cart, covered with a blanket and bundles of straw, and he realised that this journey was a hazardous one for the man taking him to the coast. Baz hardly thought such a move was a good idea at night, but presumably it was preferable to doing it in daylight. He gave up speculating and settled down to the most uncomfortable and stifling journey of his life.

He had no idea which part of the coast they were heading to, but at last the cart stopped, and as he lifted his head he saw the hazy outline of the sea ahead, with several large ships tied up in the harbour. The driver removed the straw and blanket, and Baz drew in great gulps of air, as the man pointed to the harbour. Baz realised now that the dark, moving shadows ahead of him weren't bushes, but the shuffling figures of men.

Without saying a word, his saviour got back into the cart and turned it around, leaving Baz to hobble away, to merge in with the small army of servicemen all as bent as he as on reaching the ships. He was just one among hundreds now, and no one questioned his dishevelled appearance.

"Come on, you buggers, get a move on," a raucous English voice roared at them from the quay. "Get on board as quick as you can and find yourselves a space. We'll be out of here in the morning, but you can bet your boots the Jerries will be bombing at first light, so I hope you've got a few prayers up your sleeves."

His bloody cheerfulness set Baz's teeth on edge. He thought himself a survivor, and he hadn't come all this way to be bombed by Jerry planes; but nor had any of these. There were plenty worse off than he was, and with no hospital ship to tend to them either, just the rough handling of a ship's medico. His blistered feet were the least of their worries.

He squatted down on deck, wedged between a dozen soldiers, all as exhausted and stinking as himself, and waited for daylight to come. He knew that he was on a large ship, one of several in the harbour, but theirs didn't finally get under way until mid-morning. By then the whine of air-raid sirens was constantly filling the air, the smell of burning was acrid, and the cloud of enemy aircraft was blotting out the sky, bearing down on them out of the morning sunlight like angry wasps, but with far more lethal intent. Bombs were falling like rain, and there was no chance of avoiding the inevitable. A bomb struck them amidships, rocking the entire ship, throwing men and lifeboats into the sea.

"Anyone still standing, grab a lifejacket and jump," the crew were screaming now. "You'll be safer in the sea than waiting for these bastards to blow us to bits."

It was like something out of hell as lifejackets were tossed between them, many literally torn from the next man's grasp as each fought for his own. Someone thrust one at Baz.

"Here, kid, put this on and jump for it," the man yelled.

He did as he was told and rushed to the side of the ship, instinctively drawing back as he saw how very far below the water looked. There was oil spilling out of the ship now, and a thick black sludge was spreading over the sea's surface, raw and pungent. Baz was too terrified to jump, and the hard cork of the lifejacket was throttling him. But the ship was tilting badly now, and the sheer volume of men behind him was pushing him, taking away his decision to leap over the side. It was one heaving mass of men and cumbersome lifejackets.

Then, with one last strangled gasp for survival, he found himself hurtling overboard in the midst of them, and as he hit the water the lifejacket became his killer, breaking his neck on impact.

# Chapter Thirteen

"I never thought I'd say this, but I really envy my sister," Daisy said to Alice Godfrey, in a welcome ten-minute break from their ward duties.

"What? Having a baby!" Alice said in disbelief.

"No, of course not. I wouldn't want one until I've been married for years, anyway. I didn't mean Elsie. I meant Immy. It must be exciting to drive an officer around all the time and be in on everything that's going on in London."

"You wouldn't think that if you were in the middle of an air raid!"

"All the same, it's very romantic to think of her and her young man spending a weekend's leave together, even in the middle of an air raid. I shouldn't even think they'd notice the bombs falling."

Alice laughed. "Daisy, you're such an idiot. People get killed and wounded in air raids, or haven't you noticed? It's what keeps us working too," she added, as Daisy's brow puckered.

"I know, but I'm sure Immy will be all right, and the rest of us too. Did I ever tell you I sometimes think of my mother as our guardian angel keeping us all safe?" She felt her face grow hot as she saw Alice's astonished look. "Oh, forget I said that. I don't really know why I did. It's not something I tell everyone."

"Then I'm honoured that you told me. And I don't actually think you're an idiot at all. I think you're a rather special person, if you must know."

Daisy squirmed. "Well, now you're *really* making me feel soppy. And we'd better get back to work, or Sister will be after us."

It made her feel good all the same, to know that someone as sophisticated as Alice Godfrey thought of her as someone rather special.

Since she and Elsie had come back from Cornwall, and her eighteenth birthday had come and gone, she was feeling more relaxed in one way, and more restless in another. Part of her relished the knowledge that she was still doing the job she loved, and another part said it wasn't enough to be stuck here in her local hospital when other people were out there in the midst of danger, doing *really* worthwhile jobs.

She was old enough now to volunteer. Each time the thought entered her head it gave her a shivery feeling of anticipation. She wasn't Florence Nightingale, but Florence had gone out to where she was needed, and to Daisy that was what heroines were made of. But she could just imagine the hue and cry if she dared to suggest such a thing. So although she did nothing about it, it was a thought that wouldn't go away.

It wasn't such a comfortable thought to know that there were ships still trying to get servicemen out of France that were being bombed and sunk before they even left the French ports. It wasn't safe to be on the sea nowadays, any more than it was safe to be in one of the key cities that were likely to be German targets.

She wondered where her brother was now. They hadn't heard from Baz in weeks, but since that was nothing unusual, she gave up thinking about him and got on with the business of writing a letter home for the patient in her care.

This was something she enjoyed doing, because it always gave someone at the other end a bit of hope. A wife or a mother was going to get a letter written in her neat hand on behalf of their loved one; and she encouraged all her patients to let her do this for them, carefully putting the words in their heads if they were too reticent or inarticulate to think of them for themselves but making sure the sentiments seemed exactly right for each man to have said.

"Right-oh then, Private Stokes. If you're ready to dictate, I'm ready to write. And nothing too saucy this time, if you don't mind!"

He laughed back at her, trying not to cough and start his wretched wheezing again, and winking with the one good eye that wasn't heavily bandaged. Both arms were bandaged too, and it had been touch-and-go whether or not he lost his right hand in the shell blast.

It was a good thing he hadn't, since it was the one he used to lift his pint, he'd told the doctors chirpily at the time.

"Now, Nursie, you know a little bit of sauce never did anyone any harm!" he answered in reply to her comment.

"Well, I prefer to save it for putting on my chips," Daisy said smartly, knowing some of them liked to include a bit of spice in their letters, even if it meant shocking her. It didn't actually. She was only acting as a mediator, and, in the end, they were *their* words, not hers, even the more intimate ones.

"All right," Private Stokes said. "Let's start with "My dear Hilda", as usual, and ask how she is. And the kids too.

Then tell her I'm as well as can be expected, and hoping to get out of here very soon, though I shall miss my pretty nurse and her warm hands."

"Are you sure you want to say that bit?" Daisy said, pausing. "Wouldn't it be nicer to say you're missing your wife's warm hands?"

She knew he'd led her into this the minute she heard him chuckle again.

"Oh, much better. Now, you're good at anatomy, aren't you, Nursie? So where shall we say I'd like to feel them?"

"How about holding yours?" she said innocently.

"My what?"

"Hands, of course," Daisy said, seeing the ward sister approaching, and knowing there would be no nonsense out of her if she heard this one's cheek. But if it did them good and raised their morale, where was the harm in it?

Though she knew very well that if it wasn't wartime, when people were becoming far more liberal than they ever had been before, her parents would have been scandalised to hear her speak in such a provocative manner to a virtual stranger. Even her mother, with her more flamboyant life, being a stage artiste…

"Now then, we've asked your wife how she is, and enquired after the children," she said more briskly. "Do you want to tell her how well you're doing?"

Private Stokes scowled. "You can tell her that the treatment hurts a bloody sight more than nearly getting my hand blown off, if you like. Bloody doctors. More like effing butchers, if you ask me."

Daisy waited patiently, knowing this was one of Private Stokes's expected reactions. He was actually doing very well indeed, but with the usual impatience of the regular soldier, he couldn't stand any kind of inactivity. She folded her arms, and his scowl gradually turned into a grin.

"Shocked you, did I, ducks? I restrained meself from *ekchually* saying the word, of course, for fear of offending them delicate little ears of yours—"

Daisy snapped at him before she had time to think.

"Oh, shut up, Stokesey, and let's get on with this letter. I've heard worse than that in my time, so don't think you're anything special! And there's plenty in here far worse off than you too, so stop feeling sorry for yourself. It's your wife I feel sorry for, if you're going home to her with your bad temper."

His mouth dropped open with shock at her sharp retort. Daisy surprised herself, but sometimes shock tactics were better than tip-toeing around. Anyway, she did feel sorry for the families who had to put up with them on their return home when they still weren't fully fit, especially those who played on the extent of their injuries, which she knew very well some of them did. There was a lot to be said for supervised convalescent homes with properly trained staff until they were restored to full health, rather than inflicting them on their long-suffering wives.

"Ever thought of being a female prison warder, have you, Nursie?" Private Stokes snarled. But then his eyes twinkled, and his voice lowered to a more lecherous tone. "Not that I'd object to a bit of nightly bullying from the likes of you, mind, if you know what I mean."

"I haven't the slightest idea," Daisy said airily. "Now then, should I write all that to your darling Hilda, or do you have something nicer to say to her?"

He chuckled at her then. "Just tell her I hope to be getting out of here soon and then she can give me my bed–bath instead of the wicked nurse with fingernails like talons digging into my backside."

"I hope to be getting out of here soon," Daisy dictated as she wrote down her own interpretation, "and I'm looking forward to having some of your loving care instead of these nurses. They do their best, but they're not you, dear."

She looked at him. "How does that sound to you?"

"Perfect," he said, with the surprising glint of a tear in his eye. "My old woman will love that. You wouldn't care to be my personal secretary, I suppose?"

Daisy laughed, closing the notepad before copying it out properly for him to check and then having it posted.

"If the choice is between a female prison warder and personal secretary to a wicked old rogue like you, Private Stokes, I think I'll stick where I am!"

She moved on to the next man on the ward who wanted her services, knowing she had cheered his day, just as he had cheered hers. She enjoyed writing their letters for them, and the men appreciated having a young and pretty nurse to do it for them, especially one who wasn't so starchy that she couldn't indulge in a bit of banter now and then. And it wasn't going unnoticed.

She was called into the ward sister's office later on that day, and her heart skipped a beat, knowing this was never a good sign. Daisy tried frantically to remember any misdemeanours she might have committed.

"Sit down, Daisy," Sister Macintosh said, "and there's no need to look alarmed. I'm not about to give you your marching orders."

"Thank you, Sister," Daisy murmured. But she must have done something wrong, otherwise why would she be here?

"Several of your patients have shown me the letters you've written for them, and I must say you have a way with words. I don't imagine it's always exactly the way they're told to you, is it?"

"I never try to alter the sense of them, Sister, but sometimes they find it difficult to say what they mean. Sometimes the words don't come out quite right, and I just try to tidy them up a little bit."

Her own words weren't coming out quite right at that moment, Daisy thought in a panic. Had someone complained? Maybe someone's wife had thought she was putting a little too much sentimentality into a letter from a normally tough-talking soldier...

"My dear girl, don't look so flustered. I'm not condemning you for what you're doing. On the contrary. You have a rare sensitivity for one so young, especially when writing letters for some of the older patients."

Daisy felt herself blush. If Sister knew what some of those older patients dictated to her – and the younger ones – just to tease her. But a compliment couldn't be the sole reason for being called into Sister's office. She waited, knowing there had to be more.

"Your mother was once a talented entertainer, I believe," Sister went on, taking Daisy off guard.

"Why yes, she was. Frances Caldwell. She was a singer and dancer."

Sister nodded. "I seem to remember. And that must be where you get your own artistic talents from. There is a real art in writing letters, and not everyone has it. So I have the details of an opening that might interest you."

Even though she was dying to discuss it with someone, she knew it was only right to tell her family first. She had already been invited to have supper with Alice at the Godfreys' home that evening, so by the time she went home, she could hardly contain herself, and she went straight into the parlour where Aunt Rose and Uncle Bert were listening to the wireless, and thankfully the boys were already in bed.

"You'll never guess what's happened today. You could have knocked me down with the proverbial feather," she burst out.

"It must have been something monumental then," Rose said, laughing at her excitement. "Have you been promoted to chief surgeon? If so, remind me never to have my tonsils out."

"Oh, Aunt Rose, it's nothing so unlikely! Though the whole thing seems unlikely to me. Well, perhaps not, considering what brought the suggestion about; but fancy her bringing Mother into it. That was a surprise, I can tell you."

She started giggling, her voice rising almost hysterically.

"Are you going to tell us *anything*, or is this a guessing game?" Rose said.

"I'm *trying*," she gulped. "I've been offered a post in Norfolk if I want to take it. Well, not actually *offered* it, but I've been invited to apply for it, as Sister thinks I'll be so well suited to it. I have two weeks to think about it—"

"I think you'd better slow down for a start," Bert said, in his usual placid manner. "Let's see what we've learned so far. You've been offered a new job – or almost – and your mother comes into it in some way. And if you don't stop babbling and giggling, we shall start to think you've been breathing in some of that laughing gas we're always hearing about. Now take some deep breaths and start from the beginning."

Daisy tried. But hadn't she told them everything already? What more was there to tell? The post was being advertised, and Sister Macintosh thought she would be well suited to it.

The only obstacle was that it was somewhere in Norfolk, which was still little more than a bulge on the map to Daisy, and also a very long way from home. It was also much nearer to the east coast, and together with the south it was the area most likely for the Germans to invade and start their most intensive bombing campaign. She could be putting herself right in the heart of danger.

Her small *frisson* of nerves was replaced by a stab of shame. Hadn't she just traversed the English Channel a couple of dozen times in a hospital ship, helping to bring back those very patients who would hopefully be recovering now in the Norfolk military convalescent home, and other places like it? The lucky ones, anyway. The ones who had survived.

"Daisy, I don't think this is a good idea," Aunt Rose said at once, when she had finally slowed down enough to outline it properly.

"Why not? I thought I'd have you on my side, anyway, since you didn't oppose my going on the hospital ship." She was startled at this reaction, knowing very well that she needed everyone's approval, especially her father's, and that approval all started here, with Rose and Bert.

"Darling, that was different."

"How was it different? It was far more dangerous that just sitting about in a hospital ward or a military convalescent home holding some soldier's hand and writing a letter for him!"

Rose gave a slight smile. "And is that really going to satisfy your restless heart? Think about what you've just said, Daisy."

Stubbornly, she refused to be put off. "Writing letters wouldn't be my only job, and I never thought it would be. They need trained hospital staff in these places, and I'll still be using my nursing skills, so I don't see why you should object. Anyway, if I were to volunteer for one of the services like Immy, I could be sent anywhere."

"You're not thinking about that, I hope," Bert said sharply.

"I've thought about it quite a lot, as a matter of fact," she muttered.

"And I think your father would have something to say about that, Daisy," Rose said, just as sharply.

"I daresay, but I'm not a child any longer. I *am* eighteen now, and able to make decisions of my own. And right now, my decision is to go to bed and think about it, so please excuse me if I say goodnight."

"Just a minute, young lady," her aunt said more aggressively. "Aren't you forgetting something?"

"Am I?"

"You're not a fully trained nurse yet, no matter what title you give yourself, and you won't be properly qualified for a good many years. You haven't really applied yourself to lectures, have you? I sometimes think the *idea* of being a nurse is what attracted you first of all, Daisy, and I'm not saying that you haven't become someone we're all proud of; but I do wonder if it really is a vocation."

Daisy resisted the temptation to rush out of the room, upset by this censure that she hadn't wanted and hadn't expected. She was so sure Aunt Rose had been right behind her longing to be a nurse and knew she had made a good job of it so far. But Aunt Rose was right, of course, and she was still only a probationer, with choices to be made. She didn't intend to say anything more about volunteering for the forces, which would only underline the family's opinion of her butterfly mind. But the more she thought about it, the more alluring it became.

Without knowing it, her aunt had already begun to squash the idea of working at a convalescent home, prompting Daisy into questioning the static occupation of being no more than a sympathetic helper while she wrote letters for strangers. She knew very well it wouldn't be just like that, nor only that. But the questioning had made it all sound flat and unexciting, despite the fact that every unknown soldier would be grateful for her help, just as Private Stokes had been.

The pros and cons went round and round in her head, but, in the end, she admitted that Aunt Rose was right about one thing. It wouldn't satisfy her restless heart, at least not for ever. It had been good of Sister Macintosh to think she was well suited to it, but there were other things she could do. And that posed other questions. Was Sister Macintosh hinting tactfully that perhaps hospital nursing wasn't the right job for Daisy? And was she really satisfied exactly where she was? Working in a familiar environment, where she could go home each day?

She lay fully dressed on her bed, her hands behind her head, thinking of all the people she knew, who weren't doing just that. Elsie... well, Elsie had never been as adventurous as the rest of them, and she had found her destiny with Joe Preston. Joe had enlisted just before the war began, and Immy's young man, James Church, had been a soldier for much longer. She thought about Immy, her beautiful oldest sister whom she had always looked up to so much, and who hadn't wasted a precious minute in joining up with that friend of hers.

Even Baz – risking their father's anger by refusing to stand behind a shop counter in their one-time family business and doing just what he wanted from the minute he had started working for the old ferryman on the River Avon, to going to sea on a fishing trawler. With Baz's cheek and thirst for adventure, he would probably end up as Admiral of the Fleet, Daisy thought with a grin.

So that left her. Yes, she was doing a worthwhile job, and yes, she had a way with words and an artistic talent bestowed on her by her mother, if Sister Macintosh's awkward compliment was to be believed. But she knew that, anyway, Daisy thought immediately, with a touch of her old confidence. She had inherited some of her mother's performing talent and her self-assurance, and once she had desperately wanted to follow her on to the stage, until Lucy's accident had decided her on a nursing career.

God! She was so shallow… did she really know *what* she wanted? She had wanted Cal – she still thought of Jed and Glenn with guilty affection… She turned her head on the pillow, momentarily caught by the brilliance of the moon through her window throwing playful shadows over the bed as a small breeze ruffled the leaves of the trees outside. She heard it sighing through the branches, as sweetly as a whispering voice. Telling her to go where her heart took her.

She sat up slowly, hugging her knees. Despite all the time she had worked at the hospital, she knew some thought she was only playing at it, because she hadn't done much of the formal and rigid training that was required. She was still not a *proper* nurse, as young Norman had once taunted her. It took years to be properly qualified, and even though she had once had the fanciful notion of possessing healing hands, it wasn't enough. And if she could waver like this, then she wasn't dedicated enough.

She saw the moonlit shadows dancing on her bedroom wall, as light and ethereal as fairy dancers. As light and beautiful as her mother, with the voice of an angel. Her guardian angel.

"Is that what you wanted me to do all along, Mother?" she whispered slowly. "To be like you?"

Her eyes misted with tears, knowing she could never, ever emulate the stardom of her mother. She could only be herself; but she was well aware that the women's army catered for all kinds of personnel. Even entertainers had their place. Only her father could be the one to advise her now. If he was absolutely horrified at the thought, then she would abandon it for ever.

Since her aunt and uncle seemed determined to avoid the issue, and she couldn't see her father until the following weekend, Daisy decided to talk it over with Alice Godfrey, telling her about the proposed transfer first. They walked along the beach, breathing in the salt air with some relief after a day on the wards.

"It's up to you, Daisy, but I have to say I've also had the feeling that you've become restless lately. So if you're getting the opportunity to move on and work in this convalescent home, perhaps you should take it."

"Yes, but is it what I want? It won't be the same, anyway. I'll be doing far less real nursing, and more *caring* — which is all very noble, of course, but perhaps more suited to... well... to someone older," she finished lamely.

"You think our wounded boys won't be happy to see a young and pretty face when they're convalescing?"

"Oh Lord, now you're putting me in the wrong. I knew you would!"

"Daisy, you have to make up your own mind on this. It seems to me you've reached a bit of a crossroads, anyway. You don't really want to stay at Weston General, and you're not relishing the prospect of this new job in darkest Norfolk or wherever it is. So what do you want to do?"

"I'd quite like to entertain the troops," she said in a rush. "And now that I've said it I know you'll think that's a really daft idea!"

"No I don't. I can't sing for toffee, but you were wonderful when we did the carol-singing for the patients at Christmas. Everyone said you were a star in the making, so why not?"

Daisy shook her head. "I'm not a great singer. I can dance far better. And I don't want to be a star. My mother was a star. I just want to be useful."

Alice gave her shoulder an affectionate squeeze. "Well, that may be so, but I reckon you'll be a star whatever you do, Daisy."

She still hadn't mentioned any of it to her aunt and uncle before she went home on Saturday, and she was anxiously trying to think how to tell her father.

She was glad Elsie was there too, because she needed her moral support. It was an important decision she was about to make, and if either of them had their doubts — well, she wouldn't think that far ahead.

"So when are you going to tell us what's troubling you, Daisy? Out with it, girl," Quentin said, when they had finally made enough small talk.

She took a deep breath. "Several things, actually. But firstly I wanted to ask what you'd think if I was to give up nursing, would it upset you too much?"

"It all depended on what else you wanted to do," he said, knowing her too well. "But I also think you're old enough to make your own decisions now. Something tells me you've already done that, and that this is just a formal gesture to keep your father happy."

"No, it's more than that, truly. I want your approval, both of you."

"Do I take it that you don't have your aunt's?" Quentin asked shrewdly.

"Not exactly," Daisy said carefully. "She doesn't know all of it, though."

"Then wouldn't it be a good idea if we were to hear all of it?"

Elsie intervened quickly. "Daisy, what's changed your mind about nursing? You were so keen, and I always thought it was something you wanted to do because of Lucy."

"Perhaps that's all it was, and I *did* enjoy doing it and helping people, even though some of the things I have to do are too ghastly to even think about. And I never told you everything about how awful it was on the hospital ship, and seeing those poor men brought on board – I'm sorry, Elsie, I know Joe was one of them – but you had to be there to know how terrible it was – how sickeningly terrible…"

"All right, Daisy," her father said, seeing how Elsie's face had blanched. "So you've had second thoughts about your choice of career, is that it?"

"Sister Macintosh says I could apply for a post in a Norfolk convalescent home. She seems to think I'm overflowing with sensitivity, but I got the distinct idea that what she really means is I don't have what it takes to make a good nurse."

"I'm sure that's not the case, darling," Elsie said at once.

"Well, I'm beginning to think it is. And ever since she put the thought into my head, I know I don't want to spend my time writing letters for wounded soldiers or being at everyone's beck and call like a glorified maid. I'm sorry if that sounds awful, but I've been seriously thinking about something else, and now that I've got all of that off my chest, that's really what I wanted to talk to you about."

She realised she was breathing erratically. It was crazy to feel so inhibited when she was with her own family, but she *needed* their approval. She needed their blessing. Her voice was high and quick as she blurted it all out.

"I'm old enough to volunteer for the ATS, Daddy, and they have all kinds of opportunities for women in the services now. I wouldn't want to go into the catering corps like Helen Church. I'm hopeless at cooking, anyway, and I can't drive, so I couldn't do what Immy's doing. But there are other things."

As she paused, Quentin looked at her young and beautiful face, so like her mother's, the eyes the same wide velvety brown as Frances's were, the hair a mass of titian curls. He heard the breathy quality of her voice in her uncertainty, and saw the upward tilt of her chin, and the natural grace with which she moved.

And he knew.

# Chapter Fourteen

Daisy had the distinct feeling that her father didn't want to hear any of this, so that in the end she told him she was still making up her mind about joining up and said nothing about trying to follow in her mother's footsteps. On Monday morning she still hadn't made up her mind what to do.

"Sister Macintosh didn't even try to persuade me one way or the other," Daisy reported to Alice in a bit of a rage. "It's obvious she doesn't care what I do."

"I wouldn't let her worry you. Anyway, you're going to do what you wanted, aren't you? But how about your family? I bet they had something to say."

"My father had already telephoned Aunt Rose before I got home from Bristol, so she was prepared." Daisy gave a wry grin. "And there I was, all the way home in the train, wondering how I was going to break it to her that I was thinking of joining the ATS, and she didn't turn a single blessed hair!"

"Your auntie's a very progressive woman."

Daisy laughed uneasily. "Well, that's one word for it. But now what?"

"Go to an enlistment centre?" Alice said vaguely. "Tell them you're ready and waiting to dance for the troops, and available for stage and screen."

"I didn't say I was *that* good, although I knew most of my mother's routines, and after she got ill and couldn't remember half of them my father used to encourage me to do them at home to make her smile."

She wasn't smiling now, remembering. It seemed such a long time ago, and yet she could remember as if it was yesterday, how the whole family – even Baz, before he got so cocky – used to applaud her efforts to copy her mother's dances and bring some of the glittering memories back to her.

"I shall miss you, Daisy," Alice said. "I wonder where they'll send you."

"Lord knows. I've got to volunteer first, then be accepted."

"Oh, you will be. They take anyone these days."

She laughed at Daisy's indignant expression. "I'm *teasing*, you idiot. Of course they'll take you and be glad of your talents."

Daisy nodded, although she felt far less confident now than before. It would almost have been a relief if someone had opposed her idea, she thought, with a silly burst of resentment against the whole world. But nobody had. The evacuee boys were already squabbling about who was going to have her bedroom, and Teddy was boasting that his sister was going to be a film star.

"Nobody's going to have Daisy's bedroom," Aunt Rose told them firmly. "It will always be ready for Daisy when she comes home on leave."

The word had struck a note of caution in her. If she had thought she was being regimented before, she was going to be even more so now. She knew everyone at the hospital, and she was planning to work among strangers in a very grown-up world. She had a sudden attack of nerves.

Aunt Rose sensed it, following her up to the bedroom that night as she prepared for bed. "This has to be your decision, Daisy, but please think very carefully about it. And always remember your mother's motto," she advised. "No matter how much you quake inside, keep your chin up and never show it."

"I never thought Mother ever quaked before a performance!"

"That proves how clever she was, doesn't it?"

Whether it was true, or just something that Aunt Rose knew would make her feel better, she resolved to remember it. But a week later she was still dithering, feeling more unsure of herself than ever before.

By then the whole country was reeling because France had been doubly humiliated in defeat, being forced to sign the armistice with Germany in the same railway carriage in the forest of Compiègne where they themselves had been the victors in 1918. It was a cruel piece of diplomacy on Hitler's part; and to add to the threat of the British invasion being seriously felt by everyone now, the news came that German forces had occupied the Channel Islands. It seemed it could only be a matter of time before Britain, too, was overwhelmed by the enemy.

The thought of Daisy Caldwell performing a balletic dance routine for a bunch of war-toughened soldiers who just wanted to get home seemed pathetic.

She finally decided to talk things over with their Methodist minister, by whom Aunt Rose always set such store, and who knew the family well. She didn't have to take his advice, but he would be an independent observer, and it was better than rushing into things as she usually did.

He listened sympathetically, as always; and because she was nervous, she spoke more quickly than usual.

"Once I tell the recruitment people what I've been doing, I'm sure they'll put me straight into a medical unit, but that's not what I want to do. In fact, I'm not at all sure that I'm suited to nursing after all."

"I doubt that anyone else would say that, Daisy. I always hear glowing reports of you from your aunt. Do you think you're more suited to being under enemy fire should the need arise? Or would you go to pieces the moment you heard a German shell overhead?"

Daisy's face burned. "I'm not a coward, Mr Penfold. You know I worked for several weeks on a hospital ship. I don't think I would go to pieces in a crisis, but I feel I can do other things to help the war effort."

"And what would those things be?"

She bit her lip, knowing how feeble it would sound to say she could dance quite well, and she could sing a bit, and she had inherited her mother's talent; therefore she thought she could entertain the troops to keep up their morale. But she remembered what Aunt Rose had told her, stuck her chin in the air, looked him straight in the eyes, and said it anyway.

His voice held a tinge of amusement. "So you would be no use as an ambulance-driver, or a trainee motor mechanic, or—"

"No, of course not! I believe I would be of most use as an entertainer. You know my mother's reputation, Mr Penfold, and, in all modesty, I do think I have a little of her talent. I thought I could be a dancer," she finished lamely.

"I see. But you don't have any professional performing experience, do you, my dear? Stop and think what that means for a moment. I doubt that a well-brought-up young lady dancing in front of a crowd of battle-scarred soldiers would get away without a great deal of cat-calling and probably a whole lot worse. Could you deal with that?"

When she didn't answer, he went on more gently: "Apart from which, Daisy, I don't think the army is in the business of hiring unknown entertainers in the middle of a war, nor letting you pick and choose what you want to do! And you're still very young. If you really want to change direction from nursing, have you thought about working in a munitions factory, for instance?"

Daisy held on to her temper, knowing he was being calm and sensible, but making her feel a child at the same time. She tried not to react angrily, knowing you didn't do such things in front of a minister of the church.

"I've thought about it," she said evenly. "But my sister Imogen is in the ATS and I've heard good things about it, so I wanted to do my bit there too."

"Is your sister an entertainer as well?"

From his sceptical tone now, Daisy guessed that he wondered if the entire Caldwell family was about to dance its way into the war effort.

"No. She used to work for a housing agent before he left Bristol and went to live in Cornwall when the war began. Immy's a lance-corporal now. She's the official driver for a Captain Beckett, and I believe they're attached to the War Office. It's all pretty hush-hush, of course, so all I know is that my sister is based in London now."

If it was stretching it a bit to wave Immy's credentials in front of him, Daisy had no qualms about it. *Look them straight in the eye and keep your nerve*, she remembered… and she was doing just that.

He leaned forward and patted her hand like a Dutch uncle. "Daisy, why don't you give this a little more thought before you do anything at all? But I'm very glad you came to me before doing anything rash, and I want you to know that my door is always open if you want to come and talk to me about it some more."

"Thank you, Mr Penfold," she murmured.

She knew this was his way of dismissing her, and that she had really got nowhere at all. If she had expected easy answers, she hadn't got them. In fact, it had complicated matters. It had all seemed so simple when she had first thought about it, and now she didn't know where she was.

"Don't thank me. But young girls who think that wearing a uniform is glamorous won't get very far. You'll be expected to muck in with everyone else, and you won't get any favours by passing yourself off as an entertainer, nor by mentioning your mother's name as a password to fame and glory. I also suspect that her style of dancing, however beautiful in its day, is somewhat passé now."

Daisy felt a little shock at this sting in the tail, just when she thought he was being his usual benevolent self. And he could be right… but she wasn't going to let his disapproval put her off just yet. She had once thought that dancing was going to be her destiny. But she had also thought the same thing about nursing, when she'd come to Lucy's rescue at the Luckwells' annual gymkhana and known what to do about her sprained foot. Right now she was blowing hot and cold like the wind, she thought angrily.

Alice grinned knowingly when she told her she had gone to see the minister.

"So you decided against marching straight to the recruitment office and telling them that dancing was the only job you would consider?"

Daisy was tempted to say airily that that was exactly what she had planned to do, but she couldn't quite bring herself to lie so blatantly.

"I thought it was prudent to talk it over with Mr Penfold first, but for all the good it did me I might as well have consulted Teddy," she snapped. "Or *you!*"

"Oh well, pardon me, and the best of luck, whatever you choose to do," Alice said, deciding to retreat out of an argument she couldn't win, and clearly thinking Daisy had about as much chance of getting her own way as of persuading Adolph to clear out of France and let everyone get back to normal. As it was, they parted on chilly terms.

Daisy had already written to Immy, and she was longing to get a letter back to tell her she wasn't being entirely crazy; but instead of a letter she got a telephone call from her early that evening.

"I hope you know what you're doing, Daisy," Immy said. "I always thought you were happy being a nurse."

"So I was, but not enough to do it for life."

"You'd hardly be in the ATS for life – at least, I hope not. We all hope it will be over soon, but from the sound of it… well, never mind about all that now. I gather the family doesn't object."

From the way she said it Daisy knew she had already discussed it with everyone else, and it didn't improve her feeling of being a grown-up.

"Oh Immy, I thought you'd understand! You joined up the minute you could, so why shouldn't I?"

"No reason at all, darling," Immy said, after a brief pause. "But you know the army has a habit of sending people to the opposite ends of the country from where they belong and giving them the least likely jobs. You might just end up as a wireless operator."

"I doubt it. I don't know one end of a battery from the other." But it was exactly as Mr Penfold had said, she fumed. She could end up doing anything.

"They'd jolly well soon teach you if they thought you had the aptitude for it; but knowing you, little sister, you'll probably come up smiling. You and Baz usually do," she added. "Good luck, anyway, and keep me posted."

–

Immy kept the smile in her voice until she had replaced the receiver in the draughty hall of the small hotel, not wanting to put a damper on what Daisy obviously thought was her new vocation. Not wanting to tell her how London and the south-east were being seriously prepared for the invasion, with barbed wire in the streets, railway station signs blacked out and sandbags piled up around the most precious and vulnerable buildings.

The evacuation of children, which had been suspended during the early months of the year in what had been dubbed the phoney war, was in full swing again now, including the transportation of many of them to Canada. Immy couldn't imagine how terrifying it must be to be sent far away from everything that was familiar when you were so young and bewildered by it all.

As she heard James's voice behind her, she swung round into his arms, regardless of whether or not the hotel land-lady might be in the vicinity.

"Are you going to stand there staring at that telephone for ever, sweetheart, or are we going out to do the town?"

She raised the smile to her lips again. This was the start of their precious forty-eight-hour pass. She knew now that it was also James's embarkation leave – that in a few days' time he would be setting sail with his regiment – and both of them were desperate not to waste a moment of their time together, having no idea when the next time might be.

"We're going out on the town," she said huskily.

And afterwards, when they came back after dark, fumbling their way through the blacked-out streets after an evening of reckless laughter and dancing at the Hammersmith Palais, what then? *What then…?* Immy didn't dare to think that far ahead, but the thought that these two days and nights might be all they had was never far from her mind. She knew it couldn't be far from James's mind too.

He was a red-blooded young man who loved her passionately, and she adored him in return. And they weren't children. They knew what could and did happen in a war. Daisy's young man had been killed when his aircraft had been shot out of the sky, and one of James's friends had died when his tank had been blown up. Elsie's husband had been in danger of losing his foot after Dunkirk. Such things were part of the sacrifice of war. It was a knowledge that drove people to make the most of the moment, knowing it might never come again.

For all Immy and James knew, tonight, and tomorrow night, might be all the nights they would ever share.

"What are you thinking about now?" James saw the way she ran her tongue around her bottom lip as she always did when she was thinking deeply.

"Just that I love you," she said softly. "And that I don't want to waste a minute of these two days. So what shall we do tomorrow?"

"Let's decide that after tonight," he answered, his voice telling her nothing.

"You're right. So now that I've tried to put Daisy right, I'm going to see if there's any hot water, have a good wash, then go to my room and change into my dancing frock. Then you can tell me how beautiful I look!"

"You always look beautiful to me. You know that, Immy."

"Well, we'd better not stand here in the hall admiring one another any longer, or people will definitely start looking at us oddly," she said with a laugh, because when his voice deepened like that she felt a rush of love for him that almost overwhelmed her, making her weak, making her long for the kind of fulfilment she knew could only come one way. And as yet, she hadn't known it.

When they left the hotel later that evening, there were predictably no taxis to be had, but it wasn't far to walk, and as they made their way carefully to the Palais, arms around one another for safety, Immy had the certain feeling that tonight was going to be a turning point in her life.

He had once called their love his talisman. When they had realised the miracle of having fallen in love after years of being no more than friends, he had asked nothing more than to know that she belonged to him. But she didn't, not fully, not yet. Not in the biblical sense. In her mother's, and certainly in her grandmother's day, it would have been thought of as another kind of sacrifice.

Even though she was very aware that he wanted her as much as she wanted him, it was something she and James had never yet discussed, and he had never asked anything more of her than she was willing to give. A special touch, an extra caress, a deeper kiss… but tonight she was going to give him all of herself. She knew it as surely as she breathed.

Inside the dance hall, the myriad lights from the revolving chandelier were dazzling after the darkness outside, and the orchestra was already playing a waltz as she floated into his arms. No enemy threats could diminish the pleasure they found in one another. Nor even the distant sound of air-raid sirens and the dull thud of shell-fire that frequently rocked the ground like an earthquake waiting to happen.

This was their night, and when, leaving the Palais several hours later, they saw the indigo of the sky criss-crossed with searchlights seeking out enemy planes and the occasional silver flash as one of them was caught in their beams, it only added to the urgency and wantonness of scurrying back to their hotel, urged on by an air-raid warden, suggesting that they might want to get down to the shelters or the Underground for safety.

"What do you want to do, Immy? Do you fancy sharing the night with a few hundred others crammed into the Underground?"

"I do not! I only want to share this night with you!"

She spoke as recklessly as Daisy at that moment, the words leaving her lips before she could think properly, and she felt his arm tighten around her waist as she prayed that he wouldn't think her too brazen.

"My thoughts exactly, Immy darling."

She felt her heart beat faster at his words. She wanted him so much, but she was nervous that she wouldn't be all that he expected of her. She was twenty-one years old and she didn't know how to behave with a man in the most intimate situation of all. Her mind blotted out her brief fling with a brash young man who had worked on a Bristol newspaper.

Morgan Raine had wanted her too, and had been so very seductive in pursuing her, awakening her to her first heady taste of young love... and she had been so near to giving in to him, until she found out that she wasn't the only girl in his life. She had thought herself in love then, but that was before she had found the true love of her life.

How you actually behaved in that most intimate situation of all was something they never taught you at school, and she had no one to advise her. Elsie would have known, but Elsie was far away in Bristol, and besides, you couldn't ask a younger sister such basic things. It was too humiliating. It wasn't the right order of things.

She was gasping by the time they reached the hotel. She was out of breath from racing through the streets as carefully as they could, considering the black-out, but with their way partially lit by the brightness of the moon and the weaving searchlights. And she was out of breath with nerves.

"Immy," James said, catching her to him, seconds before they went indoors. "You know I would never hurt you, don't you? And you know – you do know – what I want…"

She realised that the longing in his voice was mixed with uncertainty and a kind of desperation, and she was suddenly aware that he was nervous too. Not in the same way that she was, perhaps, but nervous of her reaction.

She felt an acute sense of tenderness towards him then, realising that a man could feel this way too. That it wasn't all just rush and fumble, the way Morgan Raine had tried to seduce her on a Bristol hillside. She leaned forward and kissed James's lips, suddenly calm, and in control of her destiny.

"I know, James. And I want it too," she whispered against his mouth.

–

Immy was required to leave details of her whereabouts at all times, in case she should be needed urgently for any reason. Even a forty-eight-hour pass wasn't excluded, and when the hotel landlady told her over breakfast that mere had been a message for her to call Captain Beckett, she flew into a panic at once.

"He didn't say it was urgent," the woman said. "But I suppose you never know these days, do you?" she added, eyeing her and James with a professional and experienced look.

Not that she had any objection to what they did, providing they didn't wake up the rest of her lodgers... besides, these two were a particularly handsome couple, and she'd had a bit of a fling with a fellow or two in her time. She didn't begrudge them their fun.

"James, I'll have to call him straight away," Immy said. She was totally flustered, as gauche and guilty as a child caught stealing apples, and desperately hoping the land-lady didn't think Captain Beckett was her husband or father.

"Calm down, darling. I'll come to the telephone with you," he said, having no more appetite for breakfast, and knowing that this call could only mean that their leave was going to be cut short. They had had just one night – one spectacular night – and who knew how long it was going to have to last them?

Immy asked the operator for Captain Beckett's private number and waited for what seemed like an age before she got through.

"It's Lance-Corporal Caldwell answering your call, sir," she remembered to say formally, even though her heart was jumping, and her teeth seemed too big for her mouth.

"Imogen, I wouldn't have interrupted your leave unless it was important, but I thought you would want to know the news right away. Word came through just after midnight that Bristol has been bombed."

"*What?*" For a moment she couldn't take in what he was saying. Her eyes glazed, and she couldn't seem to hold the receiver. She felt James take it out of her hand and heard him speak rapidly into it.

"Captain Beckett, this is James Church, Imogen's fiancé. She's feeling rather unwell, so can you tell me what's happened? I gather it's something to do with Bristol, and we both have families there."

Immy grabbed the phone from him, her face on fire. She knew he had called her his fiancée for the sake of her reputation, although they weren't officially engaged yet; but such details were hardly important now. A fine soldier she would appear if she crumbled at a piece of news over a telephone. She drew a deep breath and spoke as crisply as she could, holding the receiver away from her ear so that James could hear every word clearly too.

"I'm sorry about that, sir. Can you give me the details?"

"There have been some casualties," he said cautiously, "and buildings have been flattened. I gather much of it was around the railway station area, but other than that the reports are still sketchy. But I thought you would want to check with your family, Lance-Corporal, and then contact me again."

"Thank you, sir," she said, choked. What he meant was that if her family was in any way involved, she could take a few more days' compassionate leave.

She knew the form. She knew the unspoken words. And right now, the thought whirling around in her head was that while she and James had been making love, their beloved city was being devastated by the enemy. Their families could have died. It was a reckoning – and she knew she was letting her panic take her to ridiculous places. It wasn't their fault. It wasn't their penance.

"I'll see about a train right away," James said tensely. "If not, I know some people who might find us some transport going west."

"Yes, but first of all I have to phone my father to see if he and Elsie are all right," she stammered.

His voice was strong and reassuring. "I'm sure they will be. Vicarage Street is miles away from Temple Meads, and so is Clifton."

She was dumb for a moment, and then she was flooded with guilt. His home was in Clifton, and he'd be frantic too, and she had thought only of herself.

"But James, you can't get to Bristol and back in your short embarkation leave," she almost wept, wondering how these precious few days had suddenly gone so terribly wrong. And through no fault of their own.

"I'll manage," he said grimly. "Now, do your telephoning, darling, and let me see about transport."

He was gone while she was still dithering, but when she tried to get through to their home number and then the number of Preston's Emporium, all the lines were clogged. In desperation, she called Aunt Rose's number instead, praying that someone would be there. The voice that answered was small and scared.

"Oh, Immy, thank God," Daisy gasped. "We wanted to get hold of you, but we didn't know where you were, and it's just so awful!"

## Chapter Fifteen

"Daisy, keep calm, and tell me exactly what's happened," Immy said sharply, aware that the landlady was hovering behind her with a cup of tea.

As if warm weak tea was going to solve everything, when everyone knew it should be hot and strong for shock – and also very sweet, if only there hadn't been a sugar shortage. She pulled herself together and listened to her sister's babbling words.

"It was so frightening, Immy. We could hear the bombing from here and everything was shaking. Every time we heard the sound of enemy planes the boys started screaming, and Norman was yelling that he was going home, and of course Ronnie wet the bed, and we were changing sheets in the middle of the night, and Uncle Bert was shouting at us not to panic, and Aunt Rose was practically crying and snapping at him that he should have done as Daddy always said and built a shelter in the garden, but he never would because we had the cellar here, and eventually we all went down there, and we've been up for hours—"

"For God's sake, Daisy," Immy practically screamed at her. "Stop blithering on about what you were all doing. I can't get through to Bristol on the phone, and I'm desperate to know if Daddy and Elsie are safe."

She heard Daisy's audibly deep breath before she spoke more huffily. "Well, I'm sorry, but I'm trying to tell you! Elsie phoned a couple of hours ago. She was still a bit shaky because she'd been in the house alone when the air raid started, and she had to go down to that miserable shelter in the garden that she hates. Daddy was out on fire-fighting duty and he's got a nasty gash on his forehead from some flying glass and had to have it treated, but apart from that he's all right."

Immy felt her heart clench. Even though she was in uniform, this war had seemed so far away until now. It had been a war that was mostly happening in Europe, and now it was on their own doorstep. Not just here in London and the vulnerable south-east counties, but at home in Bristol. She felt as young and confused as Daisy as that moment. No, even younger, as vulnerable as a baby.

"Where did the bombs fall, Daisy?" she asked, knowing she had to know. Even saying it felt so unreal. It was their beautiful city…

"It's all been on the wireless. Haven't you been listening?"

*No. I've been in bed with my lover…*

"No. So just tell me, will you? James and I are coming home as soon as we can get on a train, by the way. He's gone to see about it now."

"Oh, I forgot you were spending your leave with James."

There was a tiny pause, and Immy gritted her teeth, guessing that her little sister would be putting all kinds of interpretations on that statement, and knowing that she would be right.

"*Daisy!*"

"Sorry. Lower Maudlin Street was hit first, and then the bombs fell all around Temple Meads station – oh, I wonder if the trains will get through? I don't think the lines were hit, but it's all a bit bloody, isn't it? Sorry again, but you know what I mean. They say some people have been killed and there are lots of wounded, and a lot of building damage too. Daddy was out all night, and Elsie said he's exhausted, but he still went to open the shop this morning as usual."

"Is Elsie all right?" Immy said anxiously, remembering her condition.

"She says so, but I know Joe will start making her think seriously about going to his family in Yorkshire after this. I doubt that she'd leave Daddy though."

"That's up to them to sort out," Immy said. "Look, darling, I'll have to go and pack my things, but please let Elsie know I hope to see her very soon."

"All right. Oh, and Immy – I just want to tell you that as far as I'm concerned, this changes everything, of course."

"Does it? What about?" Immy said with a frown.

She couldn't think about anything else but relief that their house was still standing, and her family was safe. At least, for now. And if that was selfish, she couldn't help it. When it came right down to it, they all had to think of themselves and the people they loved.

Daisy reverted to her usual rushing words. "Well, I'm not leaving the hospital now. I can't, can I? Who knows when it might be our turn? So I've decided to stay where I am and get some proper qualifications. I may not be the world's best nurse, but I know where I'm needed."

She hung up, fighting back the tears, not wanting to hear any platitudes from Immy, whatever her feelings were on her choice. It wasn't just the bombing that had decided her, anyway; because before all the horror of learning that Bristol had been hit last night, Private Stokes had died.

War was bloody, bloody, bloody, but Stokesey had been progressing nicely, and there had been no indication of the massive ulcer that had finally burst and killed him. Daisy had just posted his last cheerful letter to his wife, and now she had voluntarily offered to write another one, which would be more sensitive and personal than the one Mrs Stokes would eventually receive from Stokesey's CO. Daisy was definitely needed here, in however small a way.

"Who was on the phone?" she heard Aunt Rose say as she went back to bundling Ronnie's soiled sheets into the copper and lighting the gas beneath it.

"It was Immy. She'd heard the news, and she and James Church are trying to get to Bristol sometime today."

"Good," Rose said, with only half her mind on what Daisy was saying.

It was only natural that Imogen would be anxious about her family, but privately she thought it a shame that her eldest niece had to curtail her few days' leave like this, especially with that nice young man of hers whom Rose liked enormously. Rose was far more canny about what went on in the world than her nieces might believe. Her generation had already been through one war in their lifetime, and she knew how intense passions could be when you never knew what tomorrow might bring.

Last night was undoubtedly a foretaste of what they could expect from now on. They were far away from the capital, but Rose had never believed they would be safe from Hitler's bombs. Bristol's docks and aircraft industry were too vital a target for the enemy to ignore. She had her own ideas about what she was going to suggest to her brother. If she and Bert could accommodate various children and dogs in this big old house, they could surely accommodate Elsie – and a baby, in due course, she reminded herself. It wouldn't be all beer and skittles, as they said, but a baby in the house would surely cheer everybody up.

She realised Daisy was fiddling with the copper stick and asked her mildly if she intended standing about all day, or if she was ever going to get on with it and tip some soap suds into the water. And then, Rose thought grimly, before she set out for the hospital Daisy could help her create a proper shelter in the cellar, instead of the makeshift arrangements they had used last night. It was time to prepare for the unimaginable.

"I've been trying to think how to tell you something," Daisy said at last. "And I don't quite know how to do it. I know you've always thought I could never make up my mind about anything, chopping and changing like the wind—"

Her aunt broke in with a small smile. "And now you've decided that perhaps you made the right choice after all, all that time ago when you told us you wanted to be a nurse."

"Sometimes I think you're a mind-reader!" Daisy said, confused and relieved, because her aunt had spoken so calmly, instead of thinking her an irresponsible idiot who couldn't think sensibly about anything.

"No, my love, I'm no mind-reader. I just had a feeling that all the passion you put into it couldn't have been a waste of time. But you had to see it for yourself. It's your life, and you can't live anyone else's."

"Not even my mother's," Daisy said, knowing it at last.

"So are we going to sweep out the cellar and get some blankets down there ready for emergencies?" Rose said briskly. "At least the boys enjoyed camping down there last night and seemed to think of it as an adventure."

"Some adventure! But I really haven't got time, Aunt Rose, honestly!"

Her aunt let her go, knowing she still had to inform Sister Macintosh of her decision, hoping that she still had a job at Weston General. She also had to make her peace with Alice, who had been decidedly stuffy towards her lately. But all such petty squabbles were forgotten in the shock news that Bristol had been bombed.

"Daisy, have you heard from your father and sister? Are they all right?" Alice greeted her anxiously.

"Yes, thank heavens. And Alice – we are still friends, aren't we?"

"Of course we are," the older girl said, giving her arm a squeeze. "It was a rum do last night thought, wasn't it? Were you scared?"

Daisy was tempted to say no, and then caught the knowing look on Alice's face. "Of course I was scared. Weren't you?"

"Of course. So now we've both admitted that we're human, let's see what we have to do today."

"I know what I have to do," Daisy said, as the memory of yesterday's happenings rushed in on her. "I have to compose a letter to Private Stokes's wife."

"It's not really your job, Daisy. You shouldn't get too attached to the patients, and you don't owe him anything."

"I think I do. And anyway, it's something I want to do – well, sort of. I've told Sister Macintosh I intend to do it, anyway, and I'm not backing out of it."

"You're a good kid, aren't you, Daisy?"

Daisy shrugged. "Not so as you'd notice! Anyway, I'd better go and see Sister before she catches us standing around gossiping."

She went off with her chin in the air. She wasn't a kid any more, and she'd done her best to calm down the three terrified young boys last night when they'd firmly believed that Adolph himself was going to come goose-stepping into the cellar and kill them all.

Sister Macintosh listened coolly to all that Daisy had to say.

"So now you've decided your place is here with us, have you, Nurse?"

"If you'll still have me," Daisy said humbly, fixing her eyes somewhere between the woman's massive shelf of a bosom and her starched collar.

"Well, I suppose we'll have to, since you've proved yourself so far," Sister said with the glimmer of a smile on her lips.

Then the smile faded. "In any case, we're expecting casualties from last night's air raid, and since this is more than likely to be a regular occurrence from now on, I can't afford to let any of my nurses go. I know you've been restless on the ward lately, so I'm going to recommend that you do a spell on ambulance duty. There will be fully trained medical staff on board, of course, but it will give you useful experience in seeing how to deal with real emergencies."

She was dismissed, feeling unsure what to make of this latest change. It was one thing to deal with changing bandages and taking temperatures, and mopping up various kinds of disgusting messes, but she had never been called to the scene of an accident before. Or the aftermath of an air raid.

Then common sense took over. Hadn't she already seen chaos in action on the hospital ship, where you never knew what you might see next? Hadn't she already observed emergency treatments without the clinical comfort of a hospital theatre, performed in crowded conditions on a rolling ship where the skill of the surgeon's hands was vital? This was one more challenge to test whether or not she really had the makings of a nurse.

-

She went home at the end of the afternoon to a new kind of chaos. Norman and Ronnie's mother had arrived from Wales with a very large man with a weather-beaten face, whom the boys were being urged to call Uncle Ivor.

"They're coming wiv us, anyway, missus," their mother was shouting to Aunt Rose. "Me sister in Cardiff don't really have room for us, but my gentleman's got a big enough place for us all, and now that the kids are in more danger 'ere than they were back in London, we might as well have 'em wiv us."

"But Mrs Turvey, it's not Weston that's been bombed," Rose said impatiently. "I assure you we're quite safe here—"

"Oh ah, for the time being! But I ain't taking any chances wiv my kids, and Ivor wants to 'ave 'em safe wiv us, don't you, Ivor?"

"That's right, love," he said in his thick Welsh accent. "We've got plenty of room on the farm and the boys will love the animals, I'm sure. It's up in mid-Wales, see, so well away from any risk of air raids."

"And don't tell me any of that other stuff about having to check with the billeting people," Mrs Turvey went on.

"Ivor's already phoned the woman at the Town Hall, and she says they're my kids and I can do what I like wiv 'em. And you want to come and live wiv me, don't you, kids?"

"*Yes!* We want to go wiv our mum!" they shouted in unison, though Ronnie still hung back suspiciously at this new uncle. He could hardly remember his dad, but he knew he didn't talk a bit like this one. But if Norman thought he was all right, he supposed he did too.

"You can't take them away just like this without giving us any warning," Bert said angrily. "It's too much of an upheaval for them."

"Yes we can. We're staying at a B&B that Ivor knows in Sand Bay for tonight, and they can bunk in wiv us," the woman said. "So they can go and get all their things and we won't be bothering you no more."

"They're no bother, and I think you're making a big mistake," Rose said stiffly, ignoring Bert's restraining hand on her arm.

Mrs Turvey stared her out defiantly, as large and blowsy as ever.

"No, I ain't. If I was taking 'em back to London it would be a big mistake, but we ain't going back there. We're staying wiv Ivor on his farm from now on."

Daisy knew better than to join in this argument. She'd tried once before, but now, with the big, burly farmer folding his arms and forming a more than solid unit with the boys' mother, she held her tongue. They all knew Mrs Turvey was in the right, anyway. They were her children, and personally, Daisy sometimes thought they had been more trouble than they were worth.

But of course, Aunt Rose had got fond of them – and so had Teddy, she realised, seeing how he was snivelling in a corner, with his arms clutching George. It would be a real blow to her brother to lose his ready-made companions like this. While they continued arguing she managed to get him out of the room by bribing him with a drink of lemonade and a slice of cake in the kitchen.

"Do you want to come and have a game of snap in my room? George can come too, if you like," she went on, making a rare concession.

He glared at her, not taken in for a minute by her tactics. "Are Norman and Ronnie going to be taken away by that lady and man?"

Daisy sighed. "The lady is their mother, Teddy, and it's only natural that they want to go and live with her."

"They've got us, so why do they want to live with her? I don't live with my mother," he said baldly, his lips starting to quiver.

"I know you don't, darling, but that's different. None of us can do that, but I'm sure you'd want to if you could. We all would."

She was on delicate ground, and she wasn't sure that she was making things any better, but she hardly knew how to deal with this. Teddy rarely mentioned their mother, and she didn't want to revive his last memory of her hurtling over the cliffs into the Avon Gorge. She never wanted to think of that terrible day – as bad in all their minds as anything Hitler could deliver.

"Can me and George sleep in your bed tonight then?" Teddy said next.

Daisy stared, forcing her mind away from her mother's death to the sudden perversity of this question.

"Why on earth would you want to do that?" she said.

His bottom lip jutted out. "I might cry all night if Norman and Ronnie aren't in the house; but if me and George can cuddle you, I prob'ly won't feel so bad."

*The devious little devil*, Daisy thought at once. So much for caring what happened to the other boys. Kids were so bloody selfish – and she certainly didn't relish the thought of having George in her bed, filling the bedroom with his doggy smells and snuffling and snorting and twitching all night… but she saw how warily Teddy was watching her now, and knew the little blighter would create all kinds of fuss if she didn't agree to this, and Aunt Rose would be upset enough at losing two of her ewe lambs…

"Just this once, then," she said firmly. "One night only, do you understand?"

-

By the time Mrs Turvey and her Ivor had done exactly what they wanted to do and packed up everything belonging to her boys, it was time for them to say goodbye. By now, Teddy had gone back downstairs and was beginning to get tearful about their departure again.

"You can have some of my old comics," Norman told him. "I've left 'em in the bedroom, and you can cut 'em up if you like."

"Will you take care of Jemima too?" Ronnie asked, sniffing anxiously.

"Who the blazes is Jemima?" his mother said, pausing as she rummaged through their cardboard suitcases to check that they had everything they had come with. "You're a bit young to be takin' up with girls, ain't you, Ronnie boy?"

She dug Ivor in the ribs as she spoke, roaring with laughter as if she had said something funny, and Ronnie's face turned crimson.

"Jemima's my hen that lays brown eggs," he shouted.

"Don't you worry, Ronnie," Uncle Bert said, seeing how important this was to him. "We'll take care of everything, and if you ever want to come and see us again, I'm sure you'll find that Jemima will remember you."

"Yes, well, I doubt that that will happen," his mother replied. "What with these air raids now, we want to get the boys as far away from here as possible."

"We shall miss you both," Aunt Rose said suddenly, having hardly said a word for the last ten minutes as she watched the preparations for departure. "You've been good boys—"

She couldn't say any more as Ronnie suddenly threw himself into her arms and hugged her, burying his face in her shoulder.

"Go on now," she said with a great effort. "You'll have your mum to tuck you up in bed tonight, and I bet there are lots more hens on the farm where you're going to live."

She silently begged Farmer Ivor to say that there were, and to her relief he wasn't slow to brag.

"Course there are, and ducks too, and lots of sheep. And there's always rabbits in the fields for your mam to make a stew."

"Auntie Rose makes rabbit pies," Ronnie muttered.

"Well, we'll make them as well," his mother said impatiently. "Now come on, you two, say goodbye nicely to the folks for looking after you, before we change our minds about taking you at all."

The house was very quiet after they had all gone. Daisy was still stunned at the speed with which their busy and noisy household had suddenly become so depleted. Her Uncle Bert had gone down to his shed, unable to think of anything useful to say, and needing to adjust in his own way. Rose did the only thing she could think of to keep her hands busy. Plunging them into flour and lard and then kneading the dough was always a good way to vent off anger or frustration.

"Do you want to help me make some jam tarts, Teddy?" she said, seeing his wan face. "And we'll make some fairy cakes too, if you like," she added.

"Can I lick the spoon?" he asked hopefully, knowing he wouldn't have to share the delicious scrapings in the bowl with anyone else now.

"Of course you can, darling. It'll be all yours."

The phone rang while she was up to her elbows in flour.

"I'll answer it," Daisy called. It was Imogen.

"Where are you?" Daisy said at once.

"At home, and everything's all right with us and with James's parents. Father's preparing to go out on fire-fighting duty again tonight, so we shall stay here with Elsie. We both have to go back to London tomorrow, I'm afraid, but I think we've almost persuaded Elsie to come down to Weston to move in with you all. She really thinks it's her duty to stay here with Father, but we've told her it's completely ridiculous when he's on call, and likely to be more so in the future. What do you think? Will Aunt Rose have any objection?"

Daisy stared at the phone, feeling the most ridiculous urge to laugh hysterically. She couldn't think that Aunt Rose would have any objection at all, since her sole aim in life seemed to be care for other people's children.

"Is everything all right?" she heard her aunt say anxiously from the kitchen.

"Hold on a minute, Immy," Daisy said. She called out the message, asking if there would be any objection to taking in another lodger.

She paused then, as the most extraordinary sound came from her aunt. For a second, it didn't register, and then she realised it was laughter. And Teddy, being Teddy, immediately joined in, clapping his hands and spraying flour around the kitchen until they were both wreathed in a fine white cloud.

"Oh, Daisy, of course it's all right. And isn't it just as I always said? The Good Lord giveth and the Good Lord taketh away. Only this time, bless His generous heart, He's done it in reverse."

"Aunt Rose says of course it's all right, Immy," Daisy repeated hastily into the phone, wondering uneasily if it always took church-minded folk like this, and if religion was finally going to her head.

"Well, you all seem to be having a jolly good time there, considering what happened here last night," she heard Immy say, a little indignantly. "Are you having a party or something?"

"Not exactly. We've just lost the last of our evacuees today, so you can tell Elsie it'll be marvellous for us to be just family again."

"I didn't say it was definite," Immy said, with what Daisy thought was complete contrariness. "I only said we think we've *almost* persuaded her. You know how long she takes to make up her mind about anything. Well, except marrying Joe. She's heard he's being sent to a convalescent home near Oxford, by the way; then he hopes to get some leave before rejoining his regiment."

"And he'll persuade her to get out of Bristol if anybody can."

"Well, he hasn't done it yet, has he? Anyway, James and I are going to see his parents now, so I'll have to go, Daisy. Take care of yourself."

"And you too," Daisy said automatically.

Immy had been unusually impatient with her, she registered. But she supposed it was reasonable, when she had had to cut short her little holiday with James to come flying down here to check that everyone was all right. They hadn't *had* to, of course – unless it was a touch of guilty conscience that had pushed them into it, she thought with a suspicious thrill.

For a moment, Daisy wondered exactly when it was that they had heard the news of the Bristol bombing and, more importantly, just what they had been doing at the time. It was so *daring* for them to have spent their few days' leave together, and although Daisy was perfectly sure they would have booked separate rooms, as any respectable couple would in a respectable hotel, it didn't mean they had to *stay* separate at all times, did it?

Since she had never actually experienced such excitement herself, she couldn't really think *what* they had been doing, and she gave up imagining, and went back to the kitchen, where Teddy's face was already plastered with pastry and jam.

It didn't take much to cheer you up when you were only eight years old, she thought, though it might be a different matter tonight when he started missing Norman and Ronnie properly; and she resigned herself to sharing her bed with him and the exuberant George.

Soon, if all went according to Sister Macintosh's suggestion, she was going to start a new phase in her nursing career, when she went out on rescue patrol in the ambulance.

# Chapter Sixteen

One of Aunt Rose's favourite sayings was that one swallow didn't make a summer – and it was just as obvious that one air raid didn't make a war. Bristol became used to the almost nightly sound of the air-raid sirens, even when little came of them. Reading the local newspaper reports, Bert said caustically that he reckoned Hitler was just trying out his planes to see how far into England they could get over the Channel before dropping their bombs wildly.

Besides which, the swift retaliation of the RAF and the south-east defences were doing a sterling job in warding off the enemy attacks. When they reached the south-west, some of their bombs fell harmlessly into fields and ditches and only scared the cattle, and whenever such events were reported people cheered and jeered and said it only showed the incompetence of the German Air Force.

"That's not such a good thing," Rose reminded Bert. "If they start dropping bombs indiscriminately because they can't find their targets, then next time it could be a school or a row of houses. If they're aiming for the docks and know what the target is supposed to be, they're not so likely to hit ordinary people going about their daily business, are they?"

"That's true, Aunt Rose," Daisy put in, the night before she finally started her new duties, feeling more than a touch of unease at wondering just how many ordinary people were going to become part of her rescue routine in future.

Bert went on doggedly, refusing to let them stop his flow. "And you women have got blinkers on if you think it's the same for both sides, and that our boys in blue always know where to drop their bombs. We're all potential casualties in a war, Rose—"

"Well, I know that—"

"It's not just the chaps in uniform who are going to come a cropper, and we don't fight with bows and arrows any more, either. It's far more lethal these days. Anyway, I've decided I'm going to do my bit."

Rose started to laugh. "*You!* What do you think you can do at your age! You're a bit rusty on the old pins for marching, Bertie love."

"I'm not thinking of marching anywhere, but I'm not too old for joining the Civil Defence. Now that things are hotting up, it's time I did something about it."

"I think that's very patriotic, Uncle Bert," Daisy said.

"It's stupid," Rose snapped. "Your eyesight's not too good lately, and you couldn't run to catch a bus, let alone see off a few German parachutists invading Weston. Not that I think such a thing will ever happen; but really, Bert, do you honestly think you're up to staying out all night watching for enemy planes?"

"Is that all you think the CD does? Lord give me patience!"

"Well, I know they do that sort of thing, because one of our ladies at the knitting circle told me so. Her husband's in the Civil Defence, but he's twenty years younger than you, Bert. You did your bit in the last war, so you should leave this one to the younger ones."

"And I think you should stop talking as if I've got one foot in the grave! What's got into you, woman? Did you think I'd be satisfied with digging up the garden and planting vegetables for ever?"

Daisy left them to it, knowing that when they began one of their wrangling arguments it could go on for a very long time. It was part bickering, part exhilaration; but whatever mood it took, she didn't want to get involved.

Besides, she had promised that as soon as Teddy got home from school they would cycle over to the Luckwell farm, which they had done a few times now since Norman and Ronnie had gone, just to keep her brother happy.

Lucy's family always made a fuss of Teddy, letting him help with the animal feeding, and since the Luckwells still had their evacuees, it provided a sort of tiny link with his old pals. Though Daisy had to admit that Teddy had got over their departure extremely quickly, and the little wretch was revelling in the fact that he was now Aunt Rose's pet and didn't have to share her with anyone. Still, it was better than having him moping around, she thought cheerfully.

They spent an hour tramping around the farm, by which time Teddy was smelling decidedly whiffy, and was due for a bath as soon as they got back home, she told him, knowing that Rose wouldn't let him sit at the supper table until he was scrubbed spotless.

—

Daisy knew something was wrong the moment she stepped inside the front door, saw her aunt's white face, and heard the way her uncle continually cleared his throat, the way he did when he was lost for words. For these two, that in itself was an ominous sign.

"Shall I get Teddy straight into the bath?" she said quickly.

"Yes, please, Daisy; and then come back down here, please."

Once in the bathroom she filled the bath with warm water to the line that was marked around it now, for the permitted level. Though what help it was to the war effort to restrict bathwater, Daisy had no idea. She tried to keep her thoughts on inane things while she helped Teddy undress and got him in, warning him to wash himself properly or Aunt Rose would be up to scrub him. Then she went back to the parlour, her heart thumping.

"What's happened? I know it must be something awful, so please don't keep me in suspense."

"Your father called us while you were out, Daisy…"

"Is it Elsie? Has something happened to the baby?"

"It's not Elsie," Rose said in a strangled voice. "It's Baz – at least, we must assume that it's Baz. There's no real proof, of course…"

"Rose, don't build up your hopes," Bert cut in gruffly. "I don't think these people would have contacted Quentin unless they'd been sure."

"Well, I'm not giving up hope yet!"

"Will you please stop talking as if I'm not here and tell me what's happened to Baz? I have a right to know!" Daisy said, white-faced. It couldn't be anything bad. Not to Baz, the survivor…

They both looked at her, as if delaying the moment as long as possible, and then Bert nodded.

"You're right, my love. Your father has had a letter from a farmer in France. He couldn't read it himself, so he took it to someone who can speak the language. It said... it said..."

Rose continued in a monotone as Bert's voice cracked.

"It seems that Baz had been stranded in France after Dunkirk and found his way to this farm. He was taken to the coast and on to a ship at night, along with hundreds of others still trying to get out of France. The Germans were bombing the ships, and the one Baz was on was sunk before it got very far out of the harbour. Men were jumping overboard in lifejackets, but the water was very deep, and oil was spilling into it and burning, and there were no survivors. Thankfully he'd left his address with the French farmer, or we might never have known."

Daisy listened in horror as her aunt's voice went on in that strange flat tone, as if it was the only way she could say it all without breaking down. She swallowed the huge lump in her throat, unable to believe that her big, brash brother, so young and yet so full of self-confidence, could have perished in this way. She *wouldn't* believe it.

"We don't know for sure, do we? He might have got away. He could swim like a fish, and he'd know what to do..."

"Not even a fish could swim in thick oil pumping out of a broken ship, Daisy," Bert said harshly. "The farmhand who took Baz to the coast watched it all from a ditch on the shore, too scared to move while the Germans were bombing, and the ship was hit for a second time before it went down. Eventually they had the news that there were no survivors, and we have to believe it."

*So now there were four...* Daisy pushed the silly words out of her head, but she couldn't push out the fear of wondering who was going to be next. Teddy was too young to be involved in a war, thank God, but Immy was in the greatest danger in London. There was also Elsie, who was too stubborn to move out of Bristol unless she was forced into it, and even she herself might be heading into danger with the ambulance people, if they were called to the scene of an air raid.

"Put your head between your knees, Daisy," she heard her aunt's voice say sharply, and she did as she was told without question, realising she was starting to feel light-headed. She recovered quickly, though, ashamed of herself for letting go like that, when they were all feeling the shock of what had happened. A nurse should be able to rise above such panic, but right now she felt less like a nurse than like someone very young, facing a death in the family for the second time...

"Sorry," she almost gasped. "Do you think I should phone Daddy myself?"

"Not just now," Aunt Rose said. "He'll be busy on the telephone trying to contact Imogen, and then trying to find out more information from the naval authorities. I'm sure he'll call us again when he has any more news, and, in the meantime, I'm going to see Mr Penfold. Do you want to come with me, Daisy?"

"What for?" she asked blankly.

"To arrange for a small memorial service for Baz. I'm going to speak to your father about it, naturally; but it's the least we can do. In fact, my love, it's all anyone can do now. You do see that, don't you?"

"I think you could wait until you get proper confirmation before you have him dead and buried! And I don't want to talk to Mr Penfold, thank you very much. I'll go and get Teddy out of the bath before his skin is completely wrinkled, and then I'm going to my room," she said in a fury.

She bolted out of there, unable to stay and listen to her aunt's calm belief that having a small memorial service for her brother would make everything right. It wouldn't, and besides, she wasn't at all sure he had gone to his Maker, which Aunt Rose would also be firmly believing now.

Such blind belief was starting to disintegrate as far as Daisy was concerned. It was worse than that. It was almost obscene. How could any benevolent God let this happen to a young boy who wasn't yet a man, however much he thought he was? It was too cruel…

Teddy looked up enquiringly as she slammed the bathroom door behind her and leaned against it with tears flooding her eyes.

"I'm turning all white," he complained, "and there's a hole in my boat and it's sunk. When I'm bigger I'm going out in a proper boat by the pier and learn to catch fish. Is that what Baz does?" he added vaguely.

Daisy hauled him out, wrapping him in a large bath towel, and almost smothering him in the process as she hugged him close, practically cocooning them both inside it.

"Oh darling, I hope you do!" she said almost hysterically. "I hope that's the only thing you'll ever have to worry about."

"You're hurting me," he howled, and she reluctantly released him, wishing she could keep him safe like this for ever.

He would have to be told, of course. He couldn't be kept in ignorance, and it was impossible to think that they would never mention Baz's name again. When he was safely tucked up in bed that night, and she had stopped shaking, she queried it with her uncle, since Aunt Rose was still away consulting the minister.

"Should I tell him, do you think? Not that I know how to do it, but someone has to, don't they, Uncle Bert? Or to prepare him, at least. We could say that Baz was missing, and we weren't sure what had happened."

She stopped, because even that sounded so impossible. If the French farmer's story was to be believed, they knew only too well what had happened. The ship that was meant to be bringing Baz safely home to England had been bombed by the Germans, and he had drowned in a sea of burning oil. She shuddered, not wanting to picture it, and willing the images away from her mind.

"I think that, of all people, you're the right one to do it, Daisy love," her uncle said. "You write your letters for the hospital patients, and if you can't find the words to tell Teddy to his face, then why don't you write it all down in a letter or a little story that he can understand without becoming too frightened or upset?"

"It's different when I write letters for people I don't know," she said, and then stopped abruptly. Because she had just done the very same thing for Private Stokes's wife, and she had come to know the man over the weeks he had been in her care.

"Think about it, Daisy. Meanwhile, how about a cup of cocoa and a dash of sugar to calm your nerves?"

She gave a wan smile. "Didn't you know that nurses aren't supposed to have nerves, Uncle Bert?"

"Maybe so," he agreed, dropping an affectionate kiss on the top of her head as he went to the kitchen. "But nice young girls who care about their families are."

Aunt Rose came home that evening with a bundle of pamphlets from the minister, supposedly to help the bereaved come to terms with their loss. Daisy refused to look at them, knowing she had to come to terms with this in her own way. By then she had ignored her aunt's advice and telephoned her father, anyway. He had sounded grim, saying he hadn't found out any more yet, but that they must believe the worst.

Then Elsie had spoken to her, clearly upset about Baz, desperately trying to hold down her own sense of excitement in the circumstances, because she was going to Oxford to see Joe at the convalescent home in a week's time, and then they were going to spend his leave together in a small country hotel nearby.

"I know it's ghastly news about Baz, Daisy, and I probably shouldn't leave Father alone at this time, but life has to go on. And I can't help thinking it might have been Joe, so I can't refuse to do what he's arranged, can I?"

"Of course you can't," Daisy said. "I'm sure Daddy will understand."

"He's actually urging me to go. I honestly don't think he wants anyone around him at the moment, and I know he's thinking of Mother too."

"I'm sure he is," Daisy murmured. "We all are. Well, keep in touch, Elsie, and let me know if you get any more news."

Without knowing it, Elsie had given her the lead for her small story for Teddy, which she had now decided to write. A letter was too personal, and she knew she couldn't do it. Aunt Rose was still out, but she would approve, even if Daisy herself was having serious doubts about God being in His heaven and all being right with the world, when it bloody well wasn't.

Despite her undoubted grief over Baz, Aunt Rose would be quite certain that he was now somewhere with his mother in heaven, and Daisy knew that that was the only way she could explain it to a vulnerable eight-year-old boy without letting him fear that everyone he loved was being taken away from him.

It wasn't as easy as she had thought to put it into words that were at the same time deeply personal to all of them, yet as detached as she could make them for Teddy's sake. It took her more than an hour to get it right, but she had to admit it was something of a catharsis for herself to write it all out. Then she went to Teddy's bedroom and gave him the pages to read.

"What's this for? I'm reading my comic." He glared at her suspiciously, obviously sensing that something was wrong.

"This is important, Teddy. I could wait with you while you read it – or would you rather I read it aloud to you?"

"If you like," he said sullenly.

"It's a story that's a bit sad. You know that sad things happen in a war, don't you?" She swallowed. "You know about Cal."

"He got blown out of the sky in his airplane, didn't he? I told my teacher," he said, almost crowing with import-ance.

The horrible little *wretch*… Daisy gritted her teeth, but when you were only eight, she supposed, such things gave you a bit of status among your little friends. Knowing a dead hero was far better than not knowing one at all. She took a deep breath and tried again.

"Do you remember Baz when we lived in Bristol, Teddy?"

"Course I do. Well, only a bit," he said with a frown. "I can't remember his face very well, but I know he liked boats and fishing, and he used to work on the ferryboat a long time ago, didn't he?"

*Oh God, this is so difficult...* but it dawned on her that it was a very long time since Teddy had seen his brother, so perhaps the news wouldn't be so traumatic for him as it was for the rest of them.

"Is he dead as well?" Teddy said, half his attention still on his comic, and making her heart stop for a moment before it raced on.

"Teddy, leave that comic alone for a minute, will you?" she said gently. "What would you say if I told you something very sad had happened to Baz?"

She knew she was making an awful hash of this, when she was meant to be doing the opposite; but somehow, she just couldn't say the words.

"If he's dead, perhaps I can work on the ferryboat when I'm bigger," Teddy went on hopefully when she said nothing.

Oh *God...*

"Perhaps you can, darling," she said in a muffled voice.

She stared at him, seeing the eagerness in his face, his little innocent face that was a miniature of Baz's face at that moment, knowing nothing of war and death, except for the thrill of it all – and the importance of telling a teacher and his friends that he knew someone who had been blown out of the sky in an airplane.

"You go back to your comic now, love," she said, choked, "and Aunt Rose will be up soon to tuck you in."

"All right." Then he paused, his face puckered. "Daisy, when I say my prayers do I have to ask God to look after Baz as well as Mummy?"

"Yes, love, I think you should, and I'm sure they're looking after one another right now."

Somehow, she got out of the room, her eyes flooded with tears. She leaned against the door with a feeling of utter helplessness, wishing she still had the blind faith of a small child. Wishing she had Aunt Rose's faith.

Once she felt more composed she went downstairs and told her aunt and uncle what had happened.

"You handled it very well, my love."

"No I didn't! It was Teddy who somehow saw through my clumsy attempt to tell him, and, even then, I couldn't actually say it. How could I, when we don't really *know*?"

Aunt Rose was sharper than usual. "We know it in our hearts, Daisy, and you'll only make things worse by trying to keep hope alive."

"And what have you got, if you don't have hope?" she said bitterly. "Oh, I know you mean it for the best, but I can't keep on believing – about anything."

"Don't you think we all feel like that at times? It's God's way of testing our faith and our strength."

"Well, it's a pretty awful way, by killing everyone we love," Daisy muttered.

"I don't want to hear more of this," Rose said. "I'm going to tuck Teddy in and hear his prayers, and your uncle can tell you what Mr Penfold has suggested. I've spoken to your father about it, and he's in full agreement."

Daisy grimaced at her uncle when they were alone. "I suppose I'm in disgrace now," she said. "But I can't help how I feel, can I, Uncle Bert?"

"None of us can, and you mustn't think too harshly of your auntie's ways, love. She wants to do her best for everyone."

"I know that. So what has Mr Penfold suggested that Daddy agrees to?" she muttered, trying to be rational, and knowing she wasn't going to like it.

"It won't be a memorial service, but a small family service of dedication for Baz and a celebration of his life. It won't be a burial service either, Daisy, because – well, it can't be, can it?" he added delicately. "It will just be all of us, saying our private goodbyes to Baz within the blessing of the Church."

Daisy was indignant. "And when is this service going to be? It's all happening too soon, Uncle Bert. It's too hasty, as if we can't wait to wipe him out of our lives. As if we can't wait to say goodbye!"

They were still discussing it when Rose came downstairs again, her eyes slightly damp.

"It's not going to happen yet, Daisy. We all feel the same about that, and, in any case, we want to be sure Elsie feels up to it, and that Immy can be here too. Mr Penfold suggested we wait a while, possibly even until Elsie's baby has been born. We want Baz to feel the presence of all his family's love."

Daisy hardly knew what to say now. She could see that Aunt Rose thought this was a perfectly logical suggestion, and it was certainly a relief to think they weren't going to have the service immediately. In Daisy's opinion it would have been in almost indecent haste.

"We all want to do what we think is best for everyone, Daisy," Rose went on, echoing Bert's words. "You do see that, don't you?"

"I suppose so," she said grudgingly. "And if Daddy and Elsie think it's a sensible idea, then I suppose I'll have to, won't I?"

"I still think it's weird," she said to Alice Godfrey, when they had got over the necessary embarrassment of explanations and commiserations.

"You won't," Alice told her. "We had that kind of service for my brother, although we knew what had happened to him, of course. It was just for my parents, my aunts and grandmother, and me. And it did help. It made us all feel close, and that Roy was still part of us. It sort of brings it all to a proper conclusion. You'll feel the same when the time comes, Daisy."

She took a deep breath. "Well, I might, and I might not. In any case, I don't want to talk about it anymore. I feel as if I'm being choked with all this talk of churches and memorial services and people dying or not dying! Elsie's going to see Joe in the convalescent home; then they're going to take a short holiday together while he's on leave, and a good thing too. What's the point of being married if you can't spend time together?"

She went on babbling determinedly, trying to pull herself back into the land of the living, instead of some frightening, alien place where people died – or simply disappeared without trace, which was worse.

"I'd like to have some fun too! So before you think I'm being absolutely wicked to say such a thing, Aunt Rose told me I shouldn't sit around uselessly moping. She said I should even go to the pictures if I felt like it – and if you would come with me. So will you – please, Alice? What do you say?"

"I say your aunt is a very wise woman. But we already know that, don't we?"

# Chapter Seventeen

In one way, Daisy thought, it was a good thing that Norman and Ronnie had gone to live in Welsh Wales with their mother and her fancy-man farmer. They would have been asking far too many questions about Baz's fate – especially Norman, with his ghoulish interest in death – and scaring Teddy out of his wits in the process. But in another way, she wished they were still here, to give them all less time to think. When the boisterous East End boys had been around, nobody had had time to think about anything but what they were getting up to; and Teddy certainly missed them.

It was true what they said, though: keeping busy stopped you thinking, at least for a while. And Sister Macintosh had been true to her word and arranged for Daisy to join the ambulance crew for a spell of road experience, as she called it. She was now assigned as general helper to the driver, Thomas Peterson, and his assistant, Luke Forbes. Thomas was a burly, jovial man about her uncle's age, while Luke was more serious, and in his mid-thirties, Daisy guessed.

If there were air-raid casualties, there would also be a senior nurse on board, and a doctor in real emergencies. Otherwise, Thomas told her cheerfully, he and Luke were thoroughly trained in dealing with general care needs.

"You've never had to deliver a baby, I hope," she said cheekily, to cover her nervousness on that first morning, and thinking of Elsie.

"Not yet, but there's always a first time," he said with a wink. "My old lady has had three herself, so I know what's involved; but I reckon Luke here would probably faint right off, so we generally leave all that kind of thing to the professionals. Most ladies have the midwife at home for their confinement, of course, unless there are any complications."

"Good," Daisy muttered, wishing she had never asked, never having thought about Elsie having complications. She immediately resolved to read up a little more about midwifery.

"Got a young man, have you, Daisy?" Thomas went on, as he explained the various bits of equipment in the ambulance to her. "Thinking of getting married and having babies yourself, are you?"

"No. I'm never getting married," she snapped, unaccountably annoyed at the question. "It's not worth the trouble."

Thomas stopped showing her where the bandages and TCP were kept and stared at her in astonishment.

"Well, that's a fine thing for a pretty young lady to say, if you'll pardon my being so personal. I thought you all wanted to walk down the aisle with the man of your dreams, like them Hollywood flicks are always telling us!"

"Not when the man of your dreams has been…"

She stopped, suddenly realising what she was saying, and that her two new companions were looking at her with great interest like two old gossips. She certainly didn't intend telling them that Cal had been shot down, nor that she was still in a huge amount of confusion over her brother and refusing to give into mourning like the rest of her family. It was none of their business.

Besides, she still hadn't given up hope for Baz. She kept her feelings to herself, knowing that her family would call her completely foolish; but she still hoped that, somehow, he had got out of that terrible burning sea, and that some kindly French farmer's wife was helping him back to strength. Especially if some pretty young farmer's daughter was doing her bit to help him back to normality as well. Knowing Baz, it would be the best of all aids to his recovery.

As she felt her mouth quirk into a half-smile, Daisy was mildly shocked at her own thoughts, even though she had decided by now that this was going to be her way of dealing with losing her brother. If she made herself assume that he was merely missing, instead of being sucked under, then choked and drowned in that dreadful sticky black abyss, then she could cope.

"You lose somebody, did you, Daisy?" Luke, the younger ambulance man was saying now. "There ain't many families now that didn't, and they say it will get worse before it gets better. We just have to go on the best we can, don't we?"

"And there's your thought for today, Daisy girl," Thomas added. "So now that Luke's done his best to cheer everybody up, let's get started and see where we've got to go this morning."

The ambulance contained various information pamphlets for the use of patients and crew. Daisy's attention was drawn to the one on procedure if a pregnant woman went into labour en route to the hospital. It didn't make comfortable reading for someone who had never gone into it in any detail, but after reading the pamphlet Daisy could only think of what lay ahead of Elsie.

She tried to imagine how it must feel to be carrying a baby inside you, and even more, with a shudder, how it must feel to have to get the baby out. Thomas caught her studying it while they waited for their instructions.

"For a young lady who ain't never getting married, so she says, you don't want to be worried about none of that!" he said with a chuckle.

"I'm reading it on a professional level," she said defensively. "I might need to help – though I sincerely hope I don't! Actually, my sister's expecting a baby, so naturally I'm interested."

"Oh ah. Where's she then?"

"At our home in Bristol with my father, though at the moment she's visiting her husband. He's about to be discharged from a military convalescent home in Oxford; then they're spending his leave together," she said briefly.

"He'll soon be back to being fighting fodder then," Luke put in. "They don't keep 'em out of the firing line any longer than they can help these days."

*Well, thanks for that little bit of hope*, thought Daisy, deciding that of the two, she much preferred Thomas with his cheerful outlook on life, to Luke, the eternal pessimist.

"It's quite routine work in a way," Daisy reported to Aunt Rose later. "We had to collect some old people from their homes and take them to the hospital for their regular physiotherapy. And somebody from Bleadon had a broken leg and had to be brought in to have his plaster taken off. Things like that."

"You sound disappointed. Did you expect dramatics all day long?"

"No, but I didn't expect it to be quite so dull! Even though Thomas reckoned I was a sight for sore eyes for the old folk. He talks like that all the time, but I quite like him," she said with a grin. "He's got three children, and to hear him talk about them, you'd think they were still babies. One of them's in the army, and the other two are still at school. His wife's a semi-invalid too."

"You seem to have learned a lot about him in one day," Bert said. "Have you told him all your family history too?"

"Not much," Daisy said. "I was entertaining the patients in the ambulance."

"What, singing to them, do you mean?"

"Of course not. Just chatting, that's all, and trying to reassure them. Some of them were nervous about their treatment."

"And you'd be a sight for a lot of sore eyes, I bet," Bert said slyly, echoing Thomas's words.

Daisy shrugged. "I'm not even sure if I'm going to like this job. It doesn't feel like real nursing, just riding around in an ambulance all day."

"It's all good experience, Daisy," Rose told her. "And you won't feel like that when you're called out to an emergency."

"Like an air raid, you mean? Or bringing an expectant mother into the hospital with complications," she added, remembering Thomas's words.

"Well, let's hope you don't get any of those. It's enough of a trial bringing a baby into the world without complications," Aunt Rose, who had never had any babies of her own, said shrewdly.

Her words gave Daisy a real stab of anxiety for Elsie, who was only two months away from her confinement now. Elsie was being extraordinarily stubborn about leaving Bristol, no matter what anyone said. Even Joe. But that could all change when they spent their few weeks together, she supposed. What a lovely thought for them. Daisy liked her brother-in-law enormously, despite his clipped northern accent, though she could never imagine him as a husband and lover… which was probably just as well, seeing as he was both to her sister!

–

At that moment, Elsie was travelling on a train to Oxford to be with Joe and trying to contain her emotions at the thought of being with him again, even though she knew his recuperation would be complete as soon as these few weeks were over, and he would then be rejoining his regiment; which was why she was determined not to let the terrible thing that had happened to her brother overshadow this time with Joe. This precious time, which might be all they had.

But she wouldn't think in that way either, she thought, with savage determination. As she sat in the train, crowded with servicemen and women, she allowed her hand to rest protectively over her belly beneath her cotton coat. Her talisman, her hope for the future that she and Joe would share. Her only regret was that he would probably be far away when the time for her confinement arrived.

She caught the glance of a hefty young woman in khaki uniform sitting opposite her and gave her a little smile.

"You're very brave to be travelling," the woman said.

"I don't think bravery comes into it, compared with what you're doing."

Her companion laughed. "Oh, I'm just in the catering corps, and there's not much danger involved in preparing food for the troops!"

"That's quite a coincidence. My sister's best friend is in the catering corps too. Helen Church. I don't suppose you know her."

"'Fraid not, love. It's a big army."

Elsie nodded, feeling foolish for even asking. The two of them occupied the seats nearest the train window, which virtually isolated them from the rest of the people chatting together in the compartment, and impulsively she spoke again.

"I'm going to join my husband for a short time. He's about to leave a convalescent home after being at Dunkirk." She couldn't resist saying it with pride.

"Good for him. So is this your first?" she asked, nodding at the bump beneath Elsie's voluminous cotton coat that nobody could miss seeing.

"Oh yes, and possibly my last, if the way he keeps kicking me is anything to go by," she said conspiratorially.

The woman laughed agreeably in return. "Are you so sure it's going to be a he?"

"Not at all, but you have to call him something, don't you? I always feel it's a bit undignified to refer to a baby as it!"

"So what are you going to call him or her?"

Elsie shook her head. "We haven't decided. We thought it was bad luck to anticipate, and neither of us minds which we have. Just as long as he's healthy."

"Amen to that," the woman said with a smile, and turned back to the magazine she had been reading.

Elsie wasn't too sorry. She had the feeling that this conversation with a stranger was soon going to descend into aimless trivialities, and she knew she didn't have the social skills for small talk that her sisters did. Anyway, she would far rather think about Joe, and she also had her own book to read. She brought it out of her bag and smiled briefly at her travelling companion before pretending to concentrate on the pages.

The jolting movement of the train and the rhythmic clatter of the wheels made her eyelids droop, and she drifted off into a sleep where no wars existed, and the sound of babies cooing was the sweetest sound around. It was only when the book slid off her lap and on to the floor some time later that she awoke with a jerk to find that the train was pulling into a station.

"Is this Oxford?" she asked at once, and then felt her face flush as the servicewoman put her finger to her lips in a teasing hush–hush movement. Which was perfectly ridiculous, as far as Elsie was concerned, because if you didn't know where you were, how the dickens could you know when to get out of the train? She felt every bit as aggressive as Daisy might have been at that moment, since it was hardly likely that any German spies were going to be in the compartment taking notes!

"Yes, this is it, love," the woman went on, taking pity on her, and hauling down her kitbag from the overhead rack. Then she handed Elsie's case down to her as well, as everyone made bustling movements to leave the train. "Good luck, dear, and I hope you and your husband have a lovely time."

Which was enough to make Elsie forgive her anything. And then she forgot everything but making her way down the crowded platform, craning her neck to see a familiar figure, and forgetting for the moment that of course he wouldn't be there. She was to take a taxi to the convalescent home, and once the formalities were over, they would go to the small country hotel where Joe had already booked them in.

For a moment, Elsie felt unexpected qualms. She felt so bulky now, so much more clumsy in her movements than when she and Joe had first met, when she had been determined never to set foot again in the shop where her father had once been king, and where now the mighty Preston's Emporium had taken over. She had been so defensive, and so resistant to the reputed Preston charm.

It had certainly been easy to resist Robert Preston's so-called charm, the son of the mighty Preston himself. She hadn't liked him at all. But then the nephew had arrived in Bristol with his northern accent that they had all found so amusing, taking over as manager and quietly offering her a job – and with it his heart.

A surge of excitement filled her veins. Joe had adored her from the start, and she had no reason to think any of that had changed because she was carrying his child – their child that she carried so proudly and lovingly. It was just – she felt her face grow hot as the thought crept into her head – just that it was not going to be so easy in the circumstances to demonstrate their physical love for one another; and she wanted that intimacy every bit as much as Joe did.

"Are you wanting a taxi, ma'am?" she heard a voice say. "They're few and far between, but if you care to sit a while, me and my buddies will be happy to see what we can do for you."

She realised the speaker was one of a group of men in RAF uniform, a Canadian by the sound of him, she registered swiftly. Daisy had said there were many Canadian airmen in the country now, and she murmured her thanks as this one indicated a bench seat for her. She was more tired than she had expected after simply sitting in a train for several hours, and she didn't want to be so tired that she couldn't enjoy being with Joe.

"Do you live here or are you just visiting?" the Canadian went on.

"Just visiting – the Oxford military convalescent home, as a matter of fact. My husband is there."

"Well, say, you're really in luck. We go right past there, so if you're willing to trust yourself to our driver, we can give you a ride. Our truck should be along in a few minutes."

"Oh, I don't think that's a good idea," Elsie said in a mild panic.

"Sure it is. Anything's better than waiting around here for an hour, isn't it? I bet your husband will be mighty glad to see you."

She hardly knew what to say in reply. Her father wouldn't approve of her accepting a ride from strangers, though she knew that both Imogen and Daisy would have had no such fears. They lived in the real world now, while she was stuck at home, twiddling her thumbs while awaiting the birth of her baby.

And that was an *awful* thought to have! The moment it entered her head, she was angry at being so wicked on account of the baby, and so insipid on her own account. She accepted the airman's offer at once, and within minutes the truck had arrived. The group of men ushered her carefully on board as if she was made of Dresden china. She revised the tiniest thought that she might be being abducted, deciding that their Canadian cousins were the nicest and most gallant men she had ever met. Apart from Joe, of course.

She was taken right through the grounds of the convalescent home, and when they stopped at the front door of the grand-looking house, she was helped down again with great courtesy. While she was thanking them for their kindness, she saw Joe watching her through the large picture window that was criss-crossed with tape to ward off bomb-blasts, his arms folded.

"Oh dear," she murmured, as she was handed her suitcase. "I'm afraid this is not the best way for a lady in my condition to arrive to visit her husband, is it?"

But surrounded as she was now by large men in Air Force uniforms, the situation struck her as so comical that she began to laugh, and seconds later Joe came striding out of the front door.

"Joe, darling, what do you think of this for an escort?" she said at once, half-wondering if he was going to be irate.

But before he had a chance to say anything, the Canadian who had first spoken to Elsie had come to attention and saluted him.

"We were only too glad to be of service to your little lady, sir, and we admire all you fellows tremendously. Best of luck to you both."

They had got back into the truck and were on their way before Elsie could stammer out any more thanks; and then she turned to Joe, thankful to see that by now he was starting to laugh too.

"Well, they're certainly polite, I'll give them that," he said. "We've got a couple of them in here, as a matter of fact, so I wasn't surprised!"

"So is that all we're going to talk about?" Elsie asked him mildly.

Then she was in his arms, as close as he could reasonably get, considering her size, and uncaring of who might be watching. His mouth was kissing hers; she could feel his heartbeats and knew that he was wholly hers again.

"God, how I've missed you, sweetheart," he said huskily. "Both of you."

Elsie laughed shakily, sure of him at last, sure that any fears were unfounded, because all the love in the world was theirs for the keeping.

"We've missed you too, Joe," she whispered, bringing him into the enclosed world that still belonged only to her and the baby.

"Right then," he said more briskly. "Let's go inside and have some tea, and once I've been formally discharged we'll be on our way. I'm anxious to get to the hotel and have you all to myself. The resident bus is going to take us there since it's not too far out of the town. It's all part of the service."

He didn't add how much he had bribed the officials to do it, knowing Elsie would be exhausted from the travelling by the time they arrived. He could see it already by the mauve shadows beneath her beautiful eyes, and the slight slump in her shoulders; but tonight he was going to kiss all the tiredness away, he thought, with a surge of pleasure in his loins that had nothing to do with fighting off fatigue and more to do with the healthy lust of a man for his wife.

–

Only a fool would have assumed that the Luftwaffe would concentrate solely on the south-east coastal towns. Bristol was clearly destined to be a target, and although the air raids continued spasmodically in the early months after Dunkirk, everyone knew that sooner or later they were going to get the big one. Like most locals, Bert Painter was quite sure that this was only the beginning.

"We won't be completely safe down here either," he warned Rose. "They're talking about lighting decoy fires out on the moors to try and fool the Jerries, but they're not daft. They'll have done their homework and they'll know the difference between decoy fires and a city, especially by moonlight. So we'll make sure the cellar is as cosy as can be in case any stray bombs come our way."

"Are the Jerries going to bomb us then?" Teddy said half-hopefully.

"Not *us*, Teddy," Rose told him with a glare at Bert. "But sometimes they may lose their way, so we have to be prepared. Anyway, didn't I hear you telling George the cellar was your own special cave?"

"Yes, George liked it down there," Teddy said, perking up. "Daisy showed me what to do with a bandage in case anybody got hurt, and I practised tying up George's leg, but he chewed the bandage off again."

"That's because dogs don't understand about bandages," Bert told him solemnly. "You can practise on me if you like."

He rolled up his sleeve and to Teddy's delight he pretended to groan in pain. As he rushed off to find a bandage, Rose thought, as she had thought so many times, what a wonderful father Bert would have made.

"You should have been a teacher, love," she said instead.

"I know," he said, and they both knew what she really meant.

He glanced towards the parlour, where Teddy had gone to fetch the first-aid box and lowered his voice carefully. "He's taken the news about Baz very well, hasn't he?"

Rose's eyes clouded. "That's because he simply doesn't remember him properly, which is very sad, but a blessing as far as he's concerned, I suppose. It's not so good for the rest of us though, is it?"

"We can't dispute it now that Quentin has had official confirmation from the authorities though, Rose. It was just as that French farmer said: the ship has been named, and there were no survivors after it went down. It's a tragedy for all of us, but even Daisy has to accept it now."

He said no more as Teddy came back to the kitchen, trailing the bandage behind him, and Rose tut-tutted at once, telling him it was no way for a nurse to handle it, especially as George began barking excitedly, clearly thinking this was a new game they were playing. At least it veered their thoughts away from Baz for the moment.

Rose firmly believed that grief was best expressed privately, but that everyone's public role was to bolster one another up. They all cared for one another, but they all had their own ways of dealing with things, and she was thankful that her brother Quentin and the two older Caldwell girls seemed to be doing just that.

Daisy wasn't taking it so well, and she had found an unexpected ally in Thomas Peterson when she had snapped at him, and then found herself weeping on his shoulder. She hadn't told anyone about Baz except Alice, as if by the words not actually being spoken out loud, it hadn't happened at all. But now they all knew that it had, and the minister had even come to the house and talked to them, and she had hated having to sit there po-faced while he rattled on in his pious manner. She knew he meant well, but she simply couldn't take it.

She finally burst out everything on the ambulance-driver's shoulder, when she had hardly said anything at all about her family until now. She had been what some folk called 'keeping herself to herself' and what Aunt Rose would have called 'uppity'.

It had been a particularly harrowing day when they had been called out to a suspected heart attack on the seafront. A crowd had gathered around the elderly man out walking his dog, and they reported having seen him stagger and fall, crashing his head against an iron girder beneath the pier. The man's face had become the colour of parchment, his lips blue. There was also a lot of blood seeping into the sand, and the odious sight of the dog pathetically licking at the blood, as if to staunch it for his master, made Daisy want to vomit.

She knew she mustn't. She had seen far worse sights than a bleeding head in the hospital when the casualties had come in, but somehow this was different. This was just a man walking on the beach with his dog, and a tragic accident had led to something far worse. The man's breathing was barely perceptible, and she stood helplessly by while Luke fastened the oxygen mask around his mouth and nose, shaking his head briefly at Thomas.

For a moment Daisy thought it meant that they were giving up on the man, but then Thomas barked at the two of them to bring the stretcher from the ambulance, and her feet were slipping into the soft warm sand as fast as they would go as she raced after Luke.

"You don't think he'll make it, do you?" she panted.

"He'll be a goner before we get him back to the hospital," he replied. "I've seen 'em like this before; but we'll go through the motions anyway."

Daisy hated him passionately at that moment. This could have been her uncle, or her father, or any one of the elderly patients they regularly transported to and from the hospital for treatment. But she clamped her lips together and said nothing as they hauled the stretcher out of the ambulance and rushed back towards the pier with it.

As they reached it, Thomas shook his head.

"Too late, I'm afraid. There's a woman here who knows him. She'll take his dog home and inform his sister what's happened, so we'll just get him back to the hospital and let them do the business."

Daisy looked on, horrified. Seconds ago the man had been alive and now he was dead, and the crowd had scattered, leaving them to get on with their job. It was what they did, and this part of it was a harsh and clinical job. At least the man had what her brother hadn't. His family would be shocked, but at least they could give him a proper burial and a proper goodbye.

She moved like an automaton on the short journey back to the hospital, and it was only when they had delivered the man to the side ward to be attended to that she stumbled outside, tears blinding her eyes. That was where Thomas Peterson found her and spoke sharply.

"Come on now, Daisy; don't let me down. You've done well so far, and I didn't expect you to give way like this."

"Didn't you?" she snapped back, almost hysterical. "But you don't know – you don't know…"

And then she was blabbing out all the hurt and the pain in his accommodating arms.

## Chapter Eighteen

By the weekend she couldn't stay away from home any longer: it had been a long, long week. She needed to be with her father, and she knew he needed to be with someone, despite what Elsie might have thought, or Aunt Rose advised, or the kindly Thomas Peterson offered in his own brand of counselling.

If her father had decided that his shop and his fire-fighting duties were more important than spending time with his youngest daughter, he was about to find out differently. Daisy was up in arms, she had some time off, and on Friday afternoon she caught the train to Bristol and went straight to Preston's Emporium.

Quentin turned from serving his last customer of the day and gaped in astonishment at the sight of his daughter, clearly distraught.

"Daisy, what's wrong?" he said at once.

"Does something have to be wrong before I can come to see you now, Daddy?" and then the irony of what she had said swept over her, and the weak tears started to her eyes again. If it hadn't been so melodramatic she would have stamped her foot in frustration. "Oh, of course something's wrong! What could be more wrong than knowing for certain that my brother's been drowned?"

Through her tears she saw the several shop assistants shuffling awkwardly and begin muttering between themselves, and then her father came around the counter and took her in his arms.

"Come through to the back room, darling, where we can talk sensibly. Or would you rather we went home? Millie can close up the shop."

"I'd rather go home," she mumbled.

She felt suddenly tongue-tied, desperately wishing she could say how much she longed to be at home with her family all around her, the way they had always been. Her father and mother, Immy and Elsie, Baz and Teddy... They both knew those days could never come again, and she didn't know how much it would upset him to hear her say it. However close you were to someone, it was sometimes hard to say what was really in your heart, and Quentin had never invited such intimacies. It wasn't that he didn't care. It was simply that he found it hard to express his feelings in words.

They walked in silence to Vicarage Street, where the family home still stood as solid and welcoming as ever, a symbol of times past. Daisy felt a rush of nostalgia, imagining, just for a moment, that her mother was about to come running down the path to greet her with a smile and a kiss.

"I do miss her, Daddy," she said, without intending to.

He tucked her hand in the crook of his arm and squeezed it hard, not needing any explanation. "So do I, my darling. So do I."

They went inside, and to Daisy's relief everything looked the same and smelled the same, thanks to the local woman they called Mrs down-the-road who came in once a day during the week to 'do' for her father and prepare a hot meal for him. They had long since dispensed with a proper cook and housekeeper and the additional help that had been needed for Frances as her illness progressed.

They had been a decidedly middle-class family then, but largely thanks to the war, everyone seemed to be merging into the same mould nowadays, and if it was being an out and out snob to think that way, Daisy thought defiantly, then she just didn't care.

"Now then," Quentin said, when they had taken a tray of tea and biscuits into the garden on that late midsummer afternoon. "To what do I owe the delight of this visit? And it really *is* a delight to see you, darling. Your mother isn't the only one to be missed."

He forced himself to say the words, aware of how alone he must seem to them all, but alone in an aloof, self-sufficient way, when the truth was anything but that. He wasn't self-sufficient at all, except in the way that a man was supposed to be. He could still keep the stiff upper lip of the Englishman in public, and like his sister Rose, he kept his private feelings very private.

He had especially urged Elsie to join Joe instead of staying here and moping over Baz. It was her rightful place to be with her husband, and besides which, there had been a personal reason for his urging. He had needed time to be alone to grieve over his son. No man cared to let a daughter see his grief, not even this delightful one, who resembled Frances so much that it had almost made his heart stop to see her walk into the shop that afternoon.

"I keep thinking about that day when Baz came home to see us after joining the fishing fleet, Daddy," Daisy said slowly. "He was so proud of his new life, and so fearful of what you were going to say to him. We were all out here in the garden then, do you remember?"

"I remember," Quentin answered. "It was like a rite of passage for the boy, wanting to find his own feet without any assistance from me. And certainly opposing my wishes for him to join the family business in the shop." He gave a faint smile. "As it happened, it hardly mattered, since the shop was about to be taken over by Preston's."

"He'd never have been happy standing behind a shop counter all his life, would he?" Daisy said, as much for herself as for her father. It had been obvious to everyone but Quentin at the time. Or rather, he had just refused to see it.

"That he wouldn't," he agreed now. "He was never happier than being near the water, and preferably being on it in some way or other. He could never have foreseen that the life he loved would eventually kill him, though."

Daisy heard the bitterness in his voice and ached for him.

"None of us can foresee what fate has in store for us, Daddy. And if there's any comfort at all to come from this, then at least we know that Baz spent the last few years of his life doing what he really loved. How many of us can truly say that, Daddy? Only two that I can think of, and they're together now."

She felt her lips tremble, because never until that moment had she been able to share Aunt Rose's conviction that her mother and Baz were somewhere in heaven together. Maybe she still didn't truly believe it in her heart, but she had to admit that there was a great comfort in having such a belief, and if it helped her father to believe it too…

Her heart gave a sudden, frightening lurch at a sound she had never heard before. It came from her father, and he was crying. Just as swiftly, she remembered that she *had* heard it before, just once, after her mother died. It had been as appalling then as it was now, those great, racking sobs from a strong man. She had heard other men sob in the hospital, but they were strangers, wounded, and needing emotional as well as physical support. She had helped them cope. Now, she didn't know what to do. And then she simply put her arms around her father and pressed him close to her, as though she were the parent and he the child.

After a while the shaking finally stopped, and he moved away from her, embarrassed and alone again. He busied himself with pouring more tea, until Daisy felt that she would be awash with it. But she knew it gave his hands something to do, and she took the cup dutifully.

"You'll stay here tonight, won't you?" he said at last. "We can have a proper meal later, providing you're happy with spam and mash. Mrs down-the-road leaves me to it on Fridays and Saturdays."

"Well, I..." She hadn't intended to stay, but now she saw that she must. He needed her. And the odd thing was, she could never remember a time in her life before when he had done so. It had always been Immy who had shared his confidences, being the oldest daughter; and more lately, Elsie. But now he needed *her*, his youngest. "Of course I'll stay, Daddy."

She had to let Aunt Rose know, and she spoke cautiously into the phone, knowing her father was within earshot, and not wanting to admit how desperately sorry she felt for him. She had learned from her nursing experience that it was far better to be able to let your emotions out than to keep them bottled up inside you and thank God he had been able to do just that.

She couldn't help wondering if it was the first time, and if she had been the one to trigger it all off. If so, then she was glad, she thought fiercely, pushing down any guilt at witnessing his distress.

Emotional upsets had a habit of making you hungry, and preparing food gave you something else to think about. They decided to have their meal of spam and mash quite early in the evening, and it tasted surprisingly good.

"You're becoming a dab hand at cooking now, Daddy," Daisy told him. "Not that there's too much skill in bashing to death a few boiled potatoes with a drop of milk and a lick of margarine, is there?" she teased.

He laughed back. He actually laughed, Daisy thought gladly, and she determined to keep up this light-hearted tone, however much of a strain it was. For now, they had done their crying.

The summer nights were long and warm, and they didn't need to put up the blackout curtains until much later. By dusk they had already heard the whine of aircraft overhead. Searchlights were scanning the skies by the time Daisy went to bed in her old room, and she realised that the night was going to be very different here in Bristol from the comparative quiet of Weston.

"If you hear the siren," Quentin said matter-of-factly, "put on a warm coat or dressing gown and we'll go down to the shelter. I don't bother when I'm on my own, but I always insist that Elsie and I do so."

"What does Elsie do when you're on your fire duties?"

"Elsie's stubborn, like the rest of you," he said with a small smile. "She doesn't like being in there on her own, but I finally persuaded her to be sensible for the baby's sake. It's not too bad – just a bit earthy, that's all. I'm sure

Teddy would love it, and if Baz were here, he'd probably say it was like going camping."

She caught her breath in her teeth, knowing what an effort it must have been for him to bring Baz's name into it so casually, and she knew, too, that it was part of the healing process not to ignore him as if he had never existed. It was something they must all do.

She leaned forward and kissed him. "Goodnight, Daddy," she said softly. "It's good to be home."

Some of her clothes were still in her wardrobe, including an old favourite dressing gown that should have been sent to the rag-bag long ago; but it was a link with the past, and although it was a warm night, she snuggled into it on top of the bedclothes and listened to the familiarity of the house and garden settling into darkness. She hadn't drawn her curtains, since the bedroom was half-moonlit, and through the window she could see the beams of the searchlights seeking enemy aircraft; but the night remained quiet, and the siren didn't sound. It was almost an anti-climax, Daisy thought. It would have been quite something to tell Alice that she had stayed in Bristol for the night, and their street had been bombed, and that she'd been on a *real* rescue mission right here in her own back yard…

It was wicked to even think such a thing. The newspaper and wireless reports were full of praise for the spectacular way the RAF was holding off the German Luftwaffe in their dogfights now and keeping them out over the English Channel as much as possible. Even though it gave her anguish to remember that it wouldn't be Cal coming home to her from one of his RAF sorties, she kept the thought of his bravery in her heart.

Next morning her father looked decidedly better for having her in the house, and she made up her mind.

"I'd really like to stay another night if you'll have me, Daddy. I'd like to visit Mother's grave, and to take a walk down to the waterfront where Immy and Elsie and I used to go so often. I might even look in on old Enoch Bray too. Do you think that's a good idea?" she asked carefully.

"It's a very good idea, darling. I'm afraid I haven't found it in me to go and see him, and I know I should. Are you sure about this?"

"Of course I am." She could see the relief in his face, knowing he couldn't deal with telling the news to the old ferryman, who had been such a mentor and friend to Baz. But she wanted to do this. She wanted to retrace old steps where they had all been so happy in times past, and she wanted to feel that this was still home, where her mother's aura still lingered in the walls, in the stones. Just for a while.

"Oh Lord, I'd better let Aunt Rose know I'm staying until Sunday," she remembered, before her father left for the shop as usual on a busy Saturday morning. "Uncle Bert keeps saying he wants to bring Teddy to see you sometime while he's still got some petrol, so shall I suggest that they come to fetch me? If I know Aunt Rose, she'll want to bring one of her famous pies for our dinner. What do you say, Daddy?"

She willed him to say yes. It would be like old times… almost. To her surprise he wrapped his arms around her and hugged her tight.

"I say yes, of course. What more could a grateful father say to such a loving daughter?"

She watched him leave the house, her eyes troubled. He was still a comparatively young man, still upright and vital, despite all the blows that life had dealt him. He should be married – and the thought was so swift, so alien and so disloyal to her mother's memory that Daisy gasped with the shock of it. But it was true: he was never meant to be alone.

She went back inside the house, her hands shaking, wondering how she could even think of such a thing. It was this house, this lovely house that her parents had come to when they had married, and where all the Caldwell children had been born, that had always been such a happy house. It had known laughter and joy, and even when Frances had lost the ability to dance and sing in the way that had entranced her stage audiences, there had still been so much love. It was filled with memories; and love was still here, waiting to be revived.

Daisy stormed through the rooms, tidying things that didn't need tidying, furious at her own wayward thoughts. How could she even think of someone taking her mother's place? There had been two paying lady lodgers in the upper floor of the house once, when they had decided to convert it into a self-contained flat. They had both been widows, both called Mary, which was why the girls had taken to referring to them as the Marys – and one of them had developed a special rapport with Quentin.

Daisy tried to think of her name. Mary Yard, that was it. Though where she was now Daisy didn't know – and she certainly didn't want to think of her as a possible candidate for stepmother, thank you very much! She dismissed her from her mind, along with every other uneasy thought.

She telephoned her aunt and got the expected response.

"You must be psychic, Daisy! Your uncle and I were thinking exactly the same thing, and I know Teddy will be excited to be having a ride out. And tell your father not to worry about food, because I'll make one of my pies and bring it in time for dinner."

Daisy smiled into the phone. She was so predictable at times. So endearingly predictable!

"That sounds wonderful, Aunt Rose. We'll see you tomorrow then."

She began to feel more light-hearted, despite knowing just what she was going to do today. It was as she had told her father, but with a little something extra. Firstly, she was going to visit her mother's grave, talk to her the way she sometimes still talked to Lucy, and ask her what she would think if Quentin were ever to marry again. She didn't expect an answer, of course, except in feelings.

"Oh, Aunt Rose," she murmured, "perhaps there's more of you in me than I thought, if I'm starting to imagine the afterlife after all." But how could she not believe that there was something there, when she had seen it in the faces of the dying patients more than once?

She shivered, brushing aside all these noble, if slightly spooky thoughts. She was young and alive, and she had things to do today.

The first thing she did was to cut a bunch of roses from the garden to put on Frances's grave. They had always been her favourite flowers, and she had planted them herself years ago. Today, the scent of them in full bloom was almost overpowering, thought Daisy. And then she went to the small churchyard where her mother was buried and where the granite headstone said it all.

FRANCES CALDWELL
BELOVED WIFE AND MOTHER
SAFE IN THE ARMS OF JESUS

There was no indication of the tragic way she had plunged to her death nearly two years ago. Quentin had wanted no reminders of that terrible day, nor ghoulish onlookers remembering it. Daisy swallowed, arranging the roses in the pot she had filled with water; then she stared at the headstone, as if to find inspiration from it as she had so often found it in her mother.

"Do you know what I was thinking about last night, Mother?" she said in a very low voice. "I worry about Daddy being lonely without us all – without you – and if it would be right for him to... well... to..."

But she couldn't say the words. How could you ask your mother if she approved of your father marrying again, finding love again, finding happiness again? *And how could you not want that for him?* she asked herself.

The words stayed in her head, and as she slowly turned to leave, a small breeze blew through the quiet headstones, rustling leaves as sweetly as a sigh, and wafting a heavenly scent of roses into her nostrils. She turned back quickly, and a shaft of sunlight lit her mother's name for a moment before it was gone.

To Daisy it seemed symbolic. The bright light that was Frances Caldwell had faded, and perhaps it really was time to make room for someone else. It was the way she was gradually starting to feel about Cal, and the guilt that had bothered her so much over Jed, and especially Glenn, was also starting to fade. A strange sense of calm settled around her as she walked away, a sense that Frances had given her blessing to whatever future there was for all of them...

She must be going mad to let her imagination run away with her like this, Daisy thought angrily, as her ebullient nature returned. She was sane and sensible, not one of Aunt Rose's mad friends who went to seances and suchlike! In any case, the feeling of serenity was rudely interrupted as she bumped into someone outside the iron gates of the churchyard.

"Good God, by all that's holy! It's one of the Caldwell girls, isn't it?"

Daisy blinked at having her mood shattered so abruptly, and by a stranger with black curly hair and a strong Welsh voice. He stood in front of her, blocking her path as if he owned the world, and despite his arrogant good looks, she took an instant and unreasonable dislike to him.

"Do I know you?" she asked pointedly, as haughty as Helen Church.

He laughed. "Well, I used to know your sister very well, and you're the spitting image of her, my lovely, so you must be one of the younger ones. I don't think it's Elsie, so it must be Daisy. Am I right?"

Daisy stared at him, trying to place him. She didn't like the way he was looking her up and down, and she couldn't ever remember Immy having a young man before James – certainly not one as brash and coarse as this one. She was certainly *not* his lovely! But she was more than curious to know just how well he had known Immy!

"Why aren't you in uniform?" she asked inanely, simply because she couldn't think of anything else to say.

He laughed again. "The army wouldn't take me because of a heart murmur. Why? Do you fancy curing me? I could do with a bit of pampering, and I think I heard that one of you girls was a nurse. Is that you?"

"Perhaps it is and perhaps it isn't." She really didn't want to stand here gossiping with him all day. He obviously got bored with her just as quickly.

"Well, never mind. Just say hello to Immy for me the next time you see her, will you? Tell her Morgan Raine was asking after her. We were *very* friendly once, if you know what I mean," he added, winking one eye.

Daisy strode past him, disliking him even more for his smutty innuendo. She couldn't believe Immy would ever have consorted with such a rough fellow, and she intended asking her about him the first opportunity she got. She felt his gaze following her as she went down the hill to the waterfront. She had things to do that were more important than chatting with a Welshman. She had to see Enoch Bray.

The smells of fish and salt and other unmentionables assaulted her long before she neared the waterfront. They used to come here often, the Caldwell girls and their brother, Baz. He was the one who always lingered, revelling in the tales of the old fishermen, and declaring his intention of going to sea one day, filled with the adventure of it. He'd got his wish too. He'd got his adventures, including the greatest adventure of all, as the minister referred to it. To Daisy it was death, plain and simple. She deliberately avoided looking at the small groups of seamen hanging about, knowing from of old that if she once made eye contact, she was likely to get some ribald remarks.

She heard them anyway, but while she looked straight ahead to the old fishermen's cottages she could ignore them; and it wasn't far to the small cottage where old Enoch lived with his wife. She knocked on the door and when it was opened a fraction, she saw the old ferryman.

He was just as gnarled and weather-beaten as ever from his years on the river, never seeming to change as the years went on; and after a moment staring at her as if she was a vision, his old eyes lit up in recognition.

"Bless my soul, if it ain't young Baz's sister. I can't recall which of you 'tis, my pretty maid, but you'd best come inside and tell me the news."

"I'm Daisy, Mr Bray," she said. "Daisy Caldwell."

She followed him inside the one small room of the cottage, evil-smelling with his pipe and his lingering cooking odours, and she was struck dumb. This old man had been like a father to Baz and given him his first job on the ferry, and she was about to tell him the worst news of all.

"Now then, 'tis bad news, ain't it?" Enoch said calmly. "I can't think of no other reason why you'd come all this way to visit me. Now that my old woman's passed on, I don't get any visitors, so out with it, Daisy Caldwell. Bad news never did improve by being kept inside."

"It's Baz," she blurted out.

He nodded. "Of course 'tis Baz, and you've come to tell me he's dead. Why else would you want to see me? So how'd it happen?"

She thanked God that he seemed to be a mind-reader, although she supposed the look on her face must have warned him. She told him as concisely as she could, considering she hadn't been there to see it, thank God, and realised that she seemed to be thanking Him quite a lot these days.

Relating the contents of the letter her father had received from the French farmer was a trial, but by now she had discovered that the more you said it, the more believable it became. It didn't stop the hurt, but the hurt became familiar. Enoch said nothing during the telling, just nodding now and then, and then repeated what she herself had said, but putting it so much better in his simple way.

"He won't have minded going down with the fishes. It was all he lived for, so you just remember that when you're crying over him. He wouldn't have wanted to be blown up or shot at. If he had to go at all, he'd have chosen this way."

Daisy couldn't imagine that anyone would have chosen to drown in a sea of burning oil, but she couldn't argue with this simple man who had also lost his wife and got no visitors. So when he offered her some tea she accepted, while trying not to keep her nose pinched at the cottage's aroma or notice the dingy state of the cup she was offered.

"I must go, Mr Bray," she was able to say at last. "It's been a comfort to talk to you, and I'm only sorry it was with such bad news. Oh, and I'm sorry about your wife too," she remembered to add.

"These things happen, my duck, but we can't dwell on 'em, or we'd go daft, wouldn't we? You just remember that, and don't waste your pretty life mourning Baz. He wouldn't want that."

Daisy left him at last, pondering on his words, and knowing he was right. Everyone had their own opinion on how to handle a bereavement, but, in the end, you had to handle it in your own way. She walked back along the waterfront, and when a couple of the lounging sailors whistled at her, she held her head up high and squared her shoulders; unable to resist a smile, she knew she must be coming through the mist at last.

# Chapter Nineteen

A week later Daisy decided she just might be psychic after all. She had managed to resist calling her father every evening, because she knew he wouldn't appreciate being made to feel he was in need of too much attention with Elsie being away. But the following Friday evening he called her.

"You'll never guess who came into the shop today!"

She registered that he sounded cheerful, so it couldn't be bad news.

"Helen's mother?" she asked with a grin, remembering the way she had deigned to visit their 'little shop' in the past. But she was being ungenerous, and Mrs Church was a very worthy lady, involved in fund-raising and Good Works.

"Mary Yard," her father said.

Daisy felt her mouth drop open. "Good Lord, I was only thinking about her the other day. Isn't that odd?" It was the only thing she could think of to say at that moment, but she was never speechless for long. "What was she doing in Bristol?"

"She's here for a few days for the funeral of an old friend and just called in to say hello. She didn't know about Elsie expecting, of course – nor about Baz."

He paused, and Daisy finished it for him. "I'm sure she was shocked. About Baz, I mean. Not Elsie."

She bit her lip, hoping she hadn't sounded frivolous at that moment. But Mary Yard, of all people, when they had never expected to hear anything of her again, and who had come into her own thoughts only last week.

"Yes, she was upset to hear about Baz," her father went on. "We're going to have a long talk about it all tomorrow evening."

"Oh."

"It was good to see Mary again, Daisy, and it made me realise how much I've missed talking to my contemporaries. She's invited me to have dinner with her at the hotel where she's staying."

"Oh," Daisy said again.

"Is that all you can say, darling?" Quentin said, amused. "In case you're worried, we are both over twenty-one, you know."

"I'm sorry. I was just surprised, that's all. It'll be good for you to have someone to talk over old times with, Daddy. Remember me to her, won't you?"

"I will. And give my love to all."

The call ended; Daisy went back to the parlour where Uncle Bert was playing snakes and ladders with Teddy before his bedtime, and Aunt Rose was knitting yet another pair of socks for the soldiers' benevolent fund.

"Daddy sends his love to us all," she told them, "and he sounds much brighter, thank heavens."

"I'm glad," Rose said. "You can't go around with a gloomy face for ever, no matter how you feel inside."

Daisy hesitated. "Aunt Rose, do you remember the Marys who used to have the upstairs rooms in our house?"

"Of course I do. I liked them both. Widows, weren't they?"

"Yes. One of them – Mary Yard – is in Bristol for a few days, and she and Daddy are having dinner together tomorrow evening."

She was watching Teddy's progress on the snakes and ladders board at that moment, but she was perfectly aware of Rose's gaze on her, and she felt her face and neck go hot. Rose could usually guess what she was thinking, no matter how obtuse she tried to be.

"Well, as I said, you can't go around with a gloomy face for ever, no matter how you feel inside. And you can't mourn someone for ever, either. Baz certainly wouldn't want that."

And they both knew she wasn't just speaking about Baz.

Later, when Teddy was in bed and Bert had gone down to his shed for half an hour before his nightly civil defence duties, it was Rose who brought up the subject again. This time she was her usual blunt self.

"Daisy, have you ever thought about your father marrying again?"

Daisy flinched. "Well, I – I don't know…"

"I didn't ask if you approved. I asked if you had ever thought about it."

"Not seriously. It may have crossed my mind once or twice, but I always managed to ignore it," she said defensively, since she had no idea whether or not her aunt would approve.

"I don't think your mother would ignore it, if she was here."

"If she was here, there'd be no need to think of any such thing!"

Rose nodded. "Perhaps that wasn't the cleverest way to put it. What I mean is, I'm perfectly sure Frances wouldn't want your father to spend the rest of his life feeling lonely."

"He's not lonely. He's got his work, and he's got us."

"Nobody could deny that he thinks the world of his children, but if you think any of it compares with the comfort and company of being married," she said, choosing her words more carefully now, "then you've still got a lot of growing up to do, Daisy."

"That's not fair," she muttered. "I've seen a bit of the world now, Aunt Rose, and I'm not in the nursery anymore."

She could hardly say that she knew physical desire didn't end when the hair grew white or the teeth fell out, because she had written too many impassioned letters for her patients to be in any doubt about that! And Quentin Caldwell was nowhere near either of those states yet.

"Then you'll know what I'm saying," Rose went on more briskly. "Let's leave it there, shall we? Go and make some cocoa, there's a love."

She did as she was told, unable to forget the conversation, and trying to imagine how she would feel if her father did ever marry again. How any of them would feel. It was obvious that her aunt – her father's sister – wouldn't think it a bad thing at all. And Rose had loved her mother as much as any of them. But what about Imogen and Elsie?

It was too big a problem to solve on her own, and who said it was going to be a problem anyway? She asked herself crossly. One dinner didn't foretell a marriage. She shivered, but Aunt Rose had made her think about it seriously now. Did any of them want their father to be lonely? And *was* he lonely? She guessed that he often was, especially while Elsie was away, and he was in that big house all on his own, and perhaps all of them had been selfish in not staying there to give him moral support.

It had been the sensible thing for Rose and Bert to bring Teddy to Weston after their mother died. He'd been too young and bewildered to cope with the aftermath of that terrible time. Baz had already virtually left home… and nobody could prevent a war, which meant Immy had wanted to do her bit. Elsie had married Joe, so it was convenient for her to stay in Bristol and take over the upstairs flat after he had enlisted. But Daisy hadn't needed to flee down to Weston herself, had she? She could have stayed. She had truly deserted her father.

"Daisy, what on earth are you doing?" Bert's voice said close behind her as she stood rigidly in the kitchen, clasping the kettle as if it was a lifeline.

"Oh Lord, I'm sorry," she almost gasped. "I was miles away, Uncle Bert. I haven't even filled the kettle yet."

He took it out of her hands. "What's wrong, my love?"

She took a deep breath. "Will you tell me something honestly? I know it's an awful imposition of me to ask – and I know I shouldn't…"

"Well, I'll never be able to give you an answer unless you do," he said mildly, as she floundered.

"Supposing something happened to you or Aunt Rose, and one of you was left behind…"

"You mean if one of us died. There's no need to be afraid of the word, Daisy. It's something we all have to face sooner or later. So go on."

"Would you expect the one who's left to remain on their own for the rest of their life? I mean, it happens to so many people in the war, doesn't it?" she said, trying desperately to make this less personal than it had been to begin with. "I was thinking about our old lodgers, the

Marys. They were both widowed in the last war, and it's an awful long time to be alone, isn't it? Do you think it would have been disloyal to their husbands if they'd married someone else? It just made me think about these things, that's all," she finished lamely.

"I think it's up to each person to decide for themselves. There's no right or wrong about it, Daisy, but the marriage service mentions 'till death us do part", so if it's death that has brought about the separation, then I don't think it's disloyal to the first partner to think of marrying again. Not that I could imagine anyone else putting up with Rose or me, mind! Does that answer your question?"

"I think so. Yes, of course it does. Thank you, Uncle Bert."

She didn't quite know what she was thanking him for, but she kissed him impulsively. He was a dear… and although it didn't really answer anything regarding her father and Mary Yard, she decided she was probably getting things all out of proportion. It was best to forget all about it. For now, anyway.

In any case, things were becoming too hectic to think of anything but work. She was only scheduled to have four weeks with the ambulance crew, but it was far less routine now with a spate of accidents due to the black-out regulations.

"It's not so bad when there's a full moon at night," Thomas told her, "but when it's pitch-black some of these old boys out on the razzle at the local pubs can't see their way past a lamp-post. We get a lot of sore heads, especially when they miss the edge of the pavement and go crashing into the road. Next morning is when we're called out, when their old ladies have done nagging them, and realise they might have done some real damage to themselves."

"You're having me on, aren't you?"

"I am not!" He glanced at her. "Anyway, girl, I don't want to worry you, but after last night's raid on Bristol, we've been called out to bring some of the injured to Weston, since their hospitals need to be ready for more casualties soon."

"It's all right; I heard about it on the wireless," she said quickly. "My father phoned us to let us know it was over Sea Mills way and nowhere near us."

And even if it was, she had a job to do...

"Is your sister back home yet?" he went on conversationally.

"Her husband's bringing her home at the weekend; then he's got to report back to his regiment."

It would be awful for Elsie, thought Daisy. After spending these few weeks with Joe, they would be parted at an anxious time for her sister, with only weeks to go until her baby was born. She resolved to see her whenever she could, and also to find out if anything had come of her father's meeting with Mary Yard.

Luke said it was routine work to bring back some of the injured who had been caught up in the bombing raid. It was nothing to worry about... but she was more than thankful to have a senior nurse on board as well as herself, and even more relieved to discover that Alice Godfrey had asked for the job.

"I volunteered," Alice said. "I didn't see why you should have all the fun, gallivanting about with two fellows!"

"I'm not sure that's what I'd call it, but I can't tell you how glad I am that you're here," she said fervently. It would be the first time they had seen the real evidence of a German bombing raid, and they had to go through the city and report to the nearest hospital where most of the casualties had been taken for temporary treatment.

Thomas spoke sternly. "You'll both be fine, but this is a new situation to all of us, remember. It's not just dealing with someone who's come into hospital to have their tonsils out. Every day is going to be different from now on."

"But not so much for you," Daisy pointed out. "You're used to being called out to emergencies, aren't you?" And she had already learned to respect them for their way of dealing with everything that came their way.

Before they reached the bombed area, they could see the pall of grey smoke ahead, and smell the stench of burning. There was also a lingering whiff of gas in the air, and people still milled around, civilians searching for precious bits of property and missing animals, and the Civil Defence workers trying to keep everyone back until it was all made safe. They could see the skeletons of buildings in a small street that had once been family homes and businesses. Even from this one isolated attack, there was dust and rubble everywhere, and suddenly, frighteningly, the war was right here, in front of them.

According to the pompous wireless announcer that morning, it hadn't been a serious raid, just enough to flatten a few buildings and claim about thirty casualties. There hadn't been any major damage and the docks hadn't been affected – as if that was all that mattered, and these little suburban houses and shops were of far lesser importance. Daisy had hated the complacency of the man, sitting in his cosy little studio reciting the news into the microphone.

"All right, girls, let's get on with it," Thomas said, as Daisy stared into space, and she realised they had already stopped at the Casualty entrance of the hospital. "We've got work to do, and these folk would prefer to see a cheerful face to a miserable one, Miss Daisy, so *smile!*"

She tried, but it was hard to smile as she helped an old man and his wife with head wounds into the ambulance, clearly still in shock, and distraught over the loss of their home. She couldn't smile at a young couple frantic at the sight of their baby with a badly cut face from flying glass. She couldn't smile at watching Thomas and Luke carefully place a hysterical young boy on a stretcher into the ambulance, seeing from his notes that he had broken his leg in several places, and trying to block her ears to his weeping mother.

Alice was marvellous, Daisy noted. She was calm and efficient, while still showing overwhelming tenderness towards the patients. Hadn't they both done the same on the hospital ship, in a far more dangerous situation than this one, and with far worse injuries? But Daisy was beginning to wonder if she was losing her nerve, and it wasn't something she wanted to admit to anyone.

As soon as all the necessary paperwork had been done, and the patients' notes handed over, they were ready to return to Weston.

"It'll get worse before it gets better, you know," Alice said, glancing at Daisy's white face as they got into the back of the ambulance with the patients.

"I know it will," she muttered. "I'm just wondering if I was really cut out for this after all."

"Of course you are. Don't be stupid, Daisy. Everyone gets panic attacks from time to time, and you're no different from anyone else. It'll pass. Remember what we're here to do, and make sure Mr and Mrs Sage are comfortable."

Daisy glanced at the elderly couple who were sitting patients, huddled close together in blankets. They still looked dazed and bewildered, and there was dried blood and rubble in their sparse hair, but they were talking together a bit more sensibly now. She tried to smile at them encouragingly, and the old man managed a cheeky smile in return.

"That's a smile to cheer anybody up, my lover. We was just saying as how you mind my missis and me of a lady dancer we once saw on the stage years back. Can't recall her name, but she were a real smasher."

"Sam, behave yourself," his wife said. "The nurse don't want to hear none of your saucy talk."

"Was her name Frances Caldwell?" Daisy asked, her voice catching.

Sam's old eyes lit up. "By jingo, that was the name, weren't it, Mother?" he asked his wife. "Sang and danced like an angel, she did. Begging your pardon, nurse, but you've got quite a look of her about you, see?"

"I suppose I should," Daisy said. "She was my mother."

"Well, I never," the old woman exclaimed, perking up. "We never expected to be riding to hospital with a celebrity, did we, Sam?"

Daisy hardly knew what to say to that, but listening to the little exchange, she saw that the young couple were looking mildly interested at well. It was taking their minds off their injuries, and only the mother with the young boy was paying no attention. Alice gave her a meaningful nod and a nudge, and before she knew what she was doing, Daisy was elaborating on the times her mother had performed on the stage in front of big audiences in Bristol and beyond.

Minutes before, she had felt so helpless, as if she was little more than a bystander as the ambulancemen and Alice went about their business; but now she saw that her stories were really helping these people who had gone through such trauma last night. It was as good as a shot in the arm, Alice whispered to her, and if they thought Daisy was halfway to being a celebrity herself, it did no harm.

It made her think fleetingly about her one-time desire to follow in her mother's footsteps. It was a dream that would never have come true – she knew that now. She no longer wanted to leave nursing to go on the stage, nor even to join up and be one of a concert party. But she knew the hospital patients had a dreary time of it, especially those who had no family or friends near enough to visit them, and they all looked forward to the Christmas carol-singing by the nurses and the magic and puppet acts that several of the porters did.

Crazy thoughts began to whirl around in her mind as the ambulance rumbled on through the countryside between Bristol and Weston. Why should such treats for the patients just be confined to Christmas? Why not a more regular bit of entertainment? She wondered if she dared mention it to Sister Macintosh.

"My friend here sings a bit too," she heard Alice tell Sam next, just as if she was a mind-reader.

She gasped, glaring at her friend. She didn't mean here and now, for heaven's sake! It was hardly the time and place.

"Give us a song then, love," Sam's missis said.

"Oh I don't think so. These people don't want to hear me…"

"We don't mind," said the young woman, jiggling the baby up and down. "It might stop our Lucy-Belle snivelling."

"The baby's called Lucy?" Daisy exclaimed, feeling her heart lurch at hearing the name so unexpectedly. She flushed as they looked at her in surprise. "I had a friend called Lucy once. I always thought it was a pretty name."

"So what's yours then, Nursie?" old Sam asked her.

"It's Daisy."

"Come on then, give us a tune to cheer us all up," his wife encouraged, and then began a wavering tune herself. "Daisy, Daisy, give us your answer do…"

With a little laugh, Daisy took up the song. Alice joined in, and even the young woman began crooning it softly to her baby while her husband sat silently and awkwardly, the way young husbands did, until he muttered a few of the words to keep her company.

Only the woman with the young boy who was going to have his leg set in plaster of Paris remained silent, but she gave Daisy a fleeting smile at the end of the song, and nodded towards her boy, who was dozing now from his pain-killing injections and sheer exhaustion.

Thomas called out to her: "Give us another one, Daisy. You're good on the ears as well as being a sight for sore eyes. I always said we'd picked a good 'un."

Her eyes prickled at the unexpected praise. It was her mother's talent, not hers, she thought fiercely, but if a little of it had rubbed off on her, she was eternally grateful.

She sang several more songs on the way back to Weston, and the old couple did their best to join in, though by now she could see that the small burst of excitement had tired them out. The baby and the young boy were asleep by now, and she decided that enough was enough.

"I'll come and see you on the ward," she told Sam and his missis. "And you never know — we might be able to have a sing-song then."

"What are you up to, Daisy?" Alice said quietly when they were all settled.

"You'll have to wait and see, won't you?" she said with a grin, feeling considerably brighter than she had all day.

–

"It's having a purpose that does it every time," she told her aunt and uncle that evening. "It was awful going into Bristol and having to deal with those poor people and seeing how the houses had been demolished. I really felt useless, though Alice was being perfectly wonderful as usual, of course, and when Thomas told me to smile I could have hit him. But he was quite right. The patients wanted to see a cheerful smiling face, and it was just so strange that the elderly couple remembered seeing Mother on the stage."

"I don't think it was strange at all. Half of Bristol must have seen her at one time or other, so why wouldn't they have seen the likeness in you? Old people retain things in their memories far more than you might think, Daisy."

"Well, in the end it was rather a special journey back to Weston," she said. "Did I tell you the baby was called Lucy? Now *that* was a coincidence if you like!"

"Yes, it was," Rose agreed. "So what did your Sister Macintosh say when you went to her with your entertainment suggestion?"

Daisy was cautious. "I think she quite approved, but I can't always tell with her. She was going to present it to Matron, anyway, so we shall just have to wait and see."

She was more than shivery about the whole thing now, wondering if she had been far too daring. After all, a nurse's prime function was to nurse people, wasn't it? not set herself up as the prospective singing star of the ward! But she hadn't meant just herself, anyway. Between them the staff might be able to work out a small entertainment show to brighten the patients' lives on a Saturday afternoon – or whenever Matron allowed them to do it.

It might never happen; but the next day she was called into Sister Macintosh's office and told that Matron thought it was a splendid idea, providing it didn't interfere with nursing duties.

"You're to be commended for your ingenuity, Daisy," Sister said briskly. "And you may put a notice on the board asking for any likely performer who is interested to contact you."

"Oh, but I didn't intend to organise it all," she began.

"Didn't you?" Sister gave one of her rare smiles. "Well, I'm sorry, Nurse Caldwell, but it looks as though you've just been elected."

–

Elsie telephoned her when she got home from Oxford at the weekend and had said her tearful goodbyes to Joe.

"It all feels like a huge anti-climax sitting here with nothing to do," she wailed. "I'm as big as a house, and I already miss Joe terribly – and he's only been gone a few hours. I'd come and see you, but I couldn't face the train, and I've done enough travelling for a while, so when can you come home for a visit?"

Daisy was suitably sympathetic considering her underlying excitement at how her idea had been received at the hospital. "Oh Lord, not right now, I'm afraid. You'll never guess what's happened. We're starting up a kind of small hospital concert party to entertain the patients once a month, and I'm in charge. We're having meetings about it this weekend."

"What?" Elsie said. She started to laugh and then sobered up as the familiar kick of the baby brought her up short. "Well, I shouldn't be surprised, of course. You were always a bit of a bossy-boots, weren't you, sweetie?"

"Well, thank you! I didn't actually ask to be in charge, but it just happened to be my idea, and I'm landed with it now."

She didn't say it had come to her while she was transporting patients from a Bristol bombing raid to Weston General. Elsie must know the kind of danger they were all in, but she still stubbornly refused to move.

"I know you'll do a wonderful job, darling. Take no notice of my scratchiness. It's just that I never thought nine months could be so long, that's all, especially when it's so hot."

"Is it really that bad?" Daisy said quickly, unable to imagine it, and not wanting to do so anyway.

"Yes – and no – of course not. But it will all be worth it in the end, or so Mrs Woodley keeps telling me. The minute they put the baby in your arms, you're supposed to forget all that's gone before," she said delicately. "I'll believe that when it happens. For a midwife, she's disgustingly cheerful, but I suppose that's better than telling you about everything that could go wrong."

"Nothing's going to go wrong," Daisy said, aware of the apprehension in her sister's voice now. "Good Lord, people have babies every day. They'd stop doing it if they thought it was that bad, wouldn't they?"

"Oh yes, champion philosopher who knows nothing about it!" Elsie said, laughing, and with her own secret thoughts on the subject.

"Well, look, I promise I'll come up for a night or two when I can," Daisy said, relieved that she sounded more like her usual self now. "Unless you've had any thoughts about coming to Weston to have the baby?"

"What, and frighten Teddy out of his wits? Not likely. I know Mrs Woodley well by now, and she's the one I want with me when the time comes. Besides, I couldn't face moving all my things anywhere at the moment, and I wouldn't want to leave Father here all on his own."

"Oh, Elsie, that reminds me!" As her sister became more decisive, Daisy couldn't keep her curiosity at bay any longer. "Has he told you anything about having dinner with Mary Yard?"

# Chapter Twenty

To Daisy's relief it was decided to have a nurses' choir, rather than individual singers. At once time she might have felt peeved that she wasn't to be the star of the show, but now she was glad it was going to be a community activity. The hospital staff all had jobs to do, and they worked different shifts, so this way they could call on the core of the available nurses to form half a dozen songsters at each performance. The porters and other staff with various talents would provide the extra entertainment. It was going to work well.

"I think you're amazing, Daisy dear," her sister Imogen told her with a laugh on the telephone, hearing her enthusiasm. "You and Baz were always going to come up smiling, weren't you? And I'm not going to get all embarrassed over what I just said, because he got exactly what he wanted out of life, and we must never forget that. So good for you, sis!"

"Thanks," Daisy said briefly. "So how are things with you, and to what do we owe the honour of this phone call? Are you still in London?"

"For the time being," Immy said cautiously; "but once Elsie's had the baby I hope the service for Baz will go ahead fairly soon afterwards. And I'm saying no more than that."

She didn't need to, though where the army would be sending troops now that the Germans had occupied France, Daisy didn't know. And since nothing was ever given away, it was like a blessed mystery story, she thought crossly.

"What's it like being in London now then?" she said instead.

"Noisy. The sirens go off every night, and even if nothing's actually happening here, there are always aircraft overhead, and the sound of the south-east raids and the ack-ack fire," Immy said grimly. "The RAF boys are doing a grand job, of course, and did I tell you there are a lot of Australian and New Zealand servicemen around now? Interesting types."

"Types?"

Immy laughed self-consciously. "That's the way some of the officers refer to them, especially the RAF ones. They have a language all their own, Daisy."

Daisy felt her heart give a pang, because Cal had only just begun his RAF career and hadn't had much chance to pick up some of the special slang that was so delightfully RAF talk. Presumably Glenn Fraser would have done so by now, despite being a Canadian. She found herself wondering where he was now and, more importantly, if he was still safe. She had liked him a lot...

Her thoughts switched to why her sister seemed happy to talk about anything but the situation in London and where she might be posted next.

"Oh, by the way, Immy," she said casually, "I saw an old friend of yours in Bristol the last time I was there. At least, he said he was an old friend, though I thought he was rather a brash kind of fellow."

"Oh? And what do you know about my taste in young men? Not that I've ever had a large following to choose from, darling!" Immy said with a smile.

"Well, I meant the gorgeous James, of course! But let me think. It was some Welsh name – Morgan something-or-other. He implied that you'd be sure to remember him. Was it Morgan Raine?"

"Yes, it was." Immy's voice had suddenly gone flat, and she might have known Daisy would sense it, and never be able to leave it at that.

"*Well?* Who was he? I don't ever remember seeing him before. Did you have a secret admirer before you fell in love with James Church? And should he be told about this other man, I wonder?" she teased.

"He certainly should not," Immy said sharply, "because there's nothing to tell. I knew Morgan Raine long ago before Daddy had to sell out the shop to Preston's Emporium. He was going to do some leaflets for Elsie once, when she thought of doing some work at home. He's a newspaper reporter, and he's just someone I used to know."

"Well, methinks the lady doth protest too much!"

"Nonsense. I'm not protesting at all—"

"And I never knew you had such an interesting past!" Daisy went on.

"Daisy, don't be silly. If you've met him, then you'll know he's good-looking and quite charming, but also rather too fond of the ladies, and I mean that in the plural. So if he makes any advances to you, I advise you to keep well away from him. I think you know what I mean. Now, if you don't mind, I'd prefer not to talk about him any longer, and, in any case, I'll have to go, darling."

She hung up before Daisy could say any more; but not before an image of Morgan Raine's dark and dashing good looks had flashed into Immy's mind. Not before she unwillingly recalled the times they had shared on the hillside above Vicarage Street, when she had lain in his arms in the sweet grass and listened to his persuasive, seductive Welsh voice telling her that he loved her and wanted her and needed her…

Immy shivered, thanking God that she had found out before it was too late that he had also been sweet-talking another girl; before she had fallen completely for his charms and given in to him; before she had realised that it was no more than infatuation, and that her one true love was James, her best friend's brother, who had been there all along, only she had just been too blind to see it…

Daisy was intrigued more by the things Immy hadn't said than what she had, and one of these days she must remember to ask Elsie just what she knew about a news-paper reporter called Morgan Raine.

After she had assured her aunt and uncle that Immy was fine, and seemed to be enjoying her war, especially with these dark and infuriatingly hush-hush hints that she might be doing something exciting in the near future.

"Why does nobody ever tell us anything definite?" she complained.

"What would you have our people do?" Bert said. "Announce to the Jerries that we're going to bomb Berlin every Sunday night, or that we're planning to put up defences all along the south coast so that they'll sneak in around Norfolk instead? It's important to have strategies in a war, Daisy, and one of them is to keep the enemy guessing."

"The enemy, yes! But we're not the enemy."

"You're not, and neither am I, but who knows who else might be listening and passing on information to the enemy? You have to be careful who you talk to these days. Careless talk costs lives and all that!"

Rose started laughing. "For goodness' sake, Bert, you'll have our Daisy thinking there are spies around every corner. Though there might be, of course, and we can never be sure of strangers these days. You never know who you might be talking to in a queue at the butcher's, or on a train, since everyone seems free and easy in talking to people without proper introductions nowadays."

"Even in hospital," Daisy said solemnly. "Perhaps old Mr Sage was wired up to a listening device somewhere in Berlin while we were taking him to Weston General! Or the boy with the broken leg has been passing messages on his plaster to anyone who wants to see what has been written on it."

"All right, you two, I know when I'm being had," Bert said with a grin. "So let's forget it. When is your first concert to be, Daisy?"

"On Saturday afternoon. We're holding it in the main ward, and not all the patients will be able to be there, especially those who are too ill to be moved, so we're going to make it a kind of roving show, and by the end of it we'll probably all be hoarse. I'm sure we'll never be ready, and rehearsals are so haphazard it will probably be an absolute shambles."

There was far more organising involved than she had imagined, which was why it had been decided to hold it only once a month. Since she had now been given the grand title of producer of the show, she was getting butterflies in her stomach, just thinking about it.

"Nonsense, love," Bert said loyally. "In any case, think what a treat it will be for the patients. Instead of looking at four dreary walls, they'll have the chance to see our girl singing her heart out."

Daisy laughed. "And the rest of them! We do make a good sound when we're altogether, though, and Nurse Sims is wonderful on the piano. Actually, the real star is Bill Watts and his magic. He's done his act a few times on the children's ward, but I've only ever seen him pushing patients about on a trolley."

"He's obviously a man of hidden talents," Rose said. "Well, I hope it will be a great success, Daisy, and I'm sure the patients will love it."

She was very nervous when the day came, and it didn't help to settle any of them when they had an emergency admission and Bill Watts was summoned to take the elderly patient up to the ward just as the entertainment was about to begin.

Fortunately, his act was one of the last ones, and they breathed a sigh of relief when he appeared as the songsters were still in the middle of their repertoire. By then the more able patients had joined in every chorus of the well-known songs, and it was obvious that this was the highlight of their day. The roving show was an excellent idea, since it gave the patients a chance to think about something other than their ailments.

But Daisy was right, and by the time she got home that evening, she didn't have much voice left. "I'm very thankful we don't have to do it again tomorrow," she said huskily to Aunt Rose, "and that tomorrow is Sunday, so I can have a bit of a rest."

"After church, of course."

Daisy groaned. "Must I go? My throat really is quite sore, Aunt Rose."

"Then it's a dose of honey and lemon for you, some Vick to rub in your throat, and one of Bert's old woolly socks around your neck when you go to bed."

"I wonder that anyone would need to go to hospital when you're around," Daisy said, her voice cracking. "All they need is an Aunt Rose with her patent medicines."

"And they work too," Bert reminded her with a chuckle. "You do as your auntie says, my love, and you'll be as right as ninepence in the morning."

Daisy didn't doubt it, nor did she dare to dispute it. Sometimes they made her feel like a child again, but when you were feeling out of sorts, it was lovely to feel so cosseted. And after feeling so exhilarated at the success of the afternoon and basking in the congratulations the nurses and patients had heaped on her and the other members of their show, it was probably just the after-effects giving her this deflated feeling.

Next morning, she knew it was more than that. Her throat felt raw and ragged, and she had a raging headache. It hurt when she opened her eyes, and she closed them again quickly. When Teddy came and jumped up and down on her bed at what felt like the crack of dawn, she winced at his energy.

"Get up, lazy-bones. We're all having breakfast," he shouted.

"Get *off*," she croaked. "Tell Aunt Rose I don't want any breakfast and I'm staying in bed. I don't feel well."

When he said nothing for a moment, she opened her eyes a fraction and through the slits of her lids she saw him staring at her.

"Are you going to die, like Baz?" he said finally.

"Of course I'm not going to die," she said crossly, and then she saw that he really meant what he said. She was so rarely unwell, and never stayed in bed unnecessarily, and she could see the scared look in Teddy's eyes now. She caught hold of his hand.

"It's only a headache, Teddy, and I'll be fine in a little while. Go and tell Aunt Rose, will you, love?"

He slid off the bed, his face still troubled. She forced a smile to her lips.

"*Shoot!*" she said.

Minutes later Rose came into the bedroom. "I've heard of some excuses for not going to church, Daisy, but I didn't think you'd resort to this one!"

"It's no excuse, honestly," she replied weakly.

Rose felt her forehead and then her pulse.

"Probably a touch of flu. You're in the best place, and you're to stay there for a few days. Hot lemon drinks and aspirins will do the trick, and I'll let the hospital know in the morning."

"You should have been a nurse," Daisy murmured.

"Oh, I've done my bit. That, and applying common sense," Rose said with a smile. "Now, I'll bring the necessary medication up, and then you try and get some sleep. That's often the best medicine in these cases."

She stayed in bed for five days, letting the world revolve around her. There was a war on, but she was so light-headed that it meant nothing to her. The house could have fallen down, and she'd have been perfectly content to fall with it, floating in that weird sense of not being quite there at all.

Rose and Bert saw to her every need, and Teddy played the little doctor on occasion, bringing her magazines that she couldn't read, and carefully carrying her bowl of chicken soup for dinner, which was all she felt like eating, and being told strictly not to stay in the bedroom too long in case he caught it too. Hearing the instructions, she began to feel like a leper, and she didn't care...

On the sixth day, she awoke with her head clear and her eyes unfuzzy. Her throat didn't hurt every time she swallowed, and she was aware of the world outside her window for the first time in days. She could hear the sound of birds singing, and the clatter of the milk lorry going along the road. Her brain was becoming active again, and she no longer felt like a very old lady. She was eighteen and alive. She was better.

"You're awake then," Aunt Rose greeted her when she came into the room a little while later.

"And sitting up, and eager to get up," Daisy told her.

"Not so fast, young lady. Your legs won't want to move that quickly after five days in bed. Take it one step at a time."

But Daisy could tell from the relief in her voice that she was glad to see the improvement. And looking across at her reflection in the mirror on her dressing table, she could see that she looked pretty well back to normal, except for the haystack tangle of her hair.

"Can I have my comb, please?"

Rose laughed. "Of course you can, love. It's the first thing a woman wants when she's been ill, isn't it?"

"Have I been very ill? I don't remember much."

"Just a sharp bout of flu, but that can be quite nasty. Anyway, you're young and strong, and you quickly responded to treatment, as you professionals say."

"I don't feel much like a professional right now," Daisy said, tugging the comb through the knots in her hair. "I was looking forward to going back to work on Monday and having praises heaped on me from the patients after the show. What a let-down!" she mocked herself.

"You'd better have these cards then," Rose said, handing her the small pile of envelopes. "Alice brought them round last night. She knew it was best not to come up and see you until you're quite better because of taking infection back to the hospital. She's a very sensible young woman. And there are two letters for you as well."

Daisy opened the envelopes, touched that the cards came from staff and patients, and she recognised Elsie's handwriting on one of the envelopes. Her father had called every night, Rose told her, so she hadn't been forgotten while she was lying in her bed of pain.

The second letter had been forwarded from the hospital, and when she opened it her heart gave a giant leap on seeing the signature.

"Oh, my goodness," she said softly.

"I hope it's not bad news," Aunt Rose said, busily tidying the bedroom.

"No. It's from an old friend – well, just someone I met really, not exactly a friend…"

She was babbling, and she clamped her lips together before Aunt Rose thought she was going mad, and quickly read the words Glenn Fraser had written:

> You may not even remember me, Daisy, but I've never forgotten you, and I very much hope our paths will cross again someday. It's taken me a heck of a time to know where to write to you, but I put my detective nose to work and finally remembered you were at a hospital in some place called Weston-super-Mare, so I hope this reaches you. And if it does, and you feel like writing back, I'd love to hear from you.

*Yours cordially,*
*Glenn Fraser*

His image was instantly in her mind, dashing and handsome, and she was remembering how they had danced together in a wartime dance hall in Folkestone, almost floating around the floor to a slow waltz tune. He had remembered her all this time, and whether or not it was the thrill of knowing that, or the knowledge that at last she could respond without the awful feeling of guilt because of Cal, she felt suddenly, wonderfully invigorated.

The feeling was momentous, as if she had finally come out of a long, dark tunnel, and she wasn't quite ready yet to share her feelings with anyone. She needed to be alone and no longer fussed over. There was only one really private place, and she asked her aunt if she could have a bath.

"Only if you allow me to supervise, Daisy. I'll be outside the door, in case you need me."

"I'm sure it won't be necessary." But Rose was adamant, and once she had revelled in the sheer luxury of warm water for ten minutes, she was glad to be helped into her clothes and to start feeling human again. And to start feeling more positive about life than she had in ages. There was something to look forward to after all. There was Glenn... and she was thankful that Aunt Rose kept any curiosity about the letter to herself.

"So what have I been missing?" she said, after a wobbly walk downstairs and into the parlour. Bert was working in the garden and Teddy was at school, but she had to put up with George's ecstatic and very slobbery welcome.

"Well, the war's still going on, and the RAF have successfully bombed Berlin. Hitler had been assured that our boys could never reach Berlin, so that must have been a severe blow to his pride. It's not all bad news."

The way she said it alerted Daisy. "So what was the bad news?"

Rose was as casual as she dared to be. "London was bombed last weekend. Mr Churchill has praised our RAF pilots as being the finest in the world and he is assured that we shall soon fight them off."

Daisy was deflated at once, unable to stop wondering if Glenn had been involved. So much for peace of mind… but she had never believed in being negative, and everyone had to face up to these things. She swallowed her fears for Glenn and tried to sound objective.

"It still doesn't stop Hitler's planes dropping bombs on our cities, does it, Aunt Rose? And Immy's in London…"

"Now, you don't want to go worrying about Imogen. I'm sure she can take care of herself, and she has a job to do, the same as everybody else. You just worry about getting better."

"I *am* better, and I have a job to go to as well."

"Not yet you don't, Daisy. I spoke to Sister Macintosh while you were in the bath, and she says you're to stay home all next week so that you're fully recovered and won't be bringing any germs into the hospital. She's quite right."

And when Aunt Rose got that determined look in her eyes, Daisy knew there was no moving her. She and Sister Macintosh were a perfect match for one another, she thought, so she might as well be resigned to it.

But long before the next week was over her energy had returned and she was anxious to be doing something again. Inactivity didn't suit her at all. Besides which, she was beginning to feel mildly incarcerated. The summer weather was good, and she wanted to go walking on the beach, which always revived her spirits, as soon as her legs felt capable of holding her up for any length of time. But she discovered that it was going to take a few more days before that happened.

The next week dragged, and the war news was depressing. Air raids were becoming more frequent everywhere now, and once she felt more normal again, Daisy felt completely useless to be twiddling her thumbs while the rest of the country seemed embroiled in either trying to win the war or barricading themselves against possible invasion.

She had already written back to Glenn, assuring him that of course she remembered him, and that she would love to exchange letters with him. She was tempted to sign it 'with love', but that would be going just too far – it was too soon. They could be on the brink of something wonderful, or this could just be the beginning of friendship. All the same, as she posted her letter, she knew how eagerly she would be waiting for his next one. She had read that first one a dozen times by now, and each time she did, it seemed that she could hear his voice saying the words in his delicious Canadian accent, and her heart beat faster when she remembered it.

By now Teddy was forever badgering her to play with him, and he was constantly getting on her nerves, and, in the end, she suggested that she should go and spend a few days with Elsie to keep her company.

"I promised that I would at some stage, and it must be lonely for her when Daddy's out at the shop all day, and again if he's called out at night. What do you think, Aunt Rose?"

"I'm not sure if you should. You're still convalescing, remember."

"Oh, but I feel perfectly well now, and if I have to stay inactive for much longer, I shall probably go mad with boredom!"

"We wouldn't want that, would we?" Rose said drily, and they both knew this was her way of giving her assent.

Elsie was delighted to see her.

"I know Daddy will be relieved too. He's taking this second job very seriously, Daisy, and they say all little boys grow up wanting to be either engine-drivers or firemen, so I think he's in his element."

"I bet he is, but it's dangerous work too. It's not just ordinary house fires these days, is it? I know those are awful for the people concerned," she added hastily, "but it must be far worse when you're called to deal with fires in the middle of an air raid and you never know where the next bomb is going to fall."

"Well, you're a proper Job's comforter, aren't you? I thought you were here to cheer me up. I'm sure they know what to expect and what to do about it."

Elsie wasn't sure she believed it herself, because none of them knew what to expect these days, and the air-raid sirens were an almost nightly occurrence now, even if no substantial damage had been done to the city as yet. But she had other things to think about beside German bombs.

For several days now she had had the most appalling stitch in her side and it wouldn't go away. The midwife said it was just the baby lying awkwardly, and she shouldn't pay too much attention to it. It would soon be over, anyway. Sometimes she could be cheerful to the point of infuriating Elsie. It wasn't *her* pain anyway, but she trusted her implicitly.

"Why don't you stay in the flat with me while you're here, instead of in your old room?" she asked Daisy. "You can have Mary Yard's old bedroom, and we can have midnight talks if we feel like it."

"Back to our schooldays, you mean, when we crept into one another's bedrooms for a gossip, desperately trying not to disturb the parents?" Daisy said with a grin. Though she wasn't ready to tell her anything about Glenn yet, because there wasn't anything yet to tell. It was still her sweet secret, something that belonged only to her.

The memory of those old times was so wonderfully emotive, so heartbreakingly taking them back to days that could never come again, when the family had all been together, whole and alive, and there had been no talk of wars and danger. Her throat caught with the magnitude of all that had happened since then.

"I'll do that," she went on brightly, in answer to Elsie's suggestion. "And talking of Mary Yard, you still haven't told me what you know!"

Quentin came into the house just then, and the chance to quiz Elsie was gone; but Daisy wasn't an observer for nothing – a nurse always watched out for signs in the patient – and her father was showing clear signs of happiness that was possibly only partly due to his youngest daughter having come home for a few days. Well, well.

"It's good to see you, darling," he greeted her. "I'm on duty for the next few nights, so you two can get your little heads together and do your plotting without me around."

Daisy laughed. "I can't think what you mean, Daddy. When did we ever do any plotting, as you call it!" But she didn't look at Elsie as she said it.

Once darkness fell, it seemed as if the noise of aircraft went on incessantly. Elsie said knowledgeably that they were theirs, not Hitler's, and she'd soon know the difference if they had a raid. Everyone was an expert in the different engine sounds by now. Daisy brought up their bedtime cocoa and sat on the edge of Elsie's bed as her sister gave up trying to get comfortable lying down and sat gingerly on the edge of a chair.

"We can go down to the shelter if you feel nervous, Daisy."

"Do you want to?"

"No. I hate it in there. I feel as if I'm in a prison, and it smells of earth and Lord knows what else. In any case I've got no intention of stating on his birth certificate that my baby was born in an air-raid shelter at the bottom of the garden, thank you very much!"

"It's not about to be, is it? There's still two or three weeks to go, isn't there?"

Elsie gave a crooked smile as the stitch in her side became far more than that and enveloped her. "That was the plan, but apparently babies don't always arrive according to plan. When they decide they want to be born, there's no stopping them, Daisy—"

Her voice ended on a huge gasp, and she put down her cup of cocoa with shaking hands. In the gaslight, her face was white and pinched as she looked at her sister. Beneath Elsie's nightdress they saw the sudden gush of water on the floor.

"Oh God, Elsie…"

"I think you'd better telephone Mrs Woodley. Better still, run down the road and fetch her. It looks as though you're going to be in on the big event."

"Are you sure you're not mistaken…?"

Her reply was a small scream from Elsie as she clutched her stomach.

"I'm sure," she gasped. "I'm told it will take hours and hours, but it doesn't feel like it. You'd better go, Daisy, unless you want to deliver the baby yourself."

Daisy fled, only stopping to grab the torch that was kept by the front door and remembering to keep it partly covered as she raced along the road to the midwife's house. She hammered on the door. An upstairs window opened, and a voice asked who was there.

"It's Daisy Caldwell, Mrs Woodley," she gasped. "Elsie thinks the baby's on its way. Can you come, please?"

"It's probably a false alarm, but I'd better take a look," the woman said, while Daisy fumed at her easy manner. It was presumably meant to calm the patients down, but it didn't help Daisy's nerves, realising she might have to assist, or at least be on hand… and it wasn't what she had come home for.

She hopped up and down until the midwife appeared a few minutes later, fully dressed, her gas mask over one shoulder, her bag of tricks in the other hand. Her hair was a metal torment of curlers, and it might have looked comical if Daisy had felt like laughing. There were aircraft overhead now and searchlight beams picking them out, and right on cue, the air-raid siren sounded as they hurried back to the house, and the sound of retaliating gunfire shook the road.

"Don't let it bother you, Daisy. If the baby's on its way, we'll be too busy in the next few hours to pay any attention to Adolph's fly-by-nights, and neither me nor your sister want to use the blessed air-raid shelter, but if you're desperate to do so, you'll have to leave us to get on with it. All right?"

"Yes," Daisy mumbled, recognising the professional's technique of keeping her mind occupied as the harsh rumble of enemy aircraft was replaced by the scream of bombs, and then an almighty explosion as the night sky was lit up by flames. "But I am a nurse, remember? I never desert a patient."

"Good girl," Mrs Woodley said.

It seemed as if they had only taken minutes to return to Elsie's bedroom, but once they saw her it was obvious that her baby was impatient to arrive in the world and that this was no false alarm. Mrs Woodley took charge at once.

"Daisy, boil a kettle and fetch me some clean towels. And Elsie, get back in bed unless you want the child to crack its skull on the floor the minute it's born."

Daisy appreciated her brisk efficiency now. Elsie did as she was told, while she herself was a shivering bag of nerves. She knew it and couldn't stop it. She had been to Dunkirk and back. She had seen ghastly sights in the hospital. She had helped to lay out the dead. But she had never seen a baby born before, especially not one that was so close to her. It was an intimacy she had never sought.

"I'm sorry, Daisy," she heard Elsie gasp when she had done as she was told. By now they were all trying to ignore the way the house was shaking with the shattering sounds of bombs hitting their targets and the bursts of gunfire that threatened to split the eardrums.

Daisy looked down at her sister, her face contorted with pain, her lovely red hair darkened with sweat. Elsie reached out to grasp her hand, and gripped it tight, and as she did so, Daisy's fear fell away, and she saw only a patient in pain, whom she could help just by being there.

"It's all right, I'm here," she said steadily. "Grab me as hard as you like, and just think how thrilled Joe's going to be when he knows his baby's arrived. Just think how the two of you are going to show him off to the rest of us. You'll make us all jealous, because I'm sure he's going to be perfectly beautiful, and it won't be long now before we see him."

Although she was prattling on, she did it in a slow, calm voice, knowing it would make Elsie feel calmer in return. She had spoken to patients in this way so many times before, though never to a woman about to give birth, nor to an older sister; but she knew how a soothing voice helped.

Mrs Woodley evidently saw her as a medical aide now, giving her asides in how much Elsie was dilated and how soon she could expect to push. Daisy didn't particularly want to hear it, and she concentrated instead on trying not to admit how numb her fingers were becoming as Elsie gripped and clung to her.

"Do we need the doctor?" she said anxiously as the hours passed, and Elsie gave a particularly anguished cry as the contractions went on and on.

"Bless you, no. This is going very nicely," came the cheerful voice. "It's a harsh birth, but a quick one, and you can prepare to push now, Elsie love."

Daisy had never realised it was such a struggle to be born, nor that she would have to witness her sister's pain. She would surely never want to go through such agony again, not even for Joe... She was finding it hard not to cry herself, and Elsie was pushing for all she was worth now. The baby's head and shoulders had already emerged, and Daisy found it impossible not to look... and then there was a sudden slithering expulsion as the baby slid into the world, drawing air into its lungs and crying at once.

"Oh, that's the most beautiful sound in the world!" Elsie gasped, and Daisy tore her eyes away from the miracle, and looked into her sister's shimmering eyes.

"It's a beautiful sight too, and so are you," she said huskily.

"It's a girl," Mrs Woodley said, not giving them a moment to get emotional, since there was still work to be done, as she called it. "And I bet neither of you even noticed that the all-clear sounded half an hour ago."

They hadn't. And once the birth was complete, she wrapped the baby in a towel and placed her in Elsie's arms, and went to make them a cup of tea, leaving the two of them alone.

"She's just perfect," Daisy breathed, looking down at the tiny face and delicate features, and the shock of glorious red Caldwell hair. "Joe will be so proud of you, Elsie. And Mother would be too."

"I'm sure she still is," Elsie said with a tremulous smile. "My only regret is that she'll never see her – and that Joe wasn't here with me. I was proud of you too, Daisy. I couldn't have done so well without you."

"I wasn't that brave. I was scared, if you must know."

"Well, it didn't show. You're a real nurse, darling. But I never doubted that everything would be all right. Joe told me always to have faith, and so I did."

She drew in her breath. "That's what we'll call her, Daisy."

"What?" Daisy said, not following her train of thought, and still bemused by the perfection of the new little life that was now part of all of them, trying to imagine her father's face when he came home from his fire-watching to discover that their family had now expanded by one.

"We were too superstitious to think of a name, but I'm going to call her Faith, because that's something we all need these days."

As if by magical, silent approval, the baby opened her eyes. They were vacantly blue right now, although the midwife had told them they would almost certainly change to the glowing Caldwell brown. Daisy leaned forward and kissed the baby's satiny cheek, tasting her skin and feeling her sweet breath, as light as thistledown. It touched her heart as nothing else had ever done. It was their hope, and their future.

"Welcome to our world, Faith," she whispered.